SARA HOLLAND

everless

ORCHARD

ORCHARD BOOKS

First published in Great Britain in 2018 by The Watts Publishing Group
This edition published in Great Britain in 2018
by The Watts Publishing Group

1 3 5 7 9 10 8 6 4 2

A CIP catalogue record for this book is available from the British Library.

ISBN 978 1 40834 915 1

Printed and bound in Great Britain by CPI Group (UK) Ltd,
Croydon, CR0 4YY

The paper and board used in this book are
made from wood from responsible sources.

Orchard Books
An imprint of Hachette Children's Group
Part of The Watts Publishing Group Limited
Carmelite House
50 Victoria Embankment
London EC4Y 0DZ

An Hachette UK Company
www.hachette.co.uk
www.hachettechildrens.co.uk

Praise for everless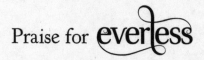

The Top Ten Bestseller

'A seductive world that reveals its secrets with every
Machiavellian twist and turn. You will want to stop
time to finish reading this book in one sitting'
South Wales Evening Post

'. . . a wonderful contribution to the YA fantasy genre
and I'd recommend it with a whole heart'
The Bookbag

'. . . everything you could possibly want from a YA fantasy'
The YA Nightstand

'I seriously loved it . . . 5/5 stars'
The Cosy Reader

'An absolute whirlwind of a reading adventure and
I loved every second of it'
Page to Stage Reviews

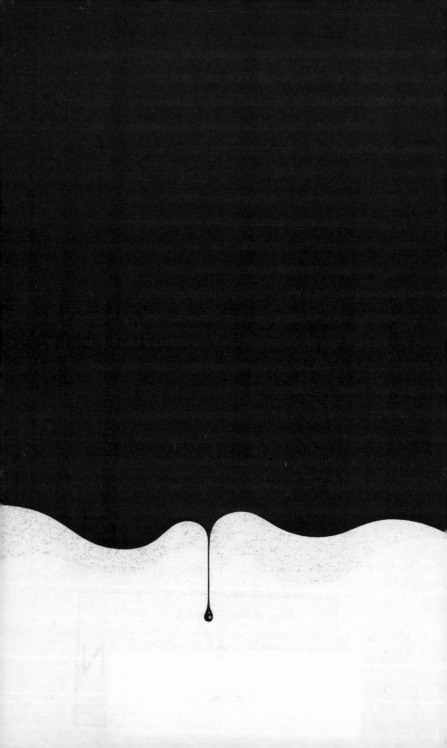

To my parents, for all the stories

1

Most people find the forest frightening, believing the old tales of fairies who will freeze the time in your blood, or witches who can spill your years out over the snow with only a whisper. Even the spirit of the Alchemist himself is said to wander these woods, trapping whole eternities in a breath.

I know better than to be afraid of stories. The forest holds real danger—thieves who lie in wait, crude knives and alchemic powder on their belts, to steal time from anyone venturing outside the safety of the village. We call them bleeders. They're why Papa doesn't like me hunting, but we have no choice. Luckily, in the winter, there's no undergrowth to hide the thieves from sight, no birdsong to muffle their footsteps.

Besides, I know these woods better than anyone else. I've always loved it here, the way the tangled branches overhead shutter out the sun and block the bitter wind. I could stay out here all day, or just keep walking through trees glittering with webs of fine ice, through the sunlight sifted into daggers. Goodbye.

Fantasy. I would never leave my father alone, especially not if he's—

He's not, I tell myself.

The lie freezes in the winter air, falls to the ground like snow. I kick at it with the toe of my boot.

Papa says some of the trees in the forest are a thousand years old. They were here before anyone alive now was born, even the Queen, even before the Alchemist and the Sorceress bound time to blood and metal—if there ever was such a time. These trees will be standing tall long after we're gone. Yet they aren't predators like wolves or people. The roots beneath my feet don't live for centuries by causing other plants to shrivel and turn gray. And their time cannot be bled from them.

If only we were more like trees.

Papa's old musket weighs heavy on my back, useless. There's been no game for miles, and in just a few hours it will be dark and the market stalls will draw their shades, one by one. Soon I'll have to go into town and face the time lender. I'd hoped hunting would calm my nerves, prepare me for what I must do. But now I only feel more afraid.

Rent is due tomorrow for Crofton. Like every month, the Gerling family will replenish its coffers with our blood-iron, claiming we owe them for their protection. Their land. Last month, when we couldn't pay, the collector let us off with a warning—Papa looked so sickly, and I so young—but it was not a kindness. This month, he'll ask for double, maybe more. Now that I'm seventeen, legally allowed to bleed my years, I know what I have to do.

Papa will be furious, if he has his wits.

Just one more try, I tell myself as I come across a small creek running through the trees. Its trickle has gone silent, frozen over—but underneath, there's a quick flicker of green and brown and gold: a trout, wriggling alone, along some invisible current. Alive under all that ice.

I kneel quickly and smash the skein of ice with the butt of the gun. I wait for the water to settle, for the flash of scales, sending up a silent plea to the Sorceress out of desperation. The blood-iron this trout would fetch wouldn't make a dent in the rent Papa owes, but I don't want to enter the market empty-handed. I won't.

I focus, willing my racing heart to calm.

And then—as sometimes happens—the world seems to slow. No, not seems. The branches really do stop whispering in the wind. Even the almost inaudible crackle of the snow melting on the ground stops, like the world is holding its breath.

I look down, at a pale glimmer in the muddy water—it too is caught in the breath of time. Before the moment can lapse, I strike, plunging my bare hand into the creek.

The shock of the cold travels up my wrist, dulling sensation in my fingers. The fish remains still—stunned—as I reach toward it, as though it wants to be caught.

When I close my hand around its slick body, time speeds up again. The fish flails in my grip, pure muscle, and I gasp, almost losing it. Before it can fling itself to freedom, I yank it from the water and dump it into my bag in one practiced motion. For a second I watch, a little nauseated, as the fish flops around inside, making the burlap twitch.

Then, the bag is still.

I don't know why time sometimes slows like that, completely at random. Heeding Papa, I keep it to myself—he once saw a man bled twenty years for simply claiming he could make an hour flow backward with a wave of his hand. Hedge witches, like Calla in our village, are tolerated as an amusement for the superstitious—as long as they pay rent. I used to go and listen to her stories about time rippling, slowing, sometimes even causing rifts or quakes in the earth, until Papa forbade me from visiting her shop, leery of drawing attention to us. I still remember its perfume—spice mingled with the blood of ancient rites. But if Papa has taught me anything, it's that keeping my head down means staying safe.

I stick my hands in my underarms to warm them and crouch over the river again, trying to slip back into focus. But no more fish come, and slowly the sun lowers its arms through the trees.

Anxiety knots my stomach.

I can't put off the marketplace any longer.

I've known for years it would eventually come to this, but still I curse under my breath. Turning back toward town, I sling my dripping satchel over my shoulder. I've gone farther out than usual, and I regret it now with the snow soaking through my worn-out boots, the trees intercepting what remains of the day's warmth.

Eventually the woods thin out and give way to the dirt road leading into town, which has been churned into frozen mud by hundreds of wagon wheels. I trudge along its side, steeling myself for the marketplace. I'm haunted by thoughts of the time lender's blade, the vials waiting to be filled with blood. And then the blood waiting to be turned to iron, the wave of exhaustion I've heard follows as he leeches time from one's veins.

Worse, though, is the thought of listening through the thin walls of the cottage as Papa tosses and turns on his straw mattress. Sorceress knows he needs the rest. This last month, I saw him waning before my eyes, like a winter moon.

I swear his eyes are graying—a sign that one's time is running out.

If only there weren't such a simple explanation for this morning, when he forgot my birthday.

Papa has never forgotten my birthday before, not once. If only he would just admit that he's been selling time, despite my begging him not to, and let me give him a few years. If only

5

the Sorceress and Alchemist were real and I could lock them up, demand that they find a way to give him lasting life.

What if—I can't look at the thought straight on—what if he only has a month, a day?

A memory floats to the top of my mind of an old beggar woman in Crofton who had bled her last week for a bowl of soup, stumbling from door to door, greeting every person in town and pleading for a day-iron or two, or even just a bit of bread. She forgot the names of the people first—then she forgot the shape of the village entirely, and wandered around the fields, raising her hand to knock on air.

Papa and I found her curled in the wheat, her skin cold as ice. Her time had run out. And it all started with the forgetting.

Thinking of her, I run. My blood urges me on, begging to be turned to coin.

Crofton announces itself first by a few spindly columns of smoke, then the patchwork of rooftops peeking out over the hills. The narrow path leading to our cottage turns east off the main road, well before the village. But I pass it by and keep walking, toward the noise and smoke of the market.

Inside the low stone wall that roughly marks the village periphery, row houses lean together like a huddling crowd, as if by being close they'll succeed in keeping out the cold, or the woods, or the slow suck of time. People hurry by me here and there, bodies hidden in layers, heads ducked against the wind.

The marketplace is nothing more than a long stretch of muddy cobblestone where three roads meet. It's crowded and noisy this afternoon: rent is due for everyone, and the space is thick with people selling. Men in rough farmers' clothes and women with babies slung across their backs haggle over bolts of cloth and loaves of bread and cattle bones thick with marrow, ignoring the handful of beggars who wander from stall to stall, their refrain—an hour? An hour?—blurring into the general hum of activity. The air is dim with smoke from the oily cook fires.

There's a long line winding from Edwin Duade's time lending shop; Papa and I are scarcely the only ones who scramble every month to make ends meet. The sight always makes my stomach hurt—dozens of people grouped up along the walls, waiting to have time drawn out from their blood and forged into blood-iron coins. I know I have to join them, but somehow, I can't force myself into the queue. If Papa finds out . . .

Better to get something to eat first, to fortify my strength before I sell my time. And I may as well sell my catch, measly as it is.

I start for the butcher's stall, where my friend Amma stands behind the counter, doling out strips of dried meat to a cluster of schoolgirls in clean pinafores. A pang of mixed nostalgia and envy goes through me. I could have been one of those children. I was, once. After Papa's expulsion from Everless, the Gerling estate—the flash of anger as I think of it is as familiar as my own heartbeat—he spent his savings on books and paper for me, so I could go to school. But as his sight worsened, the money for books and paper ran out along with his work. Papa's taught me everything he knows, but it's not the same.

I push the thought away and wave at Amma when she catches my eye. She smiles, creasing the scar that runs down one cheek. It's a relic of a bleeder raid on the village where she was born, an attack that left her father dead and her mother with only a few days left in her blood. She clung to life long enough to bring her daughters to Crofton before her time ran out completely, leaving only Amma to provide for her little sister, Alia.

To Amma—probably, to many of the schoolgirls I wade through—my hatred of the Gerlings would seem petty. They keep their towns free of bleeders and highwaymen like the ones that killed Amma's parents, and oversee trade. For their protection, they expect loyalty—and, of course, blood-irons every month. Sempera's borders are guarded to prevent anyone from slipping away with the secrets of blood-iron, which is why Papa and I stayed on Gerling lands even after we were expelled from Everless for burning down the forge all those years ago.

I remember Everless—its tapestry-lined hallways and gleaming bronze doors, its occupants flitting about in gold and silk and jewels. No Gerling would stalk you in the forest to slit your throat, but they are thieves all the same.

8

"I heard they've set the date, for the first day of spring," one of the schoolchildren gushes.

"No, it's sooner," another insists. "He's so in love, he can't wait till spring to marry her."

Only half listening, I know they're chattering about what seems like the only topic on anyone's lips these days—Roan's wedding, the joining of the two most powerful families in Sempera.

Lord Gerling's wedding, I correct myself. He's not the sticky, gap-toothed boy I knew, who would join the servant children in a game of hide-and-seek. As soon as he's married to Ina Gold, the Queen's ward, he'll be as good as Her Majesty's son. The kingdom of Sempera is divided between five families, yet the Gerlings control over a third of the land. Roan's wedding will make them even more powerful. Amma rolls her eyes at me.

"Go on," she says, shooing the schoolgirls away. "Enough chatter."

They scamper away in a swirl of too-bright colors, their faces aglow. In contrast, Amma looks exhausted, hair tied tightly back, dark circles beneath her eyes. I know she must have been up since before sunrise hanging and cutting meat. I pull out the measly trout to place on her scale.

"Long day?" Her hands are already moving to wrap the fish in paper.

I smile at her as best I can. "It'll be better in the spring."

Amma's my best friend in the world, but even she doesn't know how bad things have gotten for Papa and me. If she knew that I was about to be bled, she'd pity me—or worse, offer to help. I don't want that. She has enough troubles.

She gives me a bloodstained hour-coin for the fish and adds a strip of dried meat as a gift for me. When I accept them, she doesn't take her hand from mine. "I was hoping you'd come by today," she says, her voice lower now. "There's something I need to tell you."

Her fingers are icy and her tone too serious. "What?" I say, trying to keep my voice light. "Has Jacob finally asked you to run away with him?" Jacob is a local boy whose obvious crush on Amma has been the subject of our jokes for years.

She shakes her head and doesn't smile. "I'm leaving the village," she says, still gripping my hands tightly. "I'm going to work at Everless. They're hiring servants to help with preparations for the wedding." She smiles uncertainly.

The smile slips from my own face and cold spills through my chest. "Everless," I repeat after her numbly.

"Jules, I've heard they're paying a year on the month." Her eyes are bright now. "A whole year! Can you imagine?"

A year they've stolen from us, I think.

"But . . ." My throat is tight. Most of the time, I try to hold the memories of Everless, of my childhood, at bay. But Amma's face, full of hope, is bringing it all back to me in a flood—the labyrinthine halls, the sweeping lawn, Roan's smile. Then, the

10

memory of flames burns everything else away. My mouth suddenly tastes bitter.

"Haven't you heard the rumors?" I ask. Her smile falters, and I pause, hating to puncture her happiness. But I can't take the words back, so I plow on instead. "That they're only hiring girls. Pretty women. The elder Lord Gerling treats servants like toys, right under his wife's nose."

"That's a risk I'll have to take," she says softly. Her hands fall from mine. "Alia is going too, and Karina—her husband is gambling away their time." I can see the anger in her eyes—Karina is like a mother to her, and it enrages Amma to watch her suffer. "No one has work. Everless is the only real chance I've got, Jules."

I want to argue further, to convince her that the fate of an Everless girl is thankless and degrading, that they all just become the title without a name of their own, but I can't. Amma's right—those who serve the Gerlings are compensated well, at least by Crofton's standards, though the blood-irons they're paid are taken—stolen—from people like Amma, me, and Papa.

But I know what it is to be hungry, and Amma doesn't share my hatred of the Gerlings, or my knowledge of their cruelty. So I smile at Amma as best I can.

"I'm sure it'll be wonderful," I say, hoping she doesn't hear the doubt in my voice.

"Just think, I'll see the Queen with my own eyes," she

gushes. While Papa secretly scorns the Queen, in most families, she is little less than a goddess. She might as well be a goddess: she's been alive since the time of the Sorceress. When blood-iron spread through everyone's veins, invaders descended from other kingdoms. The Queen, then the head of the Semperan army, crushed them, and has been ruling ever since.

"And Ina Gold," Amma continues. "She's supposed to be very beautiful."

"Well, if she's marrying Lord Gerling, she must be," I reply lightly. But my stomach clenches at the thought of Lady Gold. Everyone knows her story: an orphan like so many, abandoned as an infant on the rocky beaches near the palace on Sempera's shore as a sacrifice to the Queen. In light of the many attempts on the Queen's life, especially in her early years, she refused to have her own child or take a spouse; instead, she promised to choose a child to bring up as a prince or princess— and if they were worthy, to inherit the crown when the Queen was ready to pass on the throne. Possibly Ina's parents were even more desperate than the peasants of Crofton are. She caught the eye of the Queen's lady-in-waiting, and the Queen chose Ina Gold as her daughter—and two years ago, officially named Ina as her own heir.

Now she's seventeen. The same age as Amma and me—but she'll inherit the throne, and the royal time bank, and live for centuries. And her time will be filled with feasts and balls and things I can't even imagine, unconcerned with me and everyone else burning through our little lives outside the palace walls.

I tell myself the envy that sticks in my throat is because of this, and not because she will be Roan's wife.

"You could come too, Jules," Amma says quietly. "It wouldn't be so bad if we were there to look after each other."

For a second, I imagine it—the narrow servants' halls and vast sweep of the lawn, the grand marble staircases.

But it's impossible. Papa would never stand for it. We were forced to flee Everless, flee the Gerlings. It's because of them that we're starving.

Because of Liam.

"I can't leave Papa," I say. "You know that."

Amma sighs. "Well, I'll see you when I return. I want to save up enough time to go back to school."

"Why stop there?" I tease. "Perhaps a nobleman will fall in love with you and sweep you away to a castle."

"But what would Jacob do then?" she says with a wink, and I force a laugh. Suddenly I realize just how lonely I'll be in the long months that Amma is gone. Seized by a sudden fear that I'll never see her again, I pull her into a hug. Despite the long hours spent separating bone and gristle, her hair still smells like wildflowers. "Goodbye for now, Amma."

"I'll be back before you know it," she says, "full of stories."

"I don't doubt it," I say. I don't say: *I just hope they're the happy kind.*

I tarry with Amma for as long as I can, but the sun doesn't stop sinking. My stomach heavy with dread, I trudge off to the time lender. I weave between stalls to find the end of the still-too-long line, winding toward Duade's door with its burnt-in hourglass symbol. Behind it will be the flash of the blade, the powder that turns blood and time to iron.

I keep my eyes on the ground in an effort to avoid the sight of the people who leave the shop, pale and breathless and a little bit closer to death. I try to tell myself that some of them will never visit the time lender again—that next week, after they find work, they will go home and melt a blood-iron in their tea and drink it down. But that doesn't happen here in Crofton; at least, I've never seen it. We only ever bleed, only ever sell.

After a few minutes, a commotion draws my eyes up. Three men are emerging from the store—two collectors, Everless men, the family crest gleaming on their chests and short swords swinging on their belts; and between them, the time lender, Duade, his arms pinned in their grip.

"Let me go," Duade shouts. "I didn't do nothing wrong."

The crowd murmurs, and I feel panic cinch around us all. Certainly no small number of illegal happenings go on in Duade's shop, but the Gerlings' police have always let them pass with a wink and a nod and a month-iron slipped from palm to palm. The time lender might be an oily, greedy sort, but we all need him at one time or another.

I need him today.

As Duade struggles uselessly against the officers, the sound of hooves rings out through the square. Everyone quiets at once, Duade going still in the collectors' grip as a young man on a white mare rounds the corner into the marketplace, hood drawn up against the cold.

Roan. In spite of myself, my heart lifts. Over the past few months, now that he is of age, Roan Gerling has started to pay visits to the villages his family holds. The first time he appeared, I scarcely recognized him, lean and blindingly handsome as he's become—but now, whenever I go to market, I secretly hope to see him, though I know he can never see me. I want to hate him for his fine clothes, the way he looks around with that slight, benevolent smile, reminding us that he owns every tree and cottage and pebble in the road. But my memories of Roan run too deep for hatred, no matter how I try. And besides, the collectors are more lenient when he's around. Whatever is happening with Duade, Roan will put an end to it.

But when I glance back at the storefront, the look on Duade's face as he stands pinioned between the two guards isn't relief. It's pure fear.

Confused, I turn as the boy yanks down his hood. He has the right broad shoulders, golden skin, and dark hair. But he is all severity: stormy brows; hard nose; a high, aristocratic forehead.

The breath vanishes from my lungs.

Not Roan. Liam. Liam, Roan's older brother, who I thought was safely off studying history at some ivied academy by the ocean. Liam, who for ten years has walked in my nightmares. I've dreamed so often about the night we fled, I can't separate nightmare from memory, but Papa made sure that I retained one thing: Liam Gerling was not our friend.

Liam tried to kill Roan when we were children. The three of us were playing in the forge, and Liam pushed his brother into the fire. If I hadn't pulled Roan out before the flames could catch, he would have been burned alive. And as my reward, we had to flee the only home I had ever known, because Papa was afraid of what Liam would do to me if we stayed at Everless, knowing what I had seen.

Later, when I was twelve, Liam found Papa and me in our cottage outside of Rodshire. Their scuffle woke me in the middle of the night, and when I left my bedroom, my father grabbed my hand—he'd chased Liam off—and we fled a second time.

I'm paralyzed, seized by the sense that my worst fears have come to life—after all these years, he's found me, found my father, again.

I know I should turn away, but I can't tear my eyes from him, can't stop picturing that face as it was ten years ago, staring at me in hatred through a wall of smoke, on the day we fled Everless for good.

I hear Papa's voice in my ears: *If you ever see Liam Gerling, run.*

2

Even at ten, Liam was cold and remote. He went off to boarding school less than a year after we left the estate, but rumors about him continued to travel through his family's lands. Everless servants on errands in Crofton said that his quiet exterior could turn to rage in the span of a heartbeat, that his parents feared him and sent him away. But it wasn't rage that made Liam push his brother toward the fire in the forge, or chase us to Rodshire. It was cruelty. I can't imagine how his malice might have grown in the years since.

Now, as I shrink back into the nearest doorway, I wonder how I ever mistook him for Roan. The boys share the same height, the same strong frame, the black curls—but where Roan's hair is unruly, Liam's has been wrangled and slicked back from his face. His mouth is a thin, humorless slash; his eyes

17

hooded, impossible to read. Rising above the crowd on his horse, he looks like a statue, sitting ramrod-straight in the saddle—proud, unyielding, and eternal. He surveys us, the line of people waiting to see Duade.

Too late, I reach up to raise my hood, but his gaze has already landed on me. Do I imagine that he pauses for an instant, his eyes lingering on my face? Fear has lodged in my throat, and my hands tremble as I pull my hood over my hair. I want to turn away, to flee from the line, but that would only make me more conspicuous.

Thankfully, lowly townspeople don't seem to catch Liam's interest. His eyes scan past me, and he looks down to where his guards hold Duade between them.

The old time lender looks terrified. Roan would have called off his men, but Liam has none of his kindness.

"Please . . ." The quiet is such that I can hear Duade plead from where I stand. "My lord, it was an honest mistake, nothing more."

"You broke the law. You bled time from a child." Liam's voice is deeper now, but just as cold as when he was a boy. "Do you deny it?"

All around me, shadows of remembered pain flit across faces, and I know these are the parents in the line. Children's time is unpredictable, hard to measure and hard to bind, and it's easy to take too much and accidentally kill the giver. Yet many have had no choice, and I imagine that watching your

18

child bleed is its own punishment, crueler than anything the Gerlings could dream up.

"How was I to know she was a child?" Duade stares up wildly at Liam, excuse after useless excuse tumbling from his lips. "I believe only what I'm told, my lord, I am nothing more than a servant—"

Liam's voice cuts through the air as cold and sharp as a knife. "Take him back to Everless. Bleed a year."

This stops Duade short. "A year?" For a moment, he just seems stunned. Then panic fills his face. "Lord Gerling, please—"

The collectors haul Duade toward a waiting horsecar. Liam twitches his leg, as if to dismount, and my stomach churns with nausea. I suddenly feel in danger of fainting. While Liam is distracted, I duck my head and hurry from the line, toward an alley I can take as a shortcut home.

At the edge of the market, I glance back. Immediately, I wish I hadn't. People are drifting away from the time lender's shop, but Liam is still there, looking straight at me. My heart stutters, and for a moment that lasts entirely too long, I'm frozen, trapped in his piercing gaze. If he recognizes me . . .

Run. My father's voice.

But he digs his heels into his horse and turns it away, back toward the main road, as if he can't wait to be quit of so contemptible a place as our village. My breathing is ragged in my own ears as I turn, too, and hurry homeward.

When I emerge from the village into our barren wheat field, the panic clouding my mind fades a little, leaving only the deep, inescapable dread in my stomach that Liam put there with his look. I've had nightmares since the night we were banished from Everless—smoke-filled night terrors of the fire grew into dreams of being pursued by a faceless killer. Dreams of fire and terror and the acrid smell of hot metal and burning straw, which fills my nostrils again as I picture Liam's eyes.

Ten years have passed since he last saw me, I remind myself again and again. Papa and I were only servants, me a knobby-kneed seven-year-old girl in a servant's cap. He might recognize Papa, but there is no reason he would know me.

It's not until the cottage comes into view, a paltry wisp of smoke drifting from the chimney, that I remember I meant to bring home our dinner. Amma's strip of dried venison will have to do for tonight. For Papa's sake, I hope the hour-coin I fetched for the trout will be worth the empty belly.

The sun sinks lower. I look west, toward the horizon, where the sky is laced with gray and golden red. Another day spent.

A wilting evergreen wreath hangs on our back door, and a fox ornament, which I twisted together as a child with wire and nails, sits crouched in the window. My mother apparently believed in these talismans. Papa says she would spend hours tying pine boughs together with thread or polishing her ancient wooden figurine of the Sorceress—a graceful figure with a clock in one hand and a knife in the other—that sits in the windowsill for protection, longevity. A similar statue, though much larger and less beautiful, stands near Crofton's west wall, where the devout—or desperate—ask for blessings. Even though he doesn't say so, I know my father keeps these things around to honor Mother's memory. He doesn't believe in them any more than I do. If the Sorceress exists, she's not listening to our prayers.

Inside, I linger in the unlit kitchen, waiting for my eyes to adjust to the dark, dreading the moment when I will face my father empty-handed. It's not that Papa will be upset with me—he never is—but I am ever painfully conscious of his spindly frame, the tremors in his hands. What will he have forgotten while I was gone—my name? My face? In my panic over Liam Gerling and the commotion he caused, I forgot all about the rent. And now, with Duade taken to Everless to be bled by the Gerlings' time lender, what hope do I have of selling him more before the collector arrives?

An unfamiliar voice floats in from the other room, and I freeze. The words are muffled by the crackling fire, but I can tell the voice is male. Fear lances through me again. Did Liam recognize me after all? Did he send someone to come after me?

I move to the threshold and pull back the curtain. And stop.

It takes me a moment to make sense of the scene before me. The rent collector, a Crofton man who travels from cottage to cottage every month like illness, sits across from my father near the hearth. He's early, at least earlier than normal. Between them on a rough wood table is a line of objects: a small brass bowl, a glass vial, a silver knife. The same tools that litter the time lender's counter in his glass-fronted shop. The tools to withdraw time.

Papa looks up at me. His cloudy eyes widen. "Jules," he says, struggling up from the table. "I didn't expect you back until dark."

My heart hitches; it's *already* dark.

"What's going on?" I ask, voice shot through with tears, even though I know. The collector glances my way, seeming much too large for our small home.

My father sinks back into his chair. "I'm paying our rent," he says calmly. "Why don't you wait outside, enjoy the warm day?"

Before I can reply, the collector cuts in. "Four months, then." His tone is businesslike, slightly bored. "For this month's rent and the last."

"Four months?" I take a step toward the table, my voice rising. "Papa, you can't."

The Gerling man looks briefly at me, then shrugs. "That's the penalty for being late." His eyes sweep over me once more before he turns back to his tools. "Time is for burning, girl."

It's a familiar expression in the village—why hoard time when every day is dully brutal, the same as the one before and the one that will come after? To hear it from a man who's never known hunger or cold makes my fingers twitch toward a fist.

Instead, I take the hour-coin from my pocket and hold it out to him. "Take this, and I'll—"

The collector cuts me off with a short, humorless laugh.

"Save your hour, girl," he says. "And don't look so upset. After your father's time runs out, you'll inherit these debts. I'd hate to be on bad terms."

The curse I'd been about to spit at him freezes in my throat. *After Papa's time runs out.* As if he expects it to happen soon. Has he measured my father's blood?

My father looks away, his jaw working, as the man reaches for the knife, but Papa seizes it first.

He draws a line neatly across his own palm, as calmly as if it were charcoal on paper instead of knife on skin. Blood wells. "Four months, yes," he echoes as he picks up a glass vial and holds it against his palm, catching the small stream of blood. "I have plenty to spare."

But I don't think I'm imagining the way his face gets paler and paler by the second, the lines seeming to become more deeply etched; or the way he sags a little when the filled vial leaves his hand, corked, and disappears back into the Gerling man's purse. I reach out and grab his wrist before he can pick up a second vial.

"No." With my other hand, I sweep away the knife until it's out of my father's reach. The collector watches me with eyebrows raised, and I address myself to him now. "Four months for two months' rent? There has to be another way."

"Jules."

I ignore my father's soft admonition and turn to the collector. He looks bored, which infuriates me almost as much as the fact of his taking my father's time. But I push the anger down and make my voice as honey-sweet as I can, hoisting on a smile to match. "Let me sell my time, sir. You can have five months."

Interest sparks for a moment in the man's eyes, and I can imagine what he's thinking—he could pass the rent along to the Gerlings, pocket the extra month for himself. But then my father cuts in. "She's sixteen."

"I'm seventeen," I say, hating myself for how my words make Papa's brow crease in confusion. "Papa, today is the eleventh day of the month. I'm seventeen."

The collector looks back and forth between us, unsure who to believe, and then grunts and shakes his head. "No. I won't bring the Sorceress's wrath down on my head for bleeding a child."

The Sorceress's, or Liam Gerling's?

"Please." I turn halfway toward Papa, addressing both men at the same time. "I've never given time. I can earn it back later."

"Easy to say you'll earn it back," Papa says stubbornly. "Harder to actually earn it. Collector, hand me another vial."

"I'm to work at Everless." The words leave my mouth before the idea has even fully formed in my mind. My father's head snaps toward me, and he stares at me with a warning in his eyes.

The collector hasn't moved. "And?"

"And . . ." I blink, trying to remember what Amma told me in the marketplace. "They're paying a year on the month. If you forgive us a little this time, I'll pay double what we owe you. And I'll pay two more months in advance," I add, trying to hide the desperation in my voice.

A bribe. I've caught the man's interest. He looks me up and down, evaluating me in a way that makes my skin seethe, but I hold my chin high and bear his eyes on my body. I know how the Gerlings value youth and beauty. I'm no Ina Gold, but at least I inherited my mother's long legs and shining hair. In different clothes, I could pass for an Everless girl.

"Jules!" My father struggles up from the table, grabbing his cane. Standing, he towers over us, and for a painful second I see the man he used to be—proud and strong enough to give pause to any Gerling crony. I look down at the tabletop. It hurts me to ignore him like this. But I don't know how much time he's sold, how much he has left.

"Absolutely not. I forbid you to—"

"Sit down," the collector says impatiently. "I've better things to do than listen to peasants bicker."

Slowly, my father sinks back into his seat, anger and fear clouding his brow.

"I'll let the two of you sort this out," the collector says, condescension thick in his voice as he pushes back from the table. "If you plan on going to Everless, I'll see you at the market tomorrow at dawn. We'll see if you're fit. Otherwise, I'll come back tomorrow to collect the rest of the rent."

"Thank you for your patience," I reply. Papa's eyes are trained on me. "I'll see you tomorrow."

The collector grunts noncommittally. Silence rings in his wake as he walks out, the door slamming behind him.

"How much time do you have left?" The question seems to burst from my lips of its own accord.

He either doesn't hear me or chooses to ignore me. He looks down at the table, blotting the cut on his palm with a cloth. "Jules—"

"How much time?" I press.

"Enough." I can't tell if this is an answer or a rebuke. He takes a deep breath. "You're a child. You should be going back to school."

"*You* should have told me we were behind on the rent. I could have paid. I have the time."

"No," my father says, and for the first time his voice is sharp. "I won't let that happen."

"But work is scarce." The anger I've pushed down, the rage I couldn't show the rent collector, twists and churns inside me. "Where does that leave us—leave you? I need you, Papa." To my dismay, I can feel tears springing to my eyes. "Did you think of that before you let the collector bleed you?"

"There are things you don't know about the world, Jules." The confrontation has left him worn-out, slumping in his seat. Guilt pricks at me—he did just have a month bled from him, and he must be exhausted. "The Gerlings are evil, greed-driven people," he fumes. "That boy, Liam, would have seen us executed before he told the truth about the fire—"

His words are lost in an onset of coughing. The next words are so soft, so weak, that I almost think I imagine them. "I won't let them have you."

"They won't have me. They won't even notice me," I say, trying to keep the frustration out of my voice. I'm tired of hiding, of waiting. "And if I make enough time, I can go back to school."

"No." Steel runs below the surface of his voice. "You will not go back to Everless. I forbid you."

"Papa, please. No one will recognize me." I can hear how I sound—wheedling, childish. Papa's outburst has shaken me. I know he hates the Gerlings—I do too—but it's not worth bleeding his life out to keep me away from them. Has fear come to dominate his mind so much?

"I'm still your father," he says. "As long as you live under my roof, you'll do what I say."

I've opened my mouth to argue when an ugly thought skitters across the surface of my mind.

He can't stop me.

After Papa had chased Liam off that night when I was

27

twelve, he decided to shed our past. The villagers' knowing that the Gerlings' disgraced blacksmith had landed in their midst would raise eyebrows, questions: Why had Papa left such a high station for a hardscrabble life in the village? Worse— what if Liam found us again, to enact some petty revenge? Easier, Papa said, to create a dull, typical history. A farmer and his daughter, abandoning the fields after a blight. He taught me how to lie, so no one would look too closely at us.

He doesn't realize it, but he's taught me too well.

I sigh heavily. "Amma is leaving for Everless," I say. "Maybe the butcher will give me her job."

Papa's gaze softens. "Maybe." He reaches out, puts a hand over mine. "I hate that you have to work at all. But at least here, we're together."

I smile at him, wishing I could tell the truth—that the idea of returning to Everless sickens me and fills me with dread, but I'm going to do it anyway. He's smiling, relieved, and I know he doesn't see through me. I stand, kiss him on the brow, and make for the kitchen to go about dinner.

When Papa's not looking, I take the figurine of the Sorceress from the window—the one that belonged to my mother—and slip it into my dress pocket. Maybe the Sorceress can give me luck. Maybe the thought of her will give me strength.

At dawn, I'll need both.

3

I go to bed before Papa. In my cot by the fireplace beneath a thin blanket, my eyes closed, I listen to him scratch notes in his ledger. I know he's tallying up his time, as if by checking and rechecking the figures he'll suddenly find a way to pay for all the things we can't afford. Then the cottage door creaks as he goes to fetch water from the old well outside; the fire crackles as he puts on another log. Eventually, he kisses my forehead and retreats into his room, sighing as he goes.

I wait until his breathing has evened out into sleep. Then, I slip carefully from the cot and gather my things, as quietly as I can. I take a few rolls of dark bread from the cupboard, just enough for a meal or two. I pick out my nicest dress, though the threadbare blue linen will seem humble beside the ladies of Everless. I tuck my hunting knife, sheathed, into my belt and fold a few belongings into a knapsack.

My eyes settle on the wall, on a drawing of my mother that Papa made. He loved to draw, before his eyes went bad—one day, I found the drawing tucked away in his mattress, as if he couldn't bear to be reminded of what we'd lost. I had to plead with him to let me hang it up on the wall. The paper is yellow and curled with age, but the likeness is striking: a young woman with my curly hair and brown eyes looking over her shoulder and laughing. I reach out and trace my mother's face. I wonder if she would approve of the choice I'm making. Her statue of the Sorceress is still tucked in my pocket. *Luck*, I think, my heart slowing.

On the back of one of the papers he's left scattered on the table, I scribble a note, deliberately casual: *Went to see the butcher. Back before dark.*

I leave it on top of his ledger. Papa won't realize the lie right away, I hope. If he does, I wouldn't trust him not to limp into the village himself, trying to chase the Gerlings' carriages down.

When he realizes what I've done, what will he do?

If I think too long about Papa—how worried he'll be—my nerves will fail me. So I pull on my boots as silently as I can and take up my bag. I'll be gone a month, two at the most, and I'll write him a letter from Everless to reassure him that everything is fine. When I come home, the purseful of blood-irons will make up for my deceit.

It's two hours before dawn when I finally bring myself to walk away, judging by the lightening sky and dewy smell of the air. I walk fast as the sun's light bleeds into the sky from the east. It's colder than it was yesterday, and the raw wind makes me shiver. The smell of decayed earth rises through the snow. Soon, the village of Crofton looms before me, its lump of thatched roofs like lopsided mushrooms in the dawn. The only signs of life are a few beggars sleeping in doorways. As I watch, a thin hand lights a candle in a window above the bakery. I'm not afraid—the Gerlings keep us safe from external threats, if not starvation. But it's eerie.

A few blocks from the marketplace, I hear a murmur of voices. Turning the corner, I see the largest gathering of girls I've ever encountered in one place. There must be more than fifty of us crowding the open square, all clean-scrubbed and dressed in our finest clothes. Some of them I know—there's Amma with her little sister, Alia, tiny and solemn at twelve; and Nora, a seamstress, for whom I used to do some mending before she could no longer pay me. Many girls I don't recognize. Perhaps they've come from the farms that stretch for miles outside the borders of our village, drawn here by the opportunity to work at Everless.

Moving through the crowd are men with badges bearing the Gerling insignia. They're shouting, herding the girls into one long line. My stomach drops when I recognize one—Ivan Tenburn, the son of the captain of the Everless guard, now on

31

his own horse and wearing his own badge. He was vicious as a child, and constantly at Liam's heels; all the servant children were terrified of him. Once, while his father was away, he made the stableboys stand in a line, and struck their knees with a riding crop in turn. If one cried out, he'd give the boy next to him five strikes in a row. He called it a game—snaps. I remember the dark bruise across my friend Tam's shins. It remained for weeks.

I also remember Roan's voice, demanding that Ivan stop.

Fear courses through me, sharp as the blade Ivan wears at his side. Ten years have passed, but by the way Ivan barks at the girls to move, I know that nothing has changed.

I head toward where Amma and Alia are huddled on the other side of the square. Amma looks uncertain. Her own knapsack is slung over her back, and she's wearing a traveling cloak. When she sees me, a relieved smile breaks out across her face.

"I don't believe it!" She grips my arms and draws me in for a quick hug. "Convinced your father to let you come after all?"

"Just for a month or two," I fib. "If they even choose me."

"Well, I'm sure he'll be pleased enough when you come home with two years of blood-iron."

I try to take comfort in Amma's words as she tugs me toward the line. I feel her pulse, quick and light, against my palm. "I'm glad you're here. It'll be marvelous, us all together." Next to her, Alia smiles up at me.

As we take our places, Ivan and the other Gerling men hold conference, talking in low voices before turning to face the line of girls. Behind them, two large open-topped hay carts, driven by skinny, bucktoothed boys who can't be older than twelve, roll into the square and halt. Meanwhile, Ivan and his men walk down the line, examining chins and eyes and arms, spinning the girls like tops.

"What's going on?" I whisper to Amma. She just shakes her head.

Uneasiness pools in my stomach. I've heard Lord Gerling likes his servants young and pretty, but I never expected to be treated this way, to be herded like cattle and checked like a horse for good teeth and legs. I'm tempted to run, but I can't make my feet move.

Down the line, a man examines a round-faced, frizzy-haired girl I don't recognize. He frowns and shakes his head. The girl's lip trembles. She starts to speak, but the man ignores her and moves on to the next girl in line, a willowy woman in her early twenties. He smiles greedily at her and speaks a few low words. Her face turns red and she breaks from the line, hurrying toward the hay cart.

The evaluation goes on like this. About a quarter of the girls are directed into the cart, and the rest are rejected. My skin crawls every time one of the Gerling men leers or makes a girl hitch her skirts to better show off her calves, but if I want to win a place at Everless, I don't dare say anything. Amma has gone as white as the snow still piled in drifts at the edges of the square. I give her hand a reassuring squeeze, as much to comfort myself as her.

Five girls away. Three. Then one. I bite the inside of my cheek as the Gerling servant appears in front of me, hoping my disgust doesn't show on my face. I'm just thankful it's not Ivan. He's smiling, close enough that I can smell the stink of his breath. To my dismay, he takes my chin in his hand, dragging my face upward. I flinch—I can't help it. The man chuckles and goes for my breasts instead.

Reflex takes over, and I see everything happening slowly, as if we're suspended in honey. It's happening again—time pausing, even the air unmoving, though no one seems to know it. The man's grin fixed on his face. Amma's horrified expression, a gasp caught halfway from her throat. I reach for my knife in my belt and bring it in front of me, meaning only to stop him.

But then the buzzing in my ears abruptly fades, and the world catches up again.

The guard and I both look down in shock at the hair-thin red line that crosses his overhanging gut, the drop of blood gathering at its end, staining his uniform. I've barely nicked him, but still. My stomach plummets as I realize what I've done.

There's a beat of dead silence as he glares at me, and then the other men break into laughter. The man's face colors a deep, angry red.

"Little bitch," he spits, stuffing a handkerchief to the

34

scratch. "I'll bleed you ten years . . ."

I lower my knife, tears pricking at my eyes, and begin to back away. Stupid, so stupid. One moment of impulse, and I've thrown away any chance I had of getting to Everless.

But then—

"Hang on, now, Bosley." Ivan, his velvet cloak whipping behind him, saunters over to us. His mouth is twitching, and I brace myself—what if he recognizes me?

But then I realize that the sound coming from his throat is laughter, not rage. His smile is thick—oblivious. "I like this one," he chortles. "Quick thinker. Knows how to handle herself, too. It's a wonder she didn't stick you like a pig." Some of the other men laugh, and the man who tried to grope me casts me a hate-filled gaze, but he doesn't argue.

Instead, he turns his attention to Amma. "Not with that scar," he says nastily.

Amma blinks in disbelief. "I'll work hard," she says. "I swear it." She glances helplessly at me.

"We've no shortage of hard workers, girl," the man snarls. "Just pretty faces. Home with you."

Tears spring to Amma's eyes. "Please, sir . . ." But her plea is ignored, the man already moving on to Alia, who stands trembling beside her older sister.

Belatedly, I realize Ivan is still staring at me. But he's no longer smiling. My legs tense, prepared to run. "Well? Into the cart with you."

I glance at Amma, panicked. I hadn't even considered the possibility I might have to go without her. "Sir," I plead. "She's my best friend. Please, let her come." Out of the corner of my eye, I see the other man give Alia a little shove toward the cart, as she glances over her shoulder.

"I don't care if she's your bleeding mother," Ivan says lightly. "She's staying here. Do you want to stay with her?"

"Go." Amma is blinking away tears.

Even though I feel Ivan's eyes on us, I wrap my arms around my friend, pulling her close. "Look after my sister," she whispers into my hair.

When I don't break our embrace, she gives my shoulder a little push. "Go!"

Numbly, I obey, feeling the eyes of the crowd like a weight. I clamber into the cart and seat myself amid the other favored girls—all young, all pretty, but silent and stunned as we look back at our rejected friends, our sisters. The line is already half dissolved, and those who haven't been chosen drift away into the rising fog. It's only when the square starts to thin out that I see the tax collector, leaning under the grocer's awning, watching the proceedings with his arms crossed. I stare hard at him until he notices, glancing up to meet my eyes. He gives me a short nod, like a stamp on our agreement—he'll come for his time when I'm back. I let out the breath I've been holding, and murmur another prayer to the Sorceress.

Keep my father safe.

And: *May he forgive me.*

The men move through the remaining girls. Thirty-year-old Nora's sent home with a jeer. Little Alia is already in the hay cart. Suddenly, I remember that as a child, I asked my father why there were so many children at Everless. *They work harder for less,* he answered, his voice brittle. *They have no place else to go.*

When the men are finished, about twenty girls sit crammed among the two carts. I've won my place at Everless, but I don't feel favored at all. I feel like Amma has won this game, even if she doesn't know it yet.

But it's too late to turn back. The hay cart moves forward with a jolt. It smells faintly of manure. There are twelve of us inside, packed shoulder to shoulder on bales of hay. I put my arm around Alia—she's crying silently, her eyes fixed on the town receding behind us. On my other side is a woman, Ingrid, from a farm a few miles from ours. She seems determined to remain cheerful, despite the morning's nauseating selection process and the wind that bites at our faces as we trundle along the unpaved road.

"I heard Everless is five hundred years old," she chirps as the village fades behind us. I refuse to turn around and watch it disappear. I'm half afraid that if I do, I'll simply hurtle out of the cart and run home. "Imagine! They must have lesser sorcerers holding up the walls with spells."

They've no need of magic to hold up their walls, because

money serves just as well. But I have no desire to join in the girls' excited speculation, so I turn away instead and feign interest in the low, patchy green curves of the Sempera countryside. When Papa was in better health, he'd borrow a horse from a friend and take me for rides outside the village. *We should know our country*, he'd instruct, and I wonder if he'd planned to flee Crofton someday, if we ever drew the notice of the Gerlings again.

Aside from Ingrid, no one says much. I can feel the others' nervousness as the plains give way to woods, huge old pine trees that tower over us. This forest is owned by the Gerlings, but even they don't hunt here—these woods are frightening, older than the one I roamed yesterday, and much darker.

Alia finally speaks up. "Calla said there's fairies in these woods," she says. Her eyes are wide. Like most in Crofton, she hasn't ventured more than three miles outside its borders, except for the trip her mother made to save her.

"Fairies, indeed!" a girl in front calls out. "They'll lure you in with their beauty, then drink the time from your veins." She's obviously teasing, but there's a note of strain in her voice.

"It's true!" declares another girl, her red hair coiled in a way that can only be deliberate. "Happened to my aunt. She got lost in the woods one day and woke up an old woman."

"Lied about selling time, more likely," someone else mutters.

"Fairies aren't the worst of it." This girl has beautiful dark skin and vivid blue eyes: she was one of the first to be chosen.

"This forest is where the Alchemist roams. He still carries the Sorceress's heart with him in a paper bag."

"No, he ate her heart," Ingrid corrects.

"Well," the other girl says, with a roll of her eyes. "He'll take yours, too, if you wander among the trees. Even the Sorceress won't be able to save you."

Alia squeaks in alarm. "Why? Why does he take hearts?"

"He hates people, so he gives the time in their hearts back to the trees!" the girl starts.

"Stop your nonsense," someone else cuts in. Meanwhile, Alia's lip is trembling, so I lean close.

"Pay them no mind," I whisper. "The myths are only stories. The woods are nothing to fear." I sit up without finishing the thought: I don't know about the Alchemist, but the monsters she'll meet at Everless are more dangerous than any fairies.

Then, the forest abruptly peters out, and we are in Laista, the small, prosperous town surrounding the Everless walls, where no buildings are permitted to be more than a story high. I remember Papa telling me that the Gerlings' ancestors razed the trees and leveled the hills for miles around Everless so that the men who walk the parapets can see anyone who approaches. The sandstone walls come into view, each dotted with dozens of guards. From this distance, they look like figurines.

Instinctively, I slump down in my seat as we creak through Laista's narrow streets toward the gates. When we're close enough, one of the guards at the top of the wall commands us with a shout to stop.

The world is silent, still, frozen except for the beating of my heart. Next to me, Alia's mouth is open, a wisp of hair sticking to her bottom lip. At the top of the wall, the guards are stone-faced, motionless. I have a sense the whole world is coming to an end, collapsing into that single moment.

Then, there's an enormous scraping noise—the foot-thick, iron-studded slabs of wood and metal shuddering into motion— and our cart lurches forward again.

A shadow passes over us, and we are inside.

4

Everless is a thicket of towers and palisades, picture windows paned with frosted glass, and balconies hung with flags of green and gold. An alley of carefully tended trees cuts everything in half, including the estate. At one end, the path is stoppered by the gate, where we enter; though it's not visible from where we sit, I know at the other end is a lake, bounded by Everless's walls and blackened with old ice and shadows.

In spite of myself, I devour the sight—the lawn blanketed in glittering snow, the trees bare and shivering. I loved Everless best in summer, when flowers spilled from their beds and the gardeners recruited servant children to pick the dandelions marring the emerald lawn. But the pale winter light makes the estate even more beautiful, like something carved of silver and crystal.

Once all of us have unloaded and stand, shivering, in the courtyard, an older footman with a drooping face shepherds us into the narrow servants' corridor. I keep my head down, heart beating fast, convinced that at any moment someone will recognize me, but the servants barely glance at us.

We're led through a sloping corridor I don't recognize, and into the labyrinthine network of servants' halls and quarters. A sudden memory hits me: Roan discovered that if you press your ears to these walls, you can sometimes hear nobles talk in the main corridor above. Most of what we heard was tiresome, lived-too-long aristocrats amusing themselves by gossiping about so-and-so's affair or comparing their investments, though we were too young to understand what that meant—centuries bought and sold and traded the way Papa and I played jacks for sweets. But every so often Roan would speak to me through the wall, when he couldn't be down in the servants' corridors to play. Even then his voice, his laugh, made my heart race.

Now, though the halls stream with servants, we pass through in silence. I know everyone must be hard at work, preparing the castle for the Queen's visit and Roan's wedding—that, or Everless has changed, and there is even less tolerance for chatter and laughter.

Soon, we find ourselves in the kitchen, a cavernous space that would hold my entire cottage in Crofton three times over, filled with servants and ringing with shouted conversation, different accents coming together like music. Like Sempera itself, Everless plays host to people with roots in many different lands. After she ascended the throne, the Queen—finding herself leading a battered, vulnerable kingdom—offered a hundred years to every person from elsewhere who was willing to settle in Sempera permanently, but closed the borders to travelers and merchants. People could come in, but nobody could leave.

At one enormous basin, several fresh-faced young servants work to take apart a whole side of beef. I think of Amma and feel a pang. I've watched her strip and dry meat for years—compared to her expert hands, these servants are slow. At this rate, the meat will spoil before they've finished.

When I sidle closer to them, away from the group, thinking of offering to help, one boy practically snarls at me, "Find your own work."

As I move away, I catch a glimpse of the thin white line drawn across his hand. It's a scar from selling time. Are the blood-irons he earns for himself, I wonder, or someone else?

An entire wooden table is occupied by young servants standing in a line, cutting mountains of root vegetables, and at another table, white-coated in flour, servants knead, pound, and cut rolls into shape. Two massive stoves lick flame into the room, and dozens of pots simmer, stew, and spatter, filling the room with scented steam. The smells make my head spin. I haven't eaten anything since the bread I took from the cupboard this morning.

A stunning, tall girl with a mass of curls and wearing Gerling colors enters the kitchen carrying a silver tray, which she sets down on a wooden counter. Immediately, brown-clad kitchen servants fill it with plates of sun-colored pastries, a small bronze kettle, and ornately carved utensils. Waiting, the girl plucks a length of twine from the table, languidly tying her hair back with it.

"Lord Gerling pulled me aside this morning," she says, eyes bright. Her strong arms are crosshatched with freckles. "He wants me to wait on the Queen when she arrives. Lady Verissa agrees."

Another girl snorts. "We all know why that is," she says, not tearing her eyes from the onion she's chopping.

A gray-haired woman in a beautifully embroidered apron cuts through the kitchen, and several servants trot after her, like ducklings after their mother. "Addie," she says to the tall, curly-haired one. "You still serve Lady Gerling, not the Queen," she snaps. The girl—Addie—hurriedly picks up the tray. "Now, off with you."

The older woman looks familiar: her face stirs feelings of warmth and safety, though I can't remember her name. She greets each new Everless girl with a few brisk questions, then directs them to go to one station or another.

When she comes to me, she stops. For a moment, she frowns. Does she recognize me too? But then she blinks, once, twice, and the brief look of uncertainty passes.

"Your name?" she asks.

I consider giving a false name, but then remember Papa's first rule for lying: tell the truth as much as you can. "Jules," I say. It's common enough. "From Crofton."

"Jules," she repeats after me. "Have you been in service before? I need someone who can deliver trays to lords' and ladies' chambers with no fuss. And for Sorceress's sake, I need a girl who won't get nervous and drop her tray."

Behind her, one of the servants blushes all the way to her ears. She seems like the nervous type, definitely the kind to drop her tray.

I shake my head. When her brow creases, I add, "But I'm a fast learner. I don't fluster easily."

I brace myself for more questions. Instead, the woman gives me a final look-over and then nods. "Let's try you out, then, Jules from Crofton." And with an arch of her eyebrows, she turns and sweeps away.

As a child at Everless, I lived with Papa in three rooms off the blacksmith's hut. Like the ladies-in-waiting, the butler, and the underbutlers, we had rooms to ourselves. They were small, but ours to fill with little bits of metal and the smell of smoke.

Now, I realize, we were lucky. The servant women's dormitory is a long hall containing a honeycomb of stacked beds, at least two hundred to my eye. They are pushed so close together that if we lie down in them, we could easily reach out and link hands.

I'm pleased that I was right—no one seems to recognize me, even servants who I remember from the old days. Ten years of hunger and cold have stretched me out, chipped away at any softness in me, so that I doubt anyone would recognize me as the blacksmith's daughter unless Papa were by my side, ten years younger and in his apron. No one has time to study me, and I'm happy to blend into the crop of new servants who have descended on Everless for the wedding. After laying claim to one of the narrow beds and being outfitted with a simple brown kitchen uniform, I hurry back downstairs.

The head cook in the embroidered apron—Lora—speaks in a rapid-fire mix of introduction and instruction. She walks as if she's rolling up and down on invisible ocean waves. Her left leg is severed at the knee—she wears a carved wooden leg and foot, delicately whittled and neatly painted with a red shoe, which is now darkened with vegetable stains. Born in a village to the south, she came to Everless as a girl to save enough time to live longer than her mother's and father's thirty years. Although I can tell she has no great love for the Gerlings, she has done well by serving them.

She's going over the rules surrounding the Queen for the third time—don't speak to her unless spoken to, keep your eyes down, and never touch her for any reason—when she stops suddenly and makes a clucking sound with her tongue.

"You look about to fall over," she says. She plucks a small hard roll, studded with fat bits, and a large apple from a pile on the table. "Go on and eat," she says kindly. "Then take the rest down to the lads in the stables. You can find your way there?"

I nod, trying to resist the pull of memory: the smell of the horses, the wet hay, Roan laughing as he darted between stalls, daring me to catch him, knowing full well I could scarcely catch the end of his velvet cloak as it whipped around corners.

"Good." She pats my cheek.

I wolf down the bread there at the table without bothering to sit. Still, newcomers are being sorted, an endless stream of them, taken off to be seamstresses, washerwomen, and parlor maids in anticipation of the hundreds of guests who will begin arriving for the wedding. The prettiest girls are chosen to be ladies-in-waiting to the nobles. Addie has returned to the kitchen to set them to task.

When I've polished off the apple, I take up the tray and wind my way out of the kitchen. Everything looks both smaller and stranger than I remember it, as if I'm not really walking through Everless but a strange warped dream of it. There. Where I hid behind a reliquary and rolled olive pits into the hall to try and trip up the ancient butler, Girold. There. Where I scratched my initials into the stone with Roan when we were crouched here one afternoon, hiding from Liam after he called me names. Someone has subsequently sanded it down, but I can still make out, very faintly, the ghostly letters.

I touch a hand to them and smile, then quickly jerk away. Fantasy. Those years, those happy memories, have been planed down like the stone has. Now, that's all they are: impressions.

Still, I press my ear to the wall in the servants' corridor for the briefest moment, listening for Roan Gerling's voice.

Rounding a corner, I come across a young boy—nine, maybe—holding another tray, this one silver instead of tin, and laden with meat, pastries, and a porcelain teapot. He's sitting on the steps in the mouth of a staircase off to the left, looking like he's about to cry.

"Are you lost?" I ask without thinking.

The boy jumps, almost upsetting the tray, and then relaxes when he sees who I am. "Lady Sida won't let anyone up to see her but Harlowe," he says breathily. "But Harlowe's now home and pushing for her baby, so I'm to bring this up. But she don't take to boys. Thom says she'll bite my ears off." He shudders, looks down at the floor.

Harlowe, I assume, is Lady Sida's maid. I let my eyes travel up the dark, narrow staircase behind the boy, realizing where it must lead. The nobles have a tradition: the oldest among them lives in the highest place in the castle. Lady Sida has held that position since before I was born. No one knows her exact age, but the children, Gerling and servant alike, whisper that she is over three hundred years old. The thought of her sends my skin rippling into gooseflesh. She's approaching the upper limit of how long blood-iron can sustain a human heart—except for the

Queen, whose extraordinarily long life, it's said, was a gift from the Sorceress before she vanished. When blood-iron spread through the land some five centuries ago, invaders came from all over the world to try to seize what must have seemed, then, like an incredible gift. The Queen, then just a gifted young general, led the Semperan army to victory.

What has Lady Sida seen, in her three centuries? A morbid curiosity seizes me. I crouch in front of the boy. "This one is going to the stables," I say, setting my tray down on the steps. "Trade?"

He blinks. "Aren't you scared?"

Whenever I was sad or afraid as a child, Papa would distract me with a joke or a story until I'd forgotten the fear. I've never had that talent, but I offer the boy my hand. "I'm Jules. What's your name?"

"Hinton." He shakes my hand, looking doubtful.

"Don't be afraid of the old ones; they're harmless," I say, though I am afraid of them, always have been. Few of the Gerling elders appear to be over forty, but many of them are closer to a hundred and forty. You'd never know it by looking—not until you get close enough to see the blue veins pulsing beneath their skin, or the way their thoughts flee them midsentence. And when someone lives for centuries like Lady Sida, it's said they become not quite human. It's a convenient rumor, since none of us will ever know for sure. "But I'll still take the tray up for you, if you'd like."

"Thank you." Relief floods the boy's face. By the time I pick up the tray, he's already disappeared.

I climb the stairs into darkness, willing my hands not to tremble. Lady Sida is a Gerling not by blood, but by marriage— the older servants claimed her mother was a hedge witch and that her husband brought her to Everless to study the secrets of time. As a child, I only ever saw her at a great distance, when she'd come down from her tower on feast days. Lady Sida always demanded strange, intricate, old-fashioned foods: honey wine, candied rose petals, roasted songbirds. And if you displeased her, the rumors went, she could steal a year from your blood with a glance and swallow it whole.

At the top of the stairs is a wooden door carved with an ornate four-pointed star—the symbol for a century, as the moon is for a month and the sun for a year. I lift the brass knocker and drop it against the center of the star.

For a moment, there is silence.

"Enter," calls a voice, so softly I can hardly hear it. I shoulder the door open and step inside, holding the tray before me like a shield.

The room is large and shadowy, lit only by a low fire in the hearth and watery daylight from the window. It's cluttered with velvet armchairs and silk cushions, bookshelves sagging with leather tomes, and a vanity littered with strands of jewels and silver combs. But much of it is covered with a thick layer of dust, as if she hasn't let her servants touch anything for years.

"Bring the tray."

The old woman sits framed by the light of the window, looking out over Everless's snow-covered lawn—she's tall, elegant, but bloodless somehow. Her skin is dull and thin with age, and her hair long, once black and now white as bone. Her eyes are the color of weak and watery tea. She wears a straight-skirt gown of the sort that no one has worn for a hundred years, lace frothing at her wrists and throat, and I wonder if she doesn't know the fashion or has simply stopped caring to follow it.

"You're not Harlowe," she says. Her voice is scratchy, like old wool. But sharp. "What happened to Harlowe?"

"Harlowe's home to give birth, my lady," I say. Cautiously, I approach her, stepping around cushions.

She scrutinizes me without speaking, her hands folded in her lap. Maybe she's spent the entire day just staring out the window. Anger pricks at me. She's lived more years than half of Crofton put together—years paid for by land taxes like the collector bled from my father yesterday—and this is how she spends them? Staring out a window at the frozen lawns of Everless?

"Is that chamomile?" She's eyeing the carafe of tea on the tray. "Harlowe knows I don't drink it. Chamomile is bad luck, you know."

I've no idea. "No, ma'am," I say. "We've brewed it for you especially."

Her jaw moves, as if she's chewing, before she speaks. "What news do you bring?"

"N-news, my lady?"

"Useless girl," she spits, waving her hand as if to bat away a fly. "How long until the Queen arrives?"

"Two days, my lady," I answer, having heard the frantic staff below flutter about the date. One month so the Queen and Lady Gold can make preparations for the wedding, and then Roan will be married on the eve of our spring.

"And the girl? Roan's girl?"

"She'll arrive with the Queen, my lady." *Roan's girl*. My chest tightens at her words. I feel my face heat, and hope Lady Sida won't notice it.

I remind myself that I have no claim on Roan, none at all.

"None of the other children Her Majesty has adopted have lived long enough to take the throne, have they? What makes Roan think this girl will be different?" she mutters, returning her gaze to the window.

I hesitate, unsure if I should ignore her mutterings or respond. It's true that the Queen's adopted before. By historical accounts, one child died of the plague that swept through decades ago. Another in a raid on the palace. Another by drowning. All before I was born. I don't care much for royal lineage, or for anything to do with the palace—Papa always said that history and stories can't buy bread—but I am interested in the hint of accusation behind the elder Gerling's

52

words: that the Queen will never die and never pass on her throne. Feeling brave, I tell her, "But the Queen named Ina Gold her heir, my lady."

Lady Sida narrows her eyes at me, a smile spreading like oil over her features. "I say she eats their hearts to stay young."

Her words hang in the air. I've no real love for the Queen, but the wild accusation still makes my skin itch, like it's anticipating a blow. It smacks of madness, though Lady Sida does not seem mad—she's old, but her voice is firm, her mind intact. She's taunting me. Hinton was right to be afraid. As swiftly as possible, I set the tray down on the stand next to her and wait to be dismissed.

But then she does something that chills me even more.

She produces something glittering from her breast pocket. It takes me a moment to realize that it's a year-coin, almost as wide as my palm and shining gold. A year of life. It takes everything in me to stop myself from seizing it from her withered hand and running back to the cottage. To Papa.

I wonder how far I would get before Ivan caught up.

"Stir this in," she says impatiently. "Hurry, before the tea gets cold."

Hesitantly, I reach out. My hand trembles as I take the coin—the pulse in my own fingers feels as if it's coming from within the coin, all the life this little thing could give me. Give Papa.

All the life it's already cost someone else.

But the coin, so heavy and permanent in my hand, dissolves like honey when I slip it into the cup of tea. Lady Sida purses her weathered lips to the cup and takes a long, leisurely sip. I don't think I imagine the color that flows back into her cheeks.

Not waiting to be dismissed, I curtsy before hurrying from the room, rattled by the image of the old woman's throat moving as the year entered her blood. Now, more than ever, the quickening of my heart at the mention of Roan's name feels like a betrayal—of myself, of Crofton, of Papa. How can I still hold feelings for Roan, who comes from a family who treats a year of life like a cube of sugar? Whose family has destroyed mine, and so many others?

5

By the time I fall into my bottom bunk that night, my limbs are heavy with exhaustion. But whenever I close my eyes, I see Lady Sida's papery face, her strange words keeping me awake. Some are foolish enough to whisper rumors about the Queen, always under their breaths—but I didn't expect the same from a Gerling.

And yet . . . Sida's words don't seem so absurd, now that I'm turning them over in my mind. To think she was gifted life from the Sorceress is more absurd. I never cared much to think about the Queen, not when Papa and I busied ourselves surviving. But—

"Jules," a voice whispers. Alia is hanging over the side of her top bunk a few yards away. Even in the dark, I can see her eyes are wide with fear, though she already looks exhausted from a day in the laundry, where she's been assigned.

"A boy told me that the Alchemist *does* roam this forest," she says. "He said he lived here once. He said—"

But her bunkmate, an older seamstress, hushes her gently.

"Dear, if I tell you the real story, will you stop chattering and let me sleep?" The woman has a hint of mischief in her voice, but not malice. Alia nods. The woman smiles and gives me a knowing glance.

"No one knows where they came from—two children who wandered Sempera together, before blood-iron, never parting and never growing old. The Alchemist turned earth into lead and lead into gold. The Sorceress made flowers bloom in winter."

I smile to myself, thinking of how Amma would grumble if she knew Alia were staying up late to hear fairy tales. It's hard to believe that there was a world before blood-iron. Worse, there's no use in it, while we're trapped with what we have. But listening to the seamstress speak, I find myself missing that world, if it ever existed.

"But the Alchemist—who lived at this estate, like your friend said—grew jealous. So he imprisoned them here and demanded they discover a way to make him immortal as he'd seen the Sorceress do with flowers and trees."

She's a wonderful storyteller, and her tale sweeps me away like a song. Papa and I left our books behind when we were chased from Everless, and he hasn't bothered to hide his contempt for stories since then. *You can't afford to have your head in the clouds*, he told me once, after I'd begged to hear one on my cold cot in Crofton. I never asked again.

"It was deep in his forest estate that the Sorceress, locked in a tiny chamber with only crude tools, wove time into blood, and the Alchemist found a way to bind blood to iron, so that the lord could steal time from his subjects and eat it himself." Others in the room are listening now. Though I can't see it, I can feel it. "For a time, the lord was satisfied. But soon, he saw his eyes growing colorless and his memory slipping. Death crawled into his frame. Full of rage, he demanded they find a way for him to live forever."

Alia sits up, clutching her knees to her chest.

"One day, the Alchemist declared that he'd done the impossible: he'd transformed a solid lump of lead into pure time, he said. All the lord had to do was eat it."

"But the Alchemist was clever," I hear Alia whisper.

"Correct," the seamstress replies, sounding pleased. "The cruel lord was poisoned and died, allowing the Alchemist and the Sorceress to escape. They parted ways, and soon discovered that their magic was so powerful, it seeped into the blood of all the people in Sempera."

"But why did they part ways?" Alia asks.

"The Alchemist hadn't told the Sorceress that the magic they performed to create blood-iron came at a great cost—the Sorceress's immortality. She was furious at his betrayal." The seamstress's voice takes on a ringing, tragic quality.

"Though it took generations for a single dark hair of her head to turn gray, she aged. Unlike the Alchemist, she loved this life and this world, and didn't want to leave it. But eventually, she tamped down her anger and returned to her old friend, seeking her immortality back."

Across the dormitory, another woman with a frail, papery voice begins to speak. "The Alchemist told her: 'In order to make you immortal, I must have your heart for safekeeping.' So she transformed her whole heart into a word she whispered in his ear. His throat moved like he was swallowing it down. Then, he passed her a handful of pebbles and told her to eat them, and she would live forever."

Other girls chime in now with whispered shouts of *liar!* And *thief!* My eyes flutter closed, imagining what a stone would taste like.

"Girls, hush and let me finish," the old seamstress says. "But the Sorceress remembered how the Alchemist had fooled the wealthy lord. Suspecting another betrayal, she decided instead that the Alchemist should be force-fed the little rocks— twelve of them, in all—and then drowned. She did this herself."

Alia gasps.

"But something curious happened," the seamstress says in a theatrical whisper. "The Sorceress saw a silvery shadow rise from the Alchemist's broken body, and dart away across the earth, too fast to chase after. Within the silver, something glowed dark red and pulsing. Too late, the Sorceress realized that the Alchemist had indeed tricked her—he had stolen her heart."

"Could she get it back? Her heart?" Alia asks. But I don't hear the seamstress answer. I'm already falling into a fitful sleep, shadowed by nightmares I can't remember in the morning.

The next day, Lora informs me that I'll be working at a small party of nobles in one of Everless's prettiest follies: an enclosed garden courtyard heated year-round by a fire pit fed by melted blood-iron. Time makes the flame burn bright and long. I try not to retch at the thought.

All day, she's been teaching me and a few other kitchen servants the art of self-effacement: our role, she says, is to make the Gerlings think their meal has simply materialized. My task is to keep their wineglasses full.

From the cellar that feeds up into the walled gardens, I can hear the Gerlings' aristocratic, musical laughter, the chime of tinkling glasses. Friends, relatives, and other noble families linked by time, have flocked to Everless in the weeks before the wedding. Likely they all want to boast they are among the first to mingle with the Queen and her heir. The aristocrats have swollen from their usual thirty—the four Gerlings and their grandparents, great-grandparents, and most favored relatives— to almost two hundred. They fill the dining hall to the brim every evening, dazzling in silk and feathers and jewels. My nerves flutter as I think of walking among them, knowing that Papa meant never to set foot on the estate again.

What if I see Roan? Does he remember the accident—does he blame Papa, or his brother, or me?

Does he remember me at all?

"Now, now, enough with the faces." Lora gives me a nudge as she sails past me holding a massive cake, decorated with spun sugar. "Tonight they'll be too far into their wine to notice if you make a mistake."

"Or they'll just be quicker to anger," I point out. But Lora is already gone, replaced by a butler who orders the servants into the gardens.

I swallow, clutching the carafe of wine in my hands so hard I fear it'll break. I've swept my hair forward to conceal my face—though I am no longer the skinny, knobby-kneed girl of my youth, I'm terrified that Liam will remember me.

And I'm terrified that Roan will not.

The walled garden, small compared to Everless's grand staterooms, flickers with light from torches held aloft in wrought-iron sconces. Smoke drifts toward the stars overhead. Willow trees sway gently in the breeze, and the heady scents of flowers and wine float along with it. It's like I've stepped into spring, though the stars overhead still have a wintry coldness to them. Beyond the wall, I can see Everless flags shuddering in the icy wind—but it's transformed here into a gentle, cool breeze, tamed by the time fire.

In the middle of the garden, the fire—white-hot and as tall as me—snaps within a bronze enclosure, sending waves of warmth through the garden. It's beautiful, but thinking of the wasted time to feed it makes my insides burn with rage. I look quickly away.

Nobles drift through the garden, the women glittering in gowns of velvet and silk, the men tall and imposing and dark- or silver-haired. Rings of gold gleam on dozens of fingers. A trio of musicians fills the garden with treacle-sweet chords.

Instinctively, I look around for Roan. To my dismay, the first Gerling I see is Liam. He's leaning against a vine-covered wall at the opposite end of the garden, talking to his mother, Lady Verissa.

For an instant, I feel as if I've been shrunk down, turned into a child again. Liam was always on the fringes of our little band of friends, a silent and watchful contrast to outgoing Roan. He'd sometimes show up in the doorway, quiet as a shadow, and watch us play. I was wary of him even then, of his stillness and his eyes so dark they seemed to swallow light, but Roan idolized him.

It makes my teeth grind, now, to think of the kindness Roan showed him—the kindness that Liam betrayed. But to betray someone, you must first care for them. I doubt Liam Gerling knows that feeling at all.

Certainly not from his cold mother, Lady Verissa. She must be in her fifties or sixties, though she looks thirty, radiant in an emerald satin gown that leaves her arms bare. She's beautiful in an unnerving way, with glass-sharp cheekbones and deep blue-violet eyes.

I give them a wide berth as I begin to make my rounds.

The level of wine in my carafe quickly falls—another fine way to spend so many centuries, by drinking it away, though I suppose with so much time to waste, what's the difference?—and I'm about to return to the kitchen when a woman snaps her fingers at me.

"You—come here."

I turn, keeping my eyes half-lowered. An unfamiliar tanned noblewoman whose pendant bears the Renaldi crest—a dancing bear—is staring at me, expectantly holding up her wineglass. She's only a few feet from Liam and Verissa.

I know refusing to pour for her will only draw attention, so I hurry to her side, hoping my servant's cap will conceal my face, and that darkness and the influence of time will do the rest. And suddenly Lady Verissa's voice reaches me, although she's obviously doing her best to be quiet, and I freeze.

"Lord Schuyler's daughter is here," Verissa is saying. "Meet with her."

"You don't know her name, but you know she would be a good wife?" Liam's voice is scathing.

"It scarcely matters—" She catches herself, then speaks more evenly. "You can't inherit Everless without marrying."

"That's enough, you fool. Can't you tell when a glass is

62

full?" the Renaldi woman snaps, and I step quickly away from her. She spins and strides off, dropping something small and gleaming into her wine as she goes.

Still, I linger in the shadows, curious despite myself to hear the rest of Lady Verissa and Liam's conversation. It gives me pleasure to imagine Liam forced to do something he dislikes, although I feel sorry for the poor girl who will have to marry him.

"Let Roan inherit. He'll enjoy it more than I will." His voice makes a shiver race along the back of my neck. With my eyes lowered, I can't see Liam's face, but I can imagine his glare.

Lady Verissa fidgets. "You know as well as I do that Roan—"

Her words are drowned out when a drunken cheer goes up from the partygoers. Automatically, I look for its source—and almost gasp. I've seen Roan Gerling a handful of times in the past few years, when he made his visits to Crofton. But I only ever saw him from a distance, watching from the shelter of a stall while he made the rounds on his horse.

This is different. Standing at the gates of the garden with his father, Lord Nicholas, Roan is just a few yards away. He's dressed in an elegant black suit, a golden cravat encircling his throat. His blue eyes shine in the firelight like pieces of summer sky.

I forget everything at the sight of him—the fact that his family is the cause of our ruin and poverty, the fact that he's

63

engaged to be married to a girl whose beauty, some say, is proof sorcery still exists. For an instant, there's nowhere I'd rather be than in this garden, on this night, seeing Roan smile.

The next moment, a cry of distress cuts through the buzz of conversation. A red-faced nobleman has another servant girl by the wrist. Bea, who I recognize from the kitchen earlier. There's a spreading wine stain on his blue doublet, and a carafe of wine in her shaking hand.

"I—I'm sorry," she stammers.

"Stupid girl," he growls at her. "I'll bleed you a month, and maybe then you'll mind your hands." His words are slurred, his eyes bulging with rage. He yanks a small knife from his belt. Time seems to melt, to slow like an icicle unwinding in the sun.

And then, in the next heartbeat, Roan is there behind him, reaching out to grip his shoulder and at the same time gently detaching the knife. "Lord Baldwin," he says with a low laugh. "No need to scare the poor thing. It's a hideous shirt, anyway. You should be thanking her for doing you a favor."

Everyone laughs. The man blinks and it's as if a spell has been broken: he releases Bea, who throws a thankful glance at Roan. He takes the carafe from her, and she slips back into the crowd.

"There." Roan claps Baldwin on the back and pours from the carafe himself. "Wine fixes most ills, doesn't it? Drink with me, friend."

Unconsciously, I've moved closer to them, drawn by Roan's

voice, his smile, his kindness, the way a bare, hard bulb underground is drawn toward the sun in spring.

And then, Roan's eyes meet mine. I am breathless, paralyzed, bound in his gaze. He raises a glass.

He winks at me.

Then he tosses back the glass of wine to a roar of approval. Only Liam, I notice, still glowers in the corner.

As the music resumes and people begin to dance, Roan is swept up into the crowd. My heart is pounding. Fear reaches through me too, like the dark and twisting smoke of the fire.

Roan knew me.

I'm sure of it.

6

That night, I finally have the chance to write two letters, one to Amma, and one to my father. Then, on the day the Queen and her company are to arrive, in the fifteen minutes I have to eat my hard roll and cheese, I run down to the stables, hoping to catch one of the couriers who rides daily into the villages.

I've written Amma the truth, if only a sliver of it—that Lora seems to favor me, although she has a funny way of showing it: she runs me from morning until night, so that by the time I reach my cot I can barely unplait my hair before I'm asleep.

I don't tell her that new blood-iron clinks in my purse, which I never take off my belt; that Ivan leers and lingers when he hands them over at the end of every day. I withstand it along with the others, thankful it's not Liam who's distributing wages. I always wonder, briefly, what poor man or woman the Gerlings have drawn them from, remembering the line of people waiting to bleed themselves of hours, days, years, and how it snaked through the market.

I stayed up for hours, huddled over a candle in my bunk, trying to find the right words for all the things I need to tell Papa.

I settled on *I'm sorry*. It doesn't come close, though I don't regret what I've done. I've been here two days and have already earned four weeks, which I would have sent with the letter if not for thieves on the road. If anyone has recognized me, they've left me in peace. A single thought cuts through everything: Soon I will have enough to pay the rent we owe, and then spring will be here, and better hunting. When the month is out, I'll be back in Crofton, with enough blood-iron to restore what the collector already took from Papa.

I count the coins in my head. It will be only a fraction of what they've taken from us; from Crofton. But I swallow my anger, let it dissolve in me like a blood-iron in tea. For Papa.

For now.

In the stables, a broad-backed boy shoes the courier's horse. Leather bags stuffed with letters are looped to its saddle. Hearing me approach, the boy turns.

Without thinking, I cry out. "Tam!"

Too late, I realize I've given myself away. But I don't care. My old friend is the son of two Everless guards, but as a child he and I both wanted to be blacksmiths like Papa. He skulked around the forge until Papa invited him in, and we spent hours there together, our feet swinging from Papa's workbench as we watched him work the glowing iron.

He squints at me, trying to puzzle out who I am. I pull off my cap.

"It's me, Jules." When he still looks confused, I smile and point to my front teeth. "See? Told you they'd grow back." For a full four months he called me Gofer, after both of my front teeth fell out at the same time.

His face changes. When he smiles, it's like a lantern goes on beneath his skin. As he puts his arms around me, I'm enveloped in the familiar scent of metal and smoke.

"You're working the new forge." I pull back to look at him. He's massive, a foot taller than me now, but his face is the same, handsome and earnest. "I don't believe it—it's been so long!" The words bubble out of me and I find myself laughing. "How are you? Are you in charge now? Are Etta and Merril still here too?"

But Tam smiles sadly and makes a strange gesture, touching the fingers of one hand in front of his lips and then drawing his hand away. He shakes his head and repeats the gesture, and I understand: he cannot speak.

My joy dissolves in an instant. "What happened?" I blurt out, but he can't answer. We stare at each other, lost, and I feel something unraveling in me. Images flash through my eyes of Tam and Roan in one of their playacted fights, chasing each other with wooden swords all over Everless.

Tam reaches out and squeezes my shoulder. I understand he's trying to say *it's good to see you*. But even though he smiles, his eyes are full of emotion, his lips shut tight.

"I'll come back," I say lamely. Suddenly my heart is beating in my chest like a moth against a lit windowpane.

He squeezes my shoulder again and then, with a smile, takes my letters. I'd almost forgotten them. He turns his broad back to me and without another word, I retreat to the kitchen.

What happened, I wonder, to my old friend?

In the kitchen, a line of servants covered in flour knead dough furiously, as if the Queen herself were watching. I'm on my way to join them when Lora catches my arm.

"I need you to hurry down to the root cellar," she says. "Fetch me as many onions as you can carry in a basket."

I stare at her. I've already filled the pantry here with coils of onions and thick ropes of garlic, more than she could possibly need. I nod, but linger.

"There's a boy in the stables who doesn't speak," I say, careful to keep my voice casual. "What happened to him?"

"Oh. Tam." Lora's smile slips from her face as she turns out a round of dough and begins whacking it, which is how I know I've misstepped—it's only when she's upset that she seizes work herself, rather than ordering one of us to do it. "Poor boy.

He . . ." She trails off, suddenly looking much older. "He insulted the young captain and lost his tongue for it. He'll do no such thing again."

A chill shoots down my spine as I think of Ivan's cold eyes, the steel of his blade. I knew he was cruel, but this is beyond anything I imagined, and I feel a rush of hatred for him.

Lora glares at the dough as though it's Ivan. "Now mind your own business," she tells me, in the sharpest tone I've heard her use, "and your business will mind you."

Before I can beg her for more information, the boy who was so afraid to bring the dinner tray to Lady Sida careens into the kitchen, dodging cooks, and skids to a halt before us.

"Hinton Carstairs," Lora says sternly. "Slow down."

"A messenger just came for Lord Gerling." He pants, red-faced. "The Queen's company will be here soon!" He's practically squeaking now. "The Queen is coming!"

One of the boys drops a rolling pin, while a girl clutches her chest with a floured hand, gasping. Even though I usually feel little for the Queen, my skin tingles at the thought of seeing the woman who led Sempera to victory against conquest and has ruled for hundreds of years since—a woman who's said to be blessed by the Sorceress herself, even to have walked by her side.

Lady Sida's words curdle my thoughts: *I say she eats their hearts to stay young.*

I shiver. Ridiculous.

"Yes, yes, we know the Queen is coming," Lora mutters, shooting a reprimanding look at the flustered kitchen staff. Then she takes Hinton's shoulder. "How long?"

"An hour," Hinton says, still breathing hard. "Maybe less."

Around us, the kitchen erupts into chatter. But Lora scowls deeply. She releases Hinton and turns to me.

"Root cellar," she says. "Now."

"But . . ." I begin.

"Do it," she snaps, and I'm not sorry to have an excuse to leave the kitchen: there's a new, frenetic energy in the air that makes me uneasy.

The cool air on my face as I descend into the cellars is a relief after the sweltering kitchen, but the darkness and closeness of these subterranean halls puts me on edge. Or maybe it's just that they're deserted, when I've become accustomed to the press of servants around me all day and night. I take a torch from the wall and hold it above me for light.

I turn into the root cellar and move past the barrels of apples with their faint, sour smell. There's something where it shouldn't be, something new—a dark mass in the corner. I step forward and the weak, flickering light reveals the figure of a man huddled on the dirt floor, shivering in an old cloak. Even before my eyes adjust, I know him.

"Papa." My voice comes out as a whisper as he staggers to his feet, gripping a shelf for support. I rush to him and tuck an arm around his waist, holding him upright. He looks terrible—

71

pale and gaunt, his face smeared with dirt and his eyes hollow. I can feel his ribs beneath his cloak. "How— Why— What on earth are you doing here?"

He laughs, the sound a gentle rumble in his chest, and instantly begins coughing. "I had to see you."

"You shouldn't be at Everless, Papa." He is thin, so thin.

"That didn't stop you," he says. In spite of its weakness, his voice is still teasing. My smile is fleeting and tight— desperate.

"I was a child then. No one knows my face. How could you— Who knows what will happen if a Gerling sees you? You said—"

"No one will see me," he says, and even his words carry the exhaustion of his journey. "I convinced a wheat farmer to let me hide in his cart. I won't be here long."

"You could have sent me a message, Papa. I'd have come home straightaway." The thought of him trudging along the side of the road for the entire day, stooped with exhaustion, makes me sick with guilt.

He's smiling, but there's an expression behind his eyes I don't understand. "I couldn't wait for a messenger, or trust one." He brings a hand to my face. His fingers are very cold. "Jules. My practical girl. I'm telling you again: you must come home."

"Papa, it's all right," I say numbly. Already my mind is buzzing with plans to get him back to the village. I can rent a cart with the blood-iron in my purse. Lora knew who Papa was—so she'll know what a risk he's taking being here. I can't ask her to help, but perhaps I can pay Hinton to take him, or Tam. "Just a few weeks more and we won't need to worry about paying our rent for months. Don't you see? It's all going to be fine. No one knows me."

It's the worst possible time to remember Roan's wink, but I can't fight it as the memory warms my chest. I don't want to.

"No." Papa's voice is low, urgent. "This place is dangerous for you." For an instant, I'm seven years old again, clutching his hand as he drags me from Everless, the smoke still clinging to our clothes. "The Queen will arrive soon."

"We need the money," I say firmly, suddenly angry at him, at his stubbornness. I'm not seven years old; he has no right to tell me what to do.

"I'll find the money." He takes my hands and gathers them in his own. His palms are cold, his fingers hard as bone. The torchlight deepens the lines in his face and the bruise-like shadows beneath his eyes. "Please. Leave this place."

"I can't; they'll notice if I've gone," I say, not sure if it's another lie. Guilt interlaces with the anger, but I push it down. He's protected me for seventeen years—now I'm going to protect him, no matter how painful it is. "The Queen's company will be here any minute," I say. "The countryside will be crawling with guards and nobles come to watch her approach. You must leave now, before they arrive."

"So must you, Jules." His hands grip my shoulders and his eyes bore into mine. "You can't let the Queen near you. Don't let her see you. She'll know you. It's not safe."

"The Queen?" I stare at him. "Don't you mean Liam, Papa?"

He doesn't seem to hear me. "She's a thief. And very dangerous." His words come out in a rush, he's almost breathless, and only when I pick up the torch do I see how bright his eyes are, with fever or something even worse. "I'll explain on the way. But we must leave—"

"Papa, no," I interrupt. "If I don't show up to my kitchen duties, the punishment will be severe."

He continues to tug at my hand, though weakly. Questions and fears are piling on me, crushing me with their weight—my father is going mad.

"Wait here," I say. "I'll find someone to escort you home." And then, because I see him intend to argue, I add: "I'll come home tomorrow, after I speak to Lora."

Papa's brow creases. "If you swear it."

I open my mouth to make the promise, but something makes it stick in my throat.

Never swear unless you mean it, or by swearing send the Alchemist for your soul. An old singsong warning we used to say as children.

I just hope it's not true. Because the truth is that I can't leave Everless tomorrow. Papa looks half in the grave; more than ever, he needs to replenish his time. Worse—there's a part of me, small but undeniable, that wants to see if Roan will smile at me again.

"I swear." The lie twists my stomach. "I love you."

He leans forward and kisses me on the forehead, wrapping his arms around me. For a moment I lean against him, breathing in the metal-and-straw smell of home. "I love you," he murmurs into my hair. "Always remember that."

"I'll see you tomorrow, I promise," I say. Lying feels like trying to hold an eel in my stomach: the truth wants to wriggle its way out.

I'm used to the feeling by now.

7

Back in the kitchen, I look around for Lora and find her across the room, scraping scales off a fish with a long knife. She meets my eyes and looks hurriedly back down, her brow wrinkled with worry. I will have to thank her for leading me to Papa.

But first I need to get Papa out. I search the room until I see Hinton, crouched in a corner playing a game of sticks while a pot of soup bubbles unattended behind him.

When he sees me hurrying toward him, he sweeps the sticks into a pile and scuttles in front of them, looking guilty. But I hardly notice, my hands already moving to pull coins from the purse on my belt. I wish I had time to think, to come up with a better plan. But once the Queen comes within sight of Everless, the gates will close and guards will be posted on the palisades, searching every carriage that goes in and out. I won't be able to get Papa out after that.

I grab a small wooden bowl and ladle soup into it. Hinton watches me, wide-eyed, as I pull three large copper week-coins from my belt and drop them into the steaming soup.

"You can't take that soup. That's for—"

"I know," I say, dropping to my knees in front of him. He eyes me warily, so I open my purse and hold it out toward him. Another week-coin, newly minted, shines out at us. His eyes widen, and briefly I remember being twelve: how a day seemed like a gift, a week as good as forever.

"I need a favor," I say. "Before the Queen arrives. Can you help me?"

He hesitates. But the coin is too tempting to pass up. "I'll try."

"Can you find your way to the root cellar?" A nod. "Take this bowl. You'll find a man waiting there. Make sure he drinks this. He's my—my father." I stumble over the words—I'm so used to guarding my secrets from everyone—but that doesn't matter now. "He needs to leave Everless, but he's sick. He can't get out on his own."

"Why does he need to leave?" Hinton asks warily.

"It's a long story," I say. "There's some bad blood between him and . . . Captain Ivan." I don't want to say Liam's name and inspire questions that I can't answer.

It's the right thing to say. Hinton nods in understanding—

he's as afraid of Ivan as everyone else. "What do you want me to do?"

"Take him out of here," I say. "Now. To Crofton, if you can. Do you know where that is?" He nods, and I press the coin into his hand. I smile at him, hoping the strain doesn't show in my face. If this wasn't real, I could laugh at the idea of entrusting my father's life to a nine-year-old boy. But I'm desperate.

He turns the coin over, then brings it to his teeth, gnawing thoughtfully on it. "There's a shipment of leather going to Crofton tonight. I'll get the stableboys to hide him in the carriage."

We're both startled by the deep, clear peal of a bell. The bustling kitchen falls silent as the walls hum around us, vibrating with the richness of the sound. For a fleeting moment, I forget my fear, temporarily entranced. As a child, I'd heard many of Everless's bells—there are bells for weddings and deaths, New Year's and royal proclamations. I've never before heard the bell of the Crown, reserved solely for the Queen. It means that we are to assemble for Her Majesty's arrival.

It also means I am running out of time.

"We can't wait," I tell him.

"I'll go now," Hinton says, lifting his chin. "Out the south gate."

"Be careful." I can barely get the words out, my heart is pounding so hard.

Again the bell sounds, now joined by another, higher note, and another and another, until all twelve bells sing through Everless. Of all the bells I remember from my childhood at Everless, this song is the deepest and most beautiful.

I step into the hall, joining the stream of servants flowing toward the gate. Girls pick up their skirts and run, and even the older maids and sweepers hurry along with the tide. Their chatter echoes through the halls over the clanging of the bells. The clamor reaches me as though through a glass wall. My fear for my father buzzes in my ears, clouding my vision.

But I try my best to push the fear to the back of my mind. My father is strong to his core. He came all this way, didn't he? And if the wind is at his back and luck is on his side, he'll be home by nightfall.

As quickly as possible, I join a knot of servant girls in a corner in the main hall. Lora moves among them, rubbing away flour from faces and straightening dresses.

"Jules," she says tightly, when she sees me. "We've been waiting."

I duck my head. "I'm sorry, ma'am."

Lora lifts a hand to my hair, where a few strands have escaped the knot at the back of my head to fly around my face. She tucks them behind my ears, clucking her tongue in disapproval when they just spring out again.

"No help for it," she mutters, then raises her voice. "Outside, girls, and be quick."

Out on the lawn, hundreds of servants are assembling to line the path that leads from Everless's gates to the entrance hall, a small army dressed in Gerling green and gold. I catch sight of Alia amid a cluster of other servant children, standing on her tiptoes to see the path. Guards pace the path at intervals—Ivan at the front—hands resting on jeweled sword hilts. It's the biggest gathering of people I've ever seen, and it makes me feel very small.

How much time, I think, must there be among us? Centuries and centuries. Ten thousand years or more. And yet every single Gerling has as much as ten of the rest of us.

They funnel out together, the Gerlings, flowing like a beautiful liquid wealth, like molten iron, out of the front doors of Everless. Lord Gerling is flanked by his wife and sons. Behind the four of them are arrayed a dozen relatives, resplendent in gowns of silk and velvet. I shiver as I recognize the woman standing behind Lady Verissa; the duchess, Lady Corinne, hardly looks older than her daughter, though she must be sixty at least. I watch her as she slips something from her own purse into her mouth.

Anger rises in me as I imagine an hour melt on her tongue. I glance up at the tower window where I know Lady Sida must be sitting, watching the proceedings with those strange pale eyes. But I find myself wishing I could see her expression, eavesdrop on her gossip when she sees the Queen.

Liam stands a little apart from his family, eyes half-closed as though the festivities bore him. A familiar mixture of fear and anger sweeps through me as I remember seeing him force his own brother into a roaring fire. How twisted he must be, this boy who has everything, to let two innocent lives be ruined just to disguise his own cruelty.

But Roan.

Roan.

The old folk in the village say the Gerlings have ancient blood in their veins—the blood of the mad lord who imprisoned the Sorceress and the Alchemist so many centuries ago, whose greed forced them to bind time to blood and doomed us all to our lives of toil. They certainly have enough blood-iron for it to be true. It's easy to believe the Gerlings are evil to their core, that there's something in their blood that makes them that way. But looking at Roan—his dusk-blue eyes, his time-stopping smile—I see nothing that approaches evil.

He's offered his arm gallantly to his grandmother with the vacant gaze. He wears an immaculate deep-gold waistcoat, but his hair stands up in every direction as usual. I think of the argument he must have had with his mother over that hair— the same argument I overheard so many times as a child—and despite everything, I have to suppress a smile. I watch as he elbows Liam in some secret joke, and wonder how he can be so forgiving of the brother who once tried to push him into a roaring fire.

Foolish, I chide myself. Yes, Roan is beautiful and charming.

He will be beautiful when I'm an old woman, if I live long enough to age. He'll be charming long after I'm dead.

The gates creak into motion, and a reverential murmur goes up from the assembled servants. I tear my gaze from Roan to watch the Queen's company arrive.

Gleaming carriages roll in one by one. There are five of them in all, pulled by proud white horses. A handful of guards walk alongside them, their swords glinting in the afternoon sun. My pulse speeds up as the leading carriage draws close enough for me to see the woman sitting inside.

At first, the Great Queen is just a pale spot on a field of scarlet. Then, she comes closer. Like those next to me, I cannot help but suck in a breath. She is tall, strong, her face unlined, though I know she's looked like this since well before my father was born—before his father, too, and his. A small smile lifts her mouth as she looks out over the crowd and waves, and I feel the completely inappropriate desire to laugh or clap or both.

Next to me, Ingrid leans over. "I heard she was beautiful, but this—" She pauses. "I never expected this."

"My mother says a witch tends her," Bea chimes in. She's dressed for the occasion as much as we servants can, wearing a blue shawl over her kitchen dress that sets off her brown skin beautifully. The scent of lavender drifts from her clothes.

I wish Lora were here, to tell them all to hush. If Ivan hears us chatting, who knows what example he'll make of us.

Another carriage rolls along behind hers, smaller but no less grand. When it passes, I look for the first time at Roan's betrothed, Ina Gold. She wears her dark hair short; it skims her earlobes and frames her heart-shaped face. She's so lovely she practically glows. Her perfect smile is aimed directly at Roan, and her face and hands are pressed eagerly against the carriage window as if she's waiting for the glass to vanish so she can run to him. My heart contracts when I see that he's smiling back. I avert my eyes, back to the Queen's carriage, and notice the deep grooves in the wood—as if it had been assailed with arrows. Strange.

The carriages bearing the Queen and Lady Gold, and several more behind them, pull to a halt. As the Queen descends down a narrow set of pearled steps, scarlet robes cascading around her, the Gerlings kneel and bow. The servants follow, all of us sinking to the grass. The dew dampens my skirts.

After a long moment, Lord Gerling rises, signaling for the rest of us to stand. "Your Majesty," he rumbles. "What an extraordinary honor to receive you at our home."

The Queen nods curtly, scanning Lord Gerling before looking away. Even from a distance, I see him flinch under her gaze. "Thank you, Nicholas."

Her voice sounds remote, like she's speaking from down a long, dark tunnel. She's beautiful, otherworldly, elegant and radiating power. The red waterfall of her cape is held up by a dark-haired lady-in-waiting. As the Queen surveys Everless,

Papa's strange words—*Don't let her see you*—echo through my head.

What on earth could he have meant by it?

Where is he now?

Stepping forward, Roan takes Lady Gold's hand and kisses it—she throws her head back and laughs. The noise fills the air, clear and crisp as the peal of a bell.

"Jules," Bea says too loudly. "You're staring."

I start and tear my eyes away, face filling with red. Instead of Roan and Lady Gold, I watch as a stream of men and women emerge from the carriage that followed Lady Gold's. The royal entourage, I realize, dressed in the Queen's colors—the men in waistcoats and the women in long-sleeved dresses and caps, everything the dark red-purple of wine. There are far fewer than I'd expect—and something seems strange about them. Their expressions as they disembark range from wariness to relief. None is smiling. One woman clutches a mismatching linen shawl, flecked with red, around her; her dress beneath it hangs at an odd angle, as if torn. Behind her, a man is limping, his red doublet stained brown at the shoulder.

Then I snap to attention as Lady Verissa gestures with a casual flick of her hand—our cue to shuffle forward.

Ivan moves among us, positioning servants into a kind of phalanx. The royal servants in their burgundy go at the front, and take the most precious of the Queen's things: vases of blown glass, huge leather books with pages edged in gold, bottles of liquor and perfume. Ivan takes Addie greedily by the wrist and brings her to the front. On top of her head, her hair is knotted in the shape of a rose about to bloom. A few other Everless servants step up too, filling the gaps in the royal procession. I exchange a glance with Ingrid; she looks just as confused at the strangely small group.

"Look," she whispers. "They didn't bring enough people to carry her things."

Once the entourage is in place, Ivan barks at the rest of us, "Line up!" and we hurry to obey. I find myself shoved forward, ending up just behind the royal servants, a velvet hatbox pressed into my hands. Around me, other servants take up leather cases and dresses wrapped in tissue, oil paintings draped in cloth, even chairs and cushions, almost too big to carry. *Is the Queen visiting or moving in?* I think spitefully.

Eventually, we flow like ants toward the entrance, five abreast, a small army meant only to serve and serve and serve. What are these things worth, that we carry? How many years are in our arms right now?

Thinking of Papa, I have the sudden urge to dash this hatbox against the floor. But if I did, I'd be dead within the second, based on the look in Ivan's hawkish eyes.

The Queen pauses just inside the door, the Gerlings by her side, to watch the procession of servants with narrowed eyes. "I assume I'll have an escort to my rooms?" she asks, her voice carrying throughout the hall.

Immediately, Ivan calls us to a halt from the head of the column. I stop along with the rest, my skin prickling. We're too disciplined to make a sound, but I can feel the simultaneous thrill and unease ripple through the group of servants. Though she's a few heads away, I swear I catch the mint and lemon scent of Addie's hair.

Lady Verissa looks discomfited, but after a moment she nods. "Of course, Your Majesty," she says. She nods to Addie, who walks primly to her side, though I see how tightly she's clutching the decorative jewelry box in her hands. "Addie will be serving you. She knows Everless, and the staff. She'll see that you're well cared for."

The Queen gazes at Addie but says nothing. Addie smiles nervously and casts her eyes to the floor.

Lady Verissa then turns to her sons. "Roan, Liam, take Lady Gold to her suite."

As she's speaking, the Queen glides toward a place at the head of our column. A dark-haired handmaiden moves to whisper something in Ina Gold's ear. I notice that the Queen's attendants, the ones in the royal colors, are bowing and curtsying as she passes; a moment later, the Everless servants catch on and begin to do the same. Sweat pricks at my palms. As she passes a few feet from me, something seems to ripple around us, like even the air itself is turning toward her, attentive. I bend automatically into a curtsy, lowering my head. Again, Papa's warning circles in my head. *You can't let the Queen near you*, he said.

Despite his words, something in me longs for her to notice me.

As I lift myself, I flick my eyes upward—and the Queen's eyes, which shine like glass, are staring back at me. A feeling sparks in my chest. Like recognition, though I can't place it.

Then, something goes wrong. I can't tell how it starts—maybe the Queen's foot catches on something—but she's falling, tipping forward, limbs stiff, her tall form unnaturally graceful. Addie lunges out to break her fall, and the Queen collapses against her until Addie is lost in a sea of red, swirling fabric. The box that was in Addie's arms falls and bursts open on the hard floor, scattering jewels everywhere. A deep red stone rolls all the way to the toe of my boot.

It takes only a few seconds for Addie to right herself and the Queen. But instead of pulling away, Addie freezes, her hand still on the Queen's wrist—on her bare, exposed skin. Then, she releases her grip, as suddenly as if she's touched a hearthstone.

The procession goes dead silent. No one breathes as the Queen straightens, fury in her face. The girl's eyes are wide and fearful, the look of someone who's just been struck. She brings her hand—the hand that touched the Queen—to her chest. Her trembling fingers curl over her heart.

Don't touch the Queen. I hadn't paid any mind to Lora's instructions, not thinking we would get close enough for it to matter. Addie must not have not gotten the same warning. No one—not even the royal servants—has moved.

Look away from her, I want to scream. But the girl just stares at the queen of Sempera, as if she's turned to stone.

Anxious to do something, I fall to my knees and start gathering the jewels from the floor. Before long I have a handful of rubies and sapphires and emeralds set in gold, each of which, I think dizzily, must be worth a year or more. I pick up the box. The lid, carved with a design of angular leaves and berries, is hanging lopsidedly, one hinge broken. Then, a feminine pair of hands reaches toward me and plucks the box from my grip. She bends down, her hair falling like a curtain between me and the tableaux of the Queen and Addie. Looking up, I see that it's the dark-haired handmaiden.

"I've got it," she tells me softly, a sympathetic smile on her pretty, narrow face. I let go of the jewels without hesitation, and she places them into the box, which she closes and tucks under her arm. In one graceful movement, she urges me upright and back into the line of Everless girls.

Addie finally moves from her place, trying to fade into the line with me.

"Caro, bring her to me," the Queen says.

The handmaiden—Caro—takes Addie by the arm.

"Your Majesty," Lady Verissa begins, but the Queen silences her with a look. Ivan has moved up to be a few paces behind them. His sneer frightens me the most—like he smells blood. I suppress a shiver. The Queen's gaze is full of fire, and it's trained on Addie.

"What is your name?" the Queen asks.

"Addie, Your Majesty," she says, her voice barely audible.

"Tell me, Addie." The Queen's voice is deep and resonant—like a physical thing, it takes up space in the room. "You would lay hands on your Queen?"

The girl trembles. "Your Majesty—I was just trying to help—"

"Quiet," the Queen snaps. Roan and Liam and Lady Gold have stopped in their tracks to watch from an open doorway. Lady Gold chews on her bottom lip; Roan's hand is on the small of her back. Liam, though, is staring intently at the Queen with narrowed eyes.

"Take her away," the Queen orders. "I don't want to see her on the grounds again."

Addie's mouth drops open, and I feel silent shock run through the servants. "Please!" Her desperation is clear in her voice. "Everless is my home. I didn't mean anything!"

But before she can say anything else, Ivan is there, curling his fingers around her arm. Soon, a phalanx of guards closes in around them, obscuring both from sight.

I hear her weeping as they lead her away. We all do.

"My apologies, Your Majesty," Lady Verissa says to the Queen. Even she looks shaken, her face paler than usual. "We will ensure the girl is appropriately punished."

"She will be banished." The Queen makes no effort to lower her voice. It sweeps over the crowd of servants, turns my heart cold. "Then take a year for every time she protests."

Verissa hesitates a moment, but then says, "It will be done." She gives herself a tiny, almost imperceptible shake and nods at Liam. He breaks from Ina's and Roan's side, drives forward into the gathering evening at our backs. He can be counted on to enforce the harsh terms: banishment.

"But you must be exhausted," Verissa continues, the trill back in her voice. "Let us show you to your rooms."

As we move forward, deeper into the estate, a final, faint sob travels through the corridor. It's cut off by the sound of the Everless gates as they slam shut.

8

That night, still thinking of Addie and my father and longing for home, I fall into dark dreams.

There's a forest, deep and black. Leafless trees rise as high as towers. Their branches are alive, reaching out, writhing . . . tearing at my hair, my clothes.

I run. Fear burns in my throat.

Then: I see a sickening trail of blood behind me, red footprints on the dark earth. They are mine. I am wounded, clumsy. I cannot escape. The world starts to shudder, and all the trees throw up their hands, twisting into a familiar shape—

Eyes. A pair of eyes.

My own eyes fly open, and for a moment in the cold, dark dormitory, I could swear I feel the trembling of the ground beneath me, as if part of my dream has carried over into the real world. Then I make out a shadowy figure above me, and open my mouth to scream. Immediately, a hand clamps down on my mouth.

A hand that smells, very faintly, of garlic.

"Hush!" Lora whispers. "It's just me. Get up, child."

I sit upright in bed, blinking until my eyes adjust. Lora stands by my bunk in her dressing gown. All around me, the other servants on their thin cots snore and shiver and murmur in the deep night, exhausted from cooking, serving, and clearing the first feast for the Queen.

"It's too early," I say, still confused, and half entangled in the strange dream. Who was I running from? I can't remember anymore.

"Jules." Lora grips my arm, fingers digging into my skin. She drops her voice further. "Your father."

The words cut through my sleepiness like her sharpest carving knife. Seizing my dress where it hangs by my bed, I slip, shivering, out of the blankets and pull it on over my shift. I climb out too quickly, almost losing my balance. The woman next to me grumbles in her sleep as Lora catches me, pulls me past the sleeping servants into the hall.

When she's shut the door behind us, I open my mouth, a hundred questions fighting one another on my lips.

That's when I see him—Hinton, who I paid to take my father back to Crofton. He's wearing the same clothes, though they're now torn and stained with mud. He looks like he's been crying, and as I shake off the last vestiges of sleep, I realize Lora does too. Her cheeks are blotchy, her eyes red.

I go cold.

Lora lays a hand on Hinton's shoulder. "Tell her," she says gently, and then, when he hesitates, "Go on. Out with it."

Hinton stares down at his boots, avoiding my eyes.

"Tell me," I command him, but the words sound distant, as if they've been spoken by someone else.

"I found your father in the cellars, like you said." He's shivering. The hair rises along my arms and at the nape of my neck.

"I took him aboveground right when the Queen was about to come in, so no one paid us any attention. But when I went to get a cart and horse, he . . . he . . . I lost him." Hinton looks at me, his eyes pleading. "He didn't wait. I told him to wait. I'm sorry. I wanted to tell you, but the Queen . . ."

"It's all right," I say, wanting him to stop.

"I looked all over for him, then a guard stopped me, started asking questions. When the moon rose, I finally found your father just outside the south entrance, by the lake. He was hurt."

Was. Was. Was. "Hurt—how?" I choke out.

"He'd fallen down," Hinton said softly. "And his hands were stained purple too."

"Purple?" I blink, look between Lora and the boy. "I don't understand."

"Did he smell strange?" Lora asks.

Hinton nods fiercely. "A little. Sour. Like spoiled fruit."

"Mava—the dye from the fruit is used for tracking purposes. The Queen's guard coats their weapons with it, in case someone escapes them. But . . ." She pauses, eyes trained on me. "The Everless vault is painted with mava as well. So that if someone tries to get in, they are marked."

My head spins. "Are you saying he tried to steal something from the Gerling vault? He would never . . ." I trail off, remembering the pale, desperate look in his eyes in the torchlight.

Lora says nothing, though her face is full of pity.

It takes me a moment to realize that Hinton is speaking again. "I tried to get him into the cart, but he wouldn't go."

His words have gotten quieter, and I have to move closer to hear him, though every instinct is screaming at me to flee, to bury myself in my bed and pretend this is just another terrible dream. But Hinton's small voice fixes me to the spot. "He started seeing things. Talking to people who weren't there."

"Jules, how much time did he have left?" Lora's voice is gentle, and I know what she's saying—that Papa was out of time, that he went mad, that he tried to break into the Gerling vault for—for what?

I let her question hang in the air. It takes everything I have not to retch.

Hinton is so pale the circles beneath his eyes look like

bruises. "I tried to get help, but he wouldn't let me. He asked me to sit with him instead, said there was nothing I could do."

"He's stubborn," I say in a whisper. I can hear what Hinton is telling me, sense the huge, dark, terrible truth taking shape in front of me. But I can't give voice to it myself, not yet. I look at him, waiting for him to go on. His full eyes are pleading.

"I sat with him, like he asked. I thought he was sleeping. Then I realized . . ." Tears spill down Hinton's cheeks. "I didn't know what else to do."

Lora's hand tightens on his shoulder. "That's how my ma went too. All out of days and she didn't tell a soul. Went to bed early and sometime in the night her time dried up and her heart quit." She makes the sign of the clock, moving two fingers in a circle over her torso, then moves as if to embrace me, but I step back, shaking like a wounded animal.

"He had time left," I finally manage to say. "He—he had a few weeks left at least."

The both of them just look at me, Hinton's face twisted in sorrow, Lora's heavy with that terrible pity.

"I knew of your father, Jules," Lora says. "Not well, but I know he was a sensible man. Still, if he had a go at the vault . . . And the last month is volatile," she adds roughly. "You know it is. *The mind flows from the vein as well as years.*"

A common saying in Crofton. Too common. When you lose your time, you lose your sense.

I turn away from them, bringing a hand to my mouth, feeling like I might be sick.

"I covered him as best I could. They came by in the leather cart—said they'd see to him. I'll show you, if you like." He hangs his head. "There's robbers on the road who'll pick a man's teeth out of his mouth to sell them later." Hinton sounds absolutely miserable, miserable and guilty, and despite my grief I feel sorry for him: so young, and he's seen so much already. "He had this with him."

The air vanishes from my lungs. Hinton is holding Papa's charcoal drawing of my mother.

My body bucks in a dry heave, but I don't move to take it from Hinton. It can't be true. It can't be. And yet, looking at the two of them, I know that it is.

I turn and run.

By the time my legs give out, the sky has turned from black to a dull sword-metal gray. I find myself on a rocky ledge on the northern side of the Gerlings' lake. In the half-dark, the lake looks like a mirror, reflecting nothing except the mist drifting over its surface, and the estate itself, from afar—like something that might blow away in the wind.

I fall to my knees before the water. Dimly, I realize that I'm still barefoot, that my feet are cut to pieces and so frozen I can't feel them. My mind is full of thick fog, and beyond that yawns a terrible gulf of grief, threatening to swallow me up.

Something glints among the pebbles before me.

Automatically I reach for it, and for a blissful second, thoughts of my father recede as I gape at the glittering thing in the palm of my hand.

It's a coin. Gold and shining and big as a plum, with twelve notches around its edge.

A year of life.

A joyless, half-hysterical laugh rises in my throat. Only a Gerling could drop something so precious. What's a year when you have centuries?

And why couldn't I have found this yesterday, slipped it to Papa, and saved him?

I imagine the faceless Gerling who dropped this coin, who felt his silk pocket lighten and couldn't be bothered to turn back. In his place, I would have scrabbled on my knees in the mud for as long as it took. I would have dug through the stones until my fingers bled. Until they were down to bone.

They would have called me mad, too. But they would have been wrong.

I refuse to believe that Papa is—*was*—mad. He knew something about the Queen. Otherwise he wouldn't have told me to stay away from her—and he *wouldn't* have spent his last day trying to break into the Gerling vault like a thief. But the stains Hinton described, where else could they have come from? I squeeze the coin in my hand so hard, I half expect blood to flow from it. The look in his eyes when we parted—mad, yes. But mad with grief. With goodbye.

The realization sinks into me. My father was saying goodbye, in the cellar.

This time, I do retch.

Don't let her see you, I hear again.

He wouldn't have thrown his life away for nothing. He had to have a reason for it, a reason for telling me what he did.

A reason for dying in the snow, outside Everless's walls.

My sob finally breaks loose as I dash my fist against the rocks, my fingers tight around the coin. I stand up, blind with tears, and throw it as hard as I can away from me. It arcs through the morning, a tiny flash of gold, and vanishes into the dark water.

The fog burns away from my mind in a flash, leaving cold rage beneath.

My father died here. I will find out why—then, I will make those responsible pay for the pain of his loss, in any way I can.

I swear it.

9

There was a man in the village we called the Ghost, always with a shiver and a lowering of eyes. A gambler, he bled almost all the time from both himself and his small son, and beat Edwin Duade at a hand of poison—winning two hundred years, enough to restore his squandered time and more for the both of them. But when he arrived home, the heavy purse of blood-iron on his belt, the boy was crumpled on the floor. His heart had given out midbeat. For all his luck with cards and coins, the Ghost had misjudged—bled off too much of his son's time in chase of fortune.

Now he sleeps in the streets, living every single hour of his ill-gotten two centuries in view of the public, as a kind of penance—a warning—for everyone to see.

I'd written this off as one of Papa's cautionary tales until I saw the Ghost in an alleyway, a path lined with taverns and barkeeps who'd bleed your last hour, crudely, in exchange for drink—bodies appeared in the gutter every week. The wretched man looked up at me as I passed, and his eyes, sunken as the Gerling elders', made me freeze midstep. They had lived too long; combined with his gray skin and skeletal frame, he truly looked like a ghost.

And the grief. The grief in his face threatened to swallow me whole. I never set foot in that alley again.

I feel his eyes follow me now as I stare up at an unfamiliar stone ceiling. For a blissful second after I woke, I didn't remember where I was or why. I was content with the thick mattress beneath my back, rather than my usual pallet on the dirt floor of the cottage.

Then, like a slow spring flood, everything came back—how Lora bandaged my feet and guided me to her own room, begging me to rest. How my sobs echoed in the small space until I collapsed on top of Lora's quilt, which smelled of dough, and sank back into nightmares. How my face and throat are sore from weeping, how my feet burn, and how that pain pales in comparison with the gulf now yawning in my chest.

Lora takes pity on me and lets me stay in her room, where I spend the first day and night after my father's death. Huddled under the blanket, I listen to the cheerful murmuring of the servants on the other side of the wall, the talk of roasting birds, the Queen's herb preferences. My world has been torn apart, while all the Gerling estate knows is the wedding of Roan and the Queen's daughter.

The Queen. When the dormitories clear of chatter and the wind outside settles, I swear I hear her pace the halls above me.

At some point—I'm not sure what time it is—I rise from my bed with the vague desire to walk. Mechanically, I pull on my dressing gown and wander the halls, sticking to the servants' corridors so as not to cross paths with the guards who patrol Everless at night. It feels better to move, to concentrate on the motion and the chill and not on thoughts of Papa.

Lora's bindings on my feet are coming loose, spots of red appearing through the white. I sink down by the wall to rewrap them, but fail. My hands are shaking too hard. The stone walls and floor are freezing through my nightgown. Was Papa this cold when he died?

"—killed? All of them?" a voice whispers. I glance up and down the hallway, but it's dim and empty, lit only by flickering oil lamps.

"—cut down on the road like dogs," the voice comes again. Male and somehow familiar. With a shock, I realize I've slumped down right next to what Roan used to call the whispering wall—the spot where, due to some quirk of the architecture, you can press your ear to the wall in the servants' corridor and whisper to someone in the main hall. Or hear them.

I press my ear to the wall.

I think it's Roan's voice on the other side.

"Yes, but the Queen doesn't want anyone to know," a female voice pleads. "Roan—you should have seen how they came after us. The bleeders would have killed me, killed us all, if it hadn't been for Caro. She went out to speak to the bleeders, and somehow convinced them to let the rest of us go." Her voice cracks. "The Queen sent men after them once we got here, but who knows." She pauses, and I hear a hurried, muffled *goodbye* and *good night*.

Enraptured, I press my ear closer to the wall—but there's silence again. The voice could have only been Ina Gold . . . and she was discussing death. No, killing. My mind turns, wondering what she could have meant by it. Then, I remember the notches in the Queen's carriage and the royal servants' blood-soaked hems. There's only one conclusion to draw: the Queen was attacked on her way to Everless.

How many were killed? What horrors does the Queen bring, along with Papa's death?

Images of death and violence tear through me and, like a flash flood, the memory of my father's death sweeps me away. Renewed, the pain is a physical thing, like something inside has fractured. I pull my knees to my chest and begin to sob, burying my head between my legs to muffle the noise.

"Hello?" someone whispers. Roan.

I should go back to the dormitories—but Roan's hello feels like a rope thrown to a drowning person. Tenuous, and maybe leading nowhere, but I can't help grabbing on.

"Hello," I whisper back, my voice thick with tears.

"Why are you crying?" he asks.

I can't speak about Papa, not even to a disembodied voice in a wall. Not yet. So I tell him another version of the truth: "My heart is broken." Hopefully, Roan will think I'm some lovelorn maid, crying over a suitor left behind in a village. I just want to hear his voice.

"I'm sorry," comes Roan's reply. He pauses, then adds, "I understand."

"You do?" I ask, my voice shaky. "But you're . . ." I stop myself midsentence. Foolish. Privately, I don't understand how Roan—how any Gerling—could want for anything, or understand heartbreak, especially when they are marrying the Queen's daughter.

"No, go on," he urges from the other side. "I'm what?"

"A—A Gerling," I say haltingly. Anyone could tell that, from his accent. It isn't giving myself away to say so. I hope.

He laughs softly. I wish I could lean into the sound, wrap it around myself like a blanket. "Guilty as charged," he says. "But we Gerlings have hearts too, you know."

"Sometimes it doesn't seem that way," I say softly.

Roan sighs, the sound of his breath running down the walls to me like a small waterfall. "I know," he says at length. "It was so much easier, when we were younger. There was no such thing as heartbreak or death, or anything bad then."

No, I think. My heart broke when Liam ran us out of Everless. But I say nothing.

"You sound like a kind girl. Whoever broke your heart is a fool." I close my eyes—if he only knew the truth, he wouldn't say that. "Can I do something to make you feel better?"

A smile tugs automatically at my lips. Roan's voice is like a salve. "Just keep talking," I whisper back to him. "What do you mean, it was so much easier when you were young?" I add the last bit, hungry to know that he hasn't forgotten me.

"Hmm." I can imagine the look on Roan's face right now, a slow, mischievous smile as he rifles through the memories of his wild childhood. Our childhood. "Well, life was all games. I mostly ran around the grounds with the servant children, you know. I didn't—don't—disdain them like my brother and parents."

"My . . . cousin always told me that he used to tease her," I say, choosing my words carefully. "Liam, I mean. He'd call her a witch." I can hear the bitter notes in my own voice.

"I don't doubt it." He sighs. "My parents put an end to us mixing with the servants after the fire."

My heart contracts, suddenly fearful, but I press him. "The fire?"

He pauses. "I think we were playing capture the week-coin—no, fox and snake—when the old forge caught fire."

He says nothing more, but his words snag at my memory. "Fox and snake?" I whisper.

"Oh." He laughs. "A game one of the servant girls invented. One person plays the fox, and the other the snake. And the fox hunts the snake all over."

Goose bumps rise on my arms. The servant girl was me.

Before I can answer, there's a muffled voice on his side, in the distance. "Someone's coming," he whispers, "and it wouldn't do for me to be seen talking to a wall. But I hope your heart mends, and soon."

"I hope so too," I whisper back, though what he says is impossible. "Good night," I add, but it seems he's gone, and then the hall is silent once more. A drop of sweetness mixes into the grief inside me. It's only a drop in a sea, but in that moment, it feels like everything.

10

When I stumble into the kitchen the next morning, wearing a simple black dress Lora has laid out for me, Hinton finds me right away. He has a tray of bread and cheese, a mug of tea. I sit with him at a side table and eat in silence. My senses are blunted—the gossip of the kitchen servants is a dull, distant roar, and Lora's food tastes like ashes in my mouth.

"My father was killed too," Hinton offers after a while. His voice is quiet, his eyes trained on the wood whorl of the tabletop. "His name was Cormer. The ferrier for Lord Liam . . . before."

I draw in my breath, causing Hinton to look at me sideways. I knew Cormer—a compact, steady-handed man with an almost magical ability to soothe any horse, who always had a joke or tale at the ready. Had Liam killed him?

The question—the rage—must show on my face.

"Captain Ivan." Hinton's eyes return to the tabletop, but a hint of anger has entered his voice. "After my father had cared for his team of horses, he lost a chariot race to Lord Wystan, from the east. He didn't like that. So my father paid for it."

A piece of old gossip from Crofton flashes through my mind—a ferrier for the Gerlings who, after losing a race, was tied to the back of a carriage and dragged until he died. I'd never connected it to the man I'd known. For a moment, my grief recedes into the background as I stare at the boy in horror.

I'd always known that life at Everless could be cruel and arbitrary—if you outlasted your usefulness, if you got old or sick or lost a limb, the Gerlings would turn you out in a heartbeat. But this is a darker place than I ever knew as a child. I lean in and wrap my arms around him for a moment. "I'm so sorry."

After a beat, Hinton shakes himself, as if he can fling off the memories. "It was a long time ago. Anyway, I wanted to tell you—just keep busy. It's worse if you let yourself be alone." He holds out his hand to me. The coin I gave him two days ago in exchange for Papa's safe passage gleams in his palm. I see how his hand trembles.

Instead of taking the coin from him, I reach out and fold his small fingers around it. "You've done so much for me," I say, pushing a loose strand of hair behind his ear. And I mean it.

He shakes his head. His eyes—so young, still, after

everything he's lost—bloom with tears. "I'm sorry, Jules," he says, letting his head fall to his chest. I know what he's thinking—*it's my fault*. I recognize my own thoughts on his face.

I clutch him to me. "You did nothing wrong. He'd decided on his course." If I knew anything about my father, it was that. "Nothing you could have said or done would have swayed him from it."

If the blame for his death lies on anyone's shoulders, it's mine. Mine, for not leaving when he begged me to. Mine, for lying and abandoning him, for leaving Crofton in the first place.

Hinton hesitates for a moment, then nods. His tears recede and his face brightens. He's lost his father too, but he's still smiling, kind, struggling to be good.

Watching him weave through the servants' tables, greeting people as he goes, I know I will never be so lighthearted again.

The rest of the day, I lose myself in work: tearing fragrant leaves from spiny stems, salting meat, turning cream to butter. The other servants mostly avoid me. I don't mind—I don't want to talk. I don't want to feel.

When I trudge back toward the dormitory that night, I find a handful of servant girls and one boy clustered around a doorway where the servants' corridor leads into the main hall. I recognize Bea among them, and Alia's mop of hair, and hurry toward the group to see what's the matter. In her drab gray laundry clothes, Alia looks even smaller than I remember. Guilt and worry prickle through my grief. I promised Amma I'd look after her little sister, but I've scarcely given her a thought since before the Queen arrived at Everless.

Bea is just outside the dormitory, holding court in the center of the wide-eyed servants. I stand next to Alia.

"But have they caught the bleeders?" a freckled girl asks her.

Bleeders? I feel Alia shudder beside me. She tugs at my sleeve, and when I bend down, whispers to me: "Highwaymen attacked the Queen on her way here. Bea heard that over twenty of her maids and guards died, Jules."

My stomach turns. So it's true.

"Some of the bleeders were killed in the raid," she tells us. "The rest, not yet. But the Queen sent her soldiers after them, so it's only a matter of time." She wraps her arm around a whimpering girl, holding her close until the girl's shoulders stop shaking.

"I hope the Queen bleeds them for all they're worth," someone mutters darkly.

But I can't stand to hear about more death, not now. As the others' questions start in again, I squeeze Alia's shoulder and turn toward the dormitory, hurrying away with my head down.

There, I find what Hinton tried to give me the other day laid out neatly on my bedspread. The drawing of my mother. I snatch it up—at first intending to bury it in the bottom of my trunk or throw it away with the kitchen scraps, so I don't have to see it. I don't want to remember.

Something stops me. Instead, I sit down on the bed, shrinking back into the shadows so none of the other women can see the tears forming in my eyes. I look down at what's left of my father.

The paper is soft with age, and the smell that drifts off it momentarily stops my heart: I breathe in the straw-and-woodsmoke that lingers on the paper along with the sharp scent of lead. In the image, my mother looks over her shoulder, captured so deftly I wouldn't be surprised if she opened her mouth and laughed.

I put the paper facedown on the bedspread before the ache in my chest gets worse, and stop—because the back side of the drawing isn't blank.

Picking it up again, I angle it toward the candlelight and peer closer. It's covered with text, although the letters are faint with age, as if it's been torn from a very old book. The language itself is ancient too—a dated high Semperan tongue from what I can tell, something that the Queen might have spoken when she was a girl. Though some words and letters are unfamiliar, I can read enough formal, curling script to know that it's a tale about the Sorceress and her enemy, the Alchemist.

I laugh for the first time in days—of course my father would have sacrificed a page in this book for a drawing of my mother. Papa hated anything superstitious.

But stranger still than the square of text is what's scribbled in the margins: handwritten notes in a child's scrawl. The ink is so faded and smudged, and the writing so illegible, that I can only discern snippets.

fox

to the forest

snake

of lead

Fox, forest, snake, lead. Roan's game. The words drag a memory to the surface: curling before a fire in the forge, my father reading to me from a leather book about a fox and a snake who were the best of friends.

I'm not sure whether it's the words or the smell of home on the page that expand painfully in me, pressing against the inside of my ribs.

A small voice sounds at my elbow, making me jump. "What's that—a love letter?" she chirps.

I tense—but it's just Bea. Far from being the trembling girl who spilled wine on the nobleman's doublet. Instead, her whole body seems to smile, her confidence renewed by comforting the other girls. She plops onto the bed next to me.

"Nothing interesting," I say quietly, slipping the drawing underneath my pillow. A question occurs to me. Why would my father have brought his drawing of my mother with him—for luck, the same reason I carried the statue of the Sorceress with me?

"Are you going out for Addie's position?" Bea says. Her

cheer is welcome to the others but grating to me. I shake my head, but she continues. "Lady Verissa's distraught. First Addie, then the Queen's sent away every girl Verissa's tried to put in her place. Put them through some kind of test."

An idea begins to take shape. "What kind of test?"

Bea rolls her eyes. "I've no idea—she doesn't want *provincial* serving girls, I suppose. Verissa sent lots of girls to interview, but they were all rejected flat out after they answered her questions wrong. I think they did it on purpose."

"Why?" I ask, though I already know the answer.

"What happened to Addie, of course. Who wants to be banished? Or killed?" Bea says with a shiver. She turns her head to the side, considering me. "I bet the Queen would like you though, if you wanted it—you're pretty. And not timid. Besides, soon there won't be anyone else left."

She hops up and strides to her own mattress across the room without saying goodbye. Before I can lie down, Ingrid's limp blond hair and prideful face come into view, hanging upside down from the bunk above me. Since our shared carriage ride on the way to Everless, she's taken to offering me unsolicited advice. "That one's too bold," she says.

Bea's suggestion lodges itself into my thoughts. I'll never get close to the Queen in the kitchen; I'd be lucky to get even a whisper of her conversation between glasses of wine.

If I'm to find out anything about what my father wanted in the vault, and what it might have to do with his warnings about the Queen, it would help to be closer to her. A small voice inside me warns that I'm going in the exact opposite direction of Papa's wishes, but can I put aside the questions that have begun to gnaw at my heart? And besides—what do I have to lose, if I've already lost everything?

Turning over this realization, I slip between my blanket and the mattress soundlessly, like a knife into its sheath.

11

After offering me her room after Papa died, Lora gives me no concessions. It seems that she, like Hinton, believes in hard work as an antidote to grief. I try to lose myself—every time the Queen's retinue requests something from the kitchen, I volunteer to deliver it myself, only to find a closed door and the buttress of a steel-faced guard—but no matter how I run myself ragged during the day, trying to please Lora and brooding over the Queen, sleep eludes me for hours at night. The days are a blur, melting one into the next. I can't say what day of the week it is when Lora approaches me in the kitchen, her face tight with concern.

"I've arranged for you to have the afternoon off," she says quietly. When Ingrid, beside me, looks up curiously from her chopping, Lora snaps, "Back to work!"

She pulls me out into the hallway and leans close. "You'll take a cart and horse back to Crofton and—and—collect your father's things from the time lender," she finishes, patting me with a flour-caked hand.

As I make my way down to the stables, I wonder what awaits me at the time lender's—my father had nothing but debts. Will they make me watch them strip the cottage down, tile by tile, plank by plank? Will Duade—if he's recovered from having his own time taken—bleed me in the shop, to account for what my father might have owed? The thought dissolves in my grief like a blood-iron into tea. It takes all the strength I have to put one foot in front of the other.

As Lora promised, the horse and cart are waiting for me in the stables, my old friend Tam at the reins. He gives me a brief, tight hug; maybe he's heard what happened. He grasps my shoulder, steadying me as we climb into the cart, and I lean against his rough wool coat in return, wishing I could absorb some of his strength.

The day is unseasonably warm. The snow has turned to mud around us, and a few birds chirp bravely into the wind—the weak sun glitters against the slush of white and brown. It's almost beautiful.

It's been about a week since I left Crofton, but it seems like years. When we finally go through the broken gate, the low stone wall on either side strikes me as pathetic. It couldn't keep out a cow. In the streets, the town seems shrunken, small and quiet and gray. Distantly, I wonder what our lives would be like, Papa's and mine, if we had never come to this village after fleeing Everless. If we lived in a different world where the Queen had never cut Sempera off from other kingdoms to protect the secrets of blood-iron. Where we could simply walk until we reached the sea, then get on a ship and go—elsewhere. I know there must be an *elsewhere*, somewhere without bleeders or Gerlings or the Queen. But the fantasy, reaching the limits of my knowledge, dissolves into fog.

When we get into town, Tam ties the horse to a post close to the butcher's shop. I consider running to Amma—but I don't have the strength to tell her. Does she already know too?

I wave to Tam, who brushes down the mare. I'm grateful that he's understood, without my having to explain, that I need privacy.

I arrive at the time lender's store and freeze, my hand on the doorknob. The neck button on Lora's black hand-me-down dress suddenly feels too tight. After wages, even after my gift to Hinton, I have more money in my purse than I've had in years, but I'd trade away Everless and everyone in it for the chance to return to the last time I stood in this square. I'd never have left for the marketplace, the waiting cart. I'd let Papa sell a few months, or I'd convince him to let me do it. We would have survived. Just as we had always done.

I steel myself and enter the store—this store I've passed a thousand times, peered into a thousand times, but never been in. It's tight inside, drowning in the smell of copper, the packed-dirt floor spattered with old blood.

Shivering in spite of the heat from the hearth, I walk to the counter with my head high. An older couple, two women with backs curved with too much work and too few years, hunch over a small table in the corner, taking turns cutting each other's palms and letting the blood flow into empty vials. I wonder if they're putting time away for their children. They watch me as I approach—with curiosity and pity. I suppose I still look too young for a place like this.

"My father died four days ago," I tell Edwin Duade, hoping my voice doesn't crack. "I'm here for his things."

His eyes flick up to mine, then back to his ledger. "His full name an' yours."

No words of comfort, no nonsense. I notice the red line drawn across Duade's palm. Another reminder that only a week ago, everything was different, when Liam ordering Duade bled was enough to shake me.

"Pehr Ember." This time, my voice does crack. "And I'm Jules."

Duade disappears into a back room, and a tear—two tears—escape and trickle down my cheek. I wipe them quickly away when he emerges, holding only a letter and a canvas sack as big as my two fists—a sack that, by the sound it makes against the counter, I can tell is full of blood-iron.

"You got more 'an a pint of luck, girl," he says. "His debts have been paid. To the collectors."

I blink in confusion. "But . . . by whom?"

Duade's laugh is unkind. "All been paid good an' square. That's the only thing ought to concern you."

Could Lora have paid? But more important—"Where are the rest of my things?"

He cocks his head at me. "This's all."

I blink. "What do you mean?" I think of our cottage—our home. "There was the cottage. Drawings on the wall." Never enough, but . . . "A broken pocket watch. Did you take those?"

He scoffs again, jerks his hand in the air like I'm a fly he's swatting off. "Those things aren't for you."

"What—" The tears threaten to surge again. I take a deep breath, composing myself. "There must be a mistake. You said his debts were paid, which means his possessions belong to me." I grip the counter. "There was no one else. I was all he had."

Duade sighs. "Rest belongs to the Gerlings, sweet. You say Pehr Ember was your father? Well, I've no record of that. No record of you at all."

The silence rings, broken only by the couple shuffling away, emptied of their years. My voice comes out faint. "No . . . record?"

He nods at the envelope on the counter. "Just this," he says. "Nothing more I can do for you."

As soon as I'm out of sight of the shop, I duck beneath a store's ragged awning and examine the letter. My name is written across the front of the envelope in my father's careful handwriting. My hands shake as I slice it open with one finger and slide out the note inside. The dense wall of writing blurs in my vision; I wipe away the tears to read.

Jules,

I'm off to Everless this morning, to fetch you. I hope you will come home with me and that I will, at this time tomorrow, be dropping this letter unopened into the fire. But Everless is a dangerous place, now more than ever. So I have no choice but to face the possibility that I might not return.

If this is so, and you are reading this, Jules—I wish I could give you more than this letter, my girl. You deserve so much more. But I fear that now, this is all I can offer you.

By this time, you might have begun to suspect the truth—that I am not your father by blood or by law. I've asked Duade if he can pass our things along to you anyway, but I know he will not. The law is the law, as the world is so fond of reminding us. I thought of you as my daughter—you are my daughter—so I have never told anyone otherwise. I ask that you do the same, Jules. Keep our secret. Life will be a little easier with a family name, even one such as mine.

And I shall tell you this when I see you, but in case I

only live long enough to say it once, let me repeat myself here: Stay away from Everless. Stay away from the Queen. I cannot explain myself, not in a letter that can fall into anyone's hands, but you're not safe with Her Majesty there. Please—I know you must have so many questions, Jules, but trust me now.

Before you left for the estate, you said you needed me, but you're wrong. You're strong—brave—kind, and I know that you'll keep going forward when I'm gone. Every day, every hour I've given has been more than worth it. I just wish I could have seen the woman you will become.

My girl—you are my daughter, and I your father, in every way but blood. Never forget that. Keep our secret, and keep safe. I love you.

Papa

I pace the back streets of Crofton like a madwoman, avoiding the main marketplace, though I long to see Amma. Tam can stay a while longer with the cart. It's bitterly cold despite the sun hanging in the cloudless sky, but the thought of ducking into a shop or tavern, acting like nothing is wrong, makes me sick.

Instead, my feet, only half-healed from when I ran barefoot to the lake, slip on the dirty, melting snow. A few people glance my way as they pass, but they avert their eyes, giving me a wide berth. I can tell they fear me in the same way I once feared the Ghost. They must see the same desolate wildness in my face, how grief has torn away my humanity.

My hand clutches Papa's letter. Lines come back to me as if they're refrains of a song: *I am not your father by blood or by law. I am not your father by blood or by law.* And images, as Hinton described them—the stain on my father's hands, his blank stare, drained of time.

His words, so full of meaning, are not the words of a man losing his wits. Though I don't understand it, I can feel a terrible truth lurking in his sentences, curling with the ink.

I feel his hands on my shoulders, their grip tight, shaking me, demanding that I leave—until I realize that they're my own hands, my own fingers digging into flesh. I'm trembling, but it has nothing to do with the cold.

The bag of blood-iron hangs like a lead weight on my hip. Another puzzle. Perhaps Duade was wrong, and Papa had been hoarding this blood-iron, but why didn't he use it to save himself?

Someone calls out to me. "Jules!"

I know the voice. Amma. I turn around.

Amma hurries down the alley toward me, shouldering her way through the people with their heads down and coats pulled up over their cheeks. Her bloodstained butcher's apron is rolled under her arm. She stops two strides away, her other arm outstretched to embrace me, then pulls back. She studies my face.

121

"Jules," she whispers. "What—?" The color drains from her. "Did something happen at Everless?"

I can't speak, but the sympathy in her eyes starts my tears flowing again. For a second, she stares at me, horror-struck. Then she takes my elbow and guides me to a nearby doorway, where we huddle. She puts an arm around me, pulls me into her. My voice is still weak, so I hand her the letter to read.

Her eyes skim over it, filling with tears as they do. "He must have sold his time," she whispers in stunned understanding. "I'm so sorry, Jules."

My voice, raw from crying, cracks when I speak. "It's more than that," I croak. But my next words catch in my throat. How can I explain the truth to Amma—that he spent his last hours traveling to the estate, and then, when I ignored his pleas to come home, he tried to enter the Gerling vault, and I don't know why? That because of it, he died outside Everless's walls with only Hinton, a stranger, by his side?

I fear she'll tell me what Lora did: *The mind flows from the vein as well as years.*

"I need him," I say instead, the words tangled up in a sob.

Amma pulls me to her. Now, closer, I smell the animal blood on her, but it doesn't matter—she's land, and I'm drowning. Sobs rack me again, echoing down the narrow alley, until I'm too exhausted to cry any more. Amma keeps her arms around me, holding me up, as the village gradually grows dark around us.

"What does he mean, about Everless and the Queen?" she says at length.

I wipe my eyes.

"He never liked her, or the Gerlings." *And for good reason— we wouldn't be destitute if not for Liam.* But the letter in my hand weighs heavy, screaming something more. "Still, danger . . . I don't know what he means."

The truth of it tears at me—I don't know, I don't know.

Amma is quiet for a moment. Then: "Jules, maybe you shouldn't go back."

I shudder. "No. I don't have a choice." It's half true. The thought of Everless, its warm kitchen and roaring fires, is a comfort, but the idea of the Gerlings and the Queen inside is poison. *Danger*, in my father's words. Yet if I leave now, I'll never know why.

Amma nudges the bag of blood-iron at my belt. "This looks like a choice to me."

Her words hang in the air before us. Suddenly, the bag of coins feels much heavier as they take on a new meaning—a new future, perhaps. What could I do with the years inside?

"You don't have to go back," Amma says. Her face glows with possibility. "Alia wrote to me that she wants to come home. She hates it there. She's made enough money for us to get by a few months." She pauses, her voice full. I wonder if Alia is still afraid of the Alchemist's spirit chasing her through Everless's halls, or if it's something else. "I was wrong, Jules—

123

Everless isn't worth it. What good are the years, if you have to spend them like that?"

Possibilities float through my mind too, their shine dulled by grief. I could return to Crofton, rent a new cottage, use the money to get a little farm running. I could go back to the schoolhouse and learn a trade. I could travel, try my fortunes in one of the prosperous cities on Sempera's shores, finally see the ocean.

Or—I could return to Everless. Work as hard as I can, all while listening in the halls like Roan and I used to do, and hope that something can lead me to the truth in Papa's letter. After Lady Gold is married, the Queen will retreat to her palace by the sea. If I don't act now, I'll lose my chance.

The cottage would be empty and worthless without Papa. The whole village would be. And I can't imagine traveling anywhere without turning over the question of Papa's last actions. I need to know why he did what he did, and what he meant by warning me away from the Queen. In fact—a chill dances down my spine as I realize I already know the first step. Replace Addie in the Queen's retinue. And if I'm banished too—well, I've survived it before.

"I don't have to go back," I say, my voice a quiet rasp. "But I want to." I detach the bag of blood-irons from my belt, take out a handful to slip in my pocket, and hold out the rest to Amma.

Immediately, her eyes turn hard. "Jules, no."

"I don't need it anymore," I say. "Take it for Alia, if you won't take it for you."

This is what makes her accept the money. I know Amma well enough to know that she's like me—proud, but not too proud to do what is right for her family.

My family is gone. Hers is not.

Amma closes her eyes, letting the tears spill down her cheeks. "Thank you," she breathes, burying her face in the crook of my shoulder. "Thank you, Jules."

I rest my head gently against hers. I wish so badly that this were enough, that I could do as Papa wished. Let the questions buried between the flagstones of Everless stay there, or fly away like a scrap of silk in the wind. I could go on with my life here, with our cottage and garden, the schoolhouse, my friend.

But the mystery of Papa's warning, his stained hands and his death, would drive me mad.

I'll go back. I must.

I have business with the Queen.

12

When Tam and I reach Everless's gates, he drops me by the stables with a brown paper package of hard honey sweets from the baker's.

The dormitories are empty except for one woman in her bed by the far wall wrapped in a blanket and breathing lightly—she must be sick, else Lora would be down here herself, shaking her awake. It takes all my will not to crawl under my thin blanket and shut out the world. The enormity of Papa's secrets are dragging at me, overwhelming me. Short of banging down the Queen's door and demanding an answer, I have no idea what to do. My only choice is to try to pass her silly test, if I even can get an audience with her. If I do, maybe I'll be allowed to serve her.

But this day off from the kitchen is a gift. If I want to learn anything about the Queen before approaching her, I have to start now.

I put on my nicest dress—blue wool, with long sleeves, instead of the brown knee-length dresses we wear in the kitchen. Paired with my servant's cap, I hope it will allow me to pass for a maid. I swipe an apron and dusting rag from the supply closet in the hall and set off toward the library. I know if I'm found there without permission I could be beaten. Or worse.

I tell myself that if I'm lucky, no one will notice me; I try not to think about the fact that I have never been lucky.

When Papa and I lived at Everless, he had permission to use the library—he'd told them he needed to research blacksmithing techniques, and instead snuck me inside at night to read story-books by candlelight. It was one of my favorite rooms—the shelves towering two stories high, the floor of dark, shining wood inlaid with tracings of gold, the blissful quiet punctuated only by turning pages and my whispers of wonder.

It's nearly empty now, the room lit in long rays and longer shadows from the sunset outside the west-facing window. A few nobles sit scattered at the tables and armchairs, reading or writing letters. One large man is dozing in an overstuffed leather armchair. Unlike when I was a girl, the silence holds no promise of stories waiting to be told, no crackle of magic in the air, effervescent as mist in the sun after rain.

But, thankfully, the layout is still familiar. The large, open main space is surrounded by entrances to aisles and nooks, their contents proclaimed by brass plates over the doorways. I scan them, realizing as I do that I have no idea where to start. In our schoolhouse in Crofton, we only ever heard worshipful things about the Queen—her great beauty, her vanquishing of invaders, her wisdom on the throne. Nothing that could explain why Papa would fear her.

I scan the plates—*Popular Fables, The Everless Estate, Economics*—until I see *History* across the library. It seems as good a place to start as any. I skirt the room, trying to look like I have a purpose while still remaining inconspicuous, and slip down the aisle.

Books surround me on both sides, their gilt titles gleaming in the low light. I open a slim book titled *Sempera: Histories* and begin to read halfway down the page.

By the account of a commanding officer of the Royal Navy, it reads, *the Queen of Sempera cut the invaders' throats herself, with a blade that was said to absorb any magic in their blood, gifted to her by the Sorceress. She had her time lender, a darkly hooded woman who walked the battlefield beside her, bleed men where they lay, turning them into blood-iron while the fallen were made to watch—and wait their turn.*

I close the book and hold it to my chest, shivering with cold in spite of the room's heat. Papa never told me much of the invasions and rebellions that took place in the first century of the age of blood-iron, after the Sorceress's and Alchemist's magic first spread across the land. But Amma's adoptive grandfather claimed that one of their ancestors had fought in the Queen's army. I'd walk to Amma's cottage, and we'd sit in front of his chair while the old man told stories of thieves who'd let your blood in the night, of lost limbs and rolling heads, until Amma begged him to stop. The invaders, he said, would have killed everyone in Sempera and carried the blood-iron back across the seas. But instead, the Queen ordered her armies to consume the blood-iron of the fallen and grow mighty.

Still clutching the book, I scan my surroundings for somewhere I can sit and read. But then, I see him: Liam Gerling, sitting at a desk on a balcony over my head, bent over a sheaf of pages.

I'm frozen where I stand, my heart racing. If he just glanced down, he could see me through the polished wood bars of the balcony railing. Slowly, so as not to attract attention, I back away into the shadow of a tall bookcase.

Torn between fleeing and going about my business, I observe him carefully. Even if he doesn't recognize my face, he might notice a maid reading instead of dusting. But he doesn't seem to notice anything at all. His brow is furrowed in concentration and his foot taps impatiently, as if whatever he's reading frustrates him. Every few moments, he'll frown, scratch something into his notebook, then go back to reading.

At the sight of his sharp features—so long an object of my nightmares—anger rises in me, quick as the flames from the kitchen hearth. The memory of our expulsion from Everless comes back to me in scattered images, bursts of sound and heat.

I remember Liam shoving Roan toward the hearth. A moment of stillness like the space between lightning and thunder. And then the fire roaring out of the furnace like something alive, flames leaping through the air. The terror in Roan's eyes.

I close my own eyes slowly, willing the memory away, then open them again. Whatever Liam is reading so intently must be important. Since returning from the academy at the end of summer, he has taken an active hand in managing the Gerlings' fortune and Everless affairs in general—at least, so I've gathered from other servants' grumblings about him. Would the family have accepted him back so readily if they knew what he tried to do to Roan? Does Roan remember his brush with death?

A manservant—Stefan, if I remember right—breezes by me; I catch the smell of cologne. Stefan looks back at me over his shoulder, his eyes narrowed in suspicion. My breath catches in my chest, but he continues to move down the aisle, then mounts the stairs at the end. He approaches Liam's desk and taps on his shoulder.

Liam's head jerks up, irritation twisting his features, and the servant murmurs to him. He sighs and opens a drawer, laying his book and notebook inside before closing and locking it.

I'm about to turn away when something else catches my eye, a flash of strange color as Liam stands. His palms are stained, as if he's dipped them in wine.

Hinton's words float up to the surface of my mind. *His hands were stained purple.* Papa's hands.

Before I can think better of it, my feet are moving. I put the book down and trail Liam and the servant at a distance as they stride toward the library exit, Liam in the lead.

I make sure to keep half a corridor's length behind them as they pass through the halls, keeping my eyes on the tails of Liam's long coat. We're walking along one of Everless's main corridors, and the halls are populated with lords and ladies, filtering out from their evening meal back to their rooms— gleaming in silk and velvet and swaying with drink. I keep my eyes down, hoping no one barks at me. Liam ignores all their greetings.

Eventually, though, the hall narrows and empties out, and I fall farther behind the two men. My palms sweat, slick with nerves. Ahead, the men turn a corner, and a few seconds later, I hear their footsteps stop. I slow too, and risk a peek around the corner. They have halted in front of a large door of carved mahogany. I look around—the wall hangings are less luxurious than elsewhere in Everless, but also older and more elegant, with elaborate intertwined geometric patterns. My breath quickens. I've never been here before. I shouldn't be here at all. If I'm caught . . .

To calm myself, I inhale slowly, pausing at the height of my breath—like my father taught me to do when I woke, sweating, from childhood nightmares. It's a skill I've practiced more than a little in the past few days. Two old recurring nightmares seem to have resurfaced since I came back to the estate—one about the night Papa and I were banished, and another, stranger one about a girl who follows me with a knife, her face always in shadow.

Liam and Stefan are conferring with two other men in the hallway—one of whom I recognize as a tax collector, nearly indistinguishable from the one who visited me and Papa in our cottage.

This must be it—the Gerling vault, where they keep their fortune. I'd always imagined them devouring Crofton's time in one sitting each month, like pigs feeding from a trough. Of course a Gerling would have to be present when they transfer the taxes into the vault. And I shouldn't be surprised that it's Liam. Roan doesn't seem like the type to enjoy spending an afternoon in a drafty tower, counting money.

I pull back behind the corner and strain to listen to their voices, the clink of blood-iron. Then the conversation ceases for a moment, and there's a loud creak, a heavy scraping of door against ground.

"Go up," Liam commands, and I'm startled as always by how low his voice is. "I'll meet you in a moment."

I press my back against the wall, the pounding of my heart urging him to go *up, up, up,* so I can steal a look at the vault. The thought of getting inside pulls at me, filling me with a mix of horror and fascination.

Then: Liam has turned the corner and caught me, his eyes boring into mine.

I'm far enough away that I might be able to flee if I could bring myself to move, but shock freezes my limbs. In what seems like only a heartbeat, he stands in front of me.

"You've been following us since the library," he says. His voice is calm, belying the anger tightening the skin around his eyes. "Why?"

I open my mouth, but nothing comes out. Now that he's truly looking at me, my terror of being recognized resurfaces. Again memories flash, the glint of molten metal and my own scream in my ears, acrid smoke.

Even if he doesn't know me, I'm where I don't belong. There's Ivan—his blade.

I was foolish, foolish to follow him.

But I force myself to meet Liam's eyes, willing my face to be smooth and blank and unafraid. I reach into the purse at my waist and pull out the first coin my fingers touch—a month-iron, from the fund that Duade gave me in Crofton. Old instinct screams at me not to part with the money, but I reach out and drop it into Liam's hand—his palm is bandaged and fingertips stained purple.

"I saw you drop this," I say, "in the library." Then, feigning curiosity—"Do you need something for your hand, my lord? There's witch hazel in the kitchen."

Liam's eyes narrow. He closes his fist around the coin and

pockets it, never taking his eyes from mine. "I'm sure you know where we are?" he says.

For a moment, I consider lying again—then think better of it, sure that Liam would hear the deception. "The estate vault."

"And you've heard stories about this place. Am I correct?"

Slowly I nod, unsure of what he wants. Liam's voice is low, and laced with poison.

"Well," he says. "What have you heard?"

"If anyone besides a Gerling tries to enter, the door will suck all their time out through their fingers."

He laughs—the sound is harsh, a burr stuck in his throat. "Were you going to try anyway?" he asks.

"No," I say firmly, quickly, though I don't know if it's a lie.

"It does take time to enter—and you never know how much," Liam says, the threat present beneath the words like distant thunder. "It could be a day, or fifty years. And when it bleeds you, the door mechanism stains your hands, like this." He holds up his own. "It's meant to show when someone has accessed the Everless vault—or tried to. But that's the least of your worries—Captain Ivan will do worse, if you're found where you don't belong."

I hardly hear the warning—my mind is spinning, thinking of the stain on Papa's hands. So it is true that the vault takes your time. And Papa was nearly out of that. It would explain why he came to the estate, just to die at its walls . . . why the soup I gave him couldn't save his life.

134

But no. No matter how desperate he was, my father wouldn't steal blood-iron or jewels. Whatever he was trying to get from inside was worth dying for.

"What's your name?" Liam asks.

"Jules," I mutter, still thinking about my father's stained hands. Then my stomach sinks as I realize what I've given away.

I look up at Liam. I'm close enough to see that the whites of his eyes are ringed with red. *Jules is a common name*, I think desperately. He wouldn't make the connection to something that happened ten years ago.

"You were in the library too," he says. "Another place you don't belong."

His tone is casual, like he doesn't mean it as a threat, just a statement of fact. It takes me a moment to process the danger in it.

"I—I was looking for a book," I stammer, the truth escaping in spite of myself. I should have said *cleaning*, but it's just as well—he would have seen the lie on my face. "I like reading." I curse my slow-wittedness and take a step back from him, wanting to escape.

"Lord Gerling!" a voice calls down.

I take advantage of the moment to step away farther. "Good evening, my lord."

"Wait." He reaches out and catches my wrist. Now his eyes are slightly wild, the black in his pupils spreading into his eyes' dark irises. Sensing danger, I freeze, hoping he can't feel my pulse thundering under my skin.

"What book?" he asks, and when I stare in confusion, adds, "In the library."

"Oh." I cast my mind around, and the titles of every book I've ever read fly out of my head at once. I don't know what he'd make of the fact I was studying the Queen. "Nothing important—just an old children's book." I catch on a scrap of a memory. "*The Tale of Elisa*—"

"*The Traveler*," Liam finishes for me. His eyes are fixed on mine, wild still, too intent, his head cocked to one side. "I knew a girl once who loved that book." There's a current of something in his voice that raises the hair on the nape of my neck.

Then, something changes in him. His posture stiffens, and he steps back from me. "Curiosity ill befits a servant," he says. "If you're found where you don't belong again, I'll report you to Captain Ivan. I advise you not to test me."

His words are sharp. Even though a moment ago I was trying to figure out how to leave, I can't help but blink, stunned.

But I say nothing, just turn on my heel and leave.

Rage makes my hands shake as I walk—almost run—through the halls, desperate to get as far away from Liam as Everless will allow me. For a moment, when he remembered the name of that book, I almost forgot who he was—the boy who caused us to be banished from our homes to cover his own cruelty. The root of all our ruin.

I must never forget again.

I duck through one of the small doorways to the servants' corridors, eager to get out of sight. Unlike the main hallways, with their lush red carpet and sunlight streaming in through the high windows, the narrow, twisting servants' corridors are dark and protected. They're familiar, and I have a sudden feeling I want them to swallow me. I don't see the figure coming from the opposite direction until we collide at a corner, shoulders smacking painfully together. I stumble and almost lose my balance.

"Sorry," I mutter, hurrying to pick myself up. And then I catch sight of a corner of velvet coat. This is no servant I've nearly run over.

All at once, Roan Gerling's hands are on my upper arms, pulling me upright.

His eyes go wide as he registers my face, and my breath stops in my throat.

Roan's coat is askew, his cheeks flushed and eyes bright. He takes half a step back to better see me, his head tilting to one side. Then, slowly, his mouth curves in a slight smile.

I know I should duck my head and flee, but another part of me is shouting at Roan Gerling to see me, really, finally see me, and remember. His face is so crystallized in my mind that it's hard to believe he can look into my face and not remember my name as well.

"L-Lord Gerling," I say, my tongue tripping over itself.

I drop into a curtsy, feeling my cheeks burning red. "My apologies."

"No matter." His chuckle invites me to look up, so I do—it's hard not to, with his blue eyes drawing mine in like a magnet. "Where are you off to in such a hurry?"

I blink. "Nowhere, my lord."

This makes him laugh. Then he stops, abruptly, and studies my face. "You helped us with the Queen's arrival," he says. "Picked up her things when they fell."

It isn't the recognition I hoped for, especially after he winked at me at the garden party, but I consume it. Maybe he doesn't remember exactly who I am after all, but he knows my face. "Yes, sir."

"What's your name?" This he asks a little slower, his head tilted to the side, as if gazing at something half familiar.

My heart squeezes and stumbles. Do I tell him the truth?

Liam might know who I am; he's the one who hates me. If any harm is coming because of my carelessness, it's already on its way. No danger will come for my father—it already has.

"Jules," I say. I close my lips, half afraid that whatever it is fluttering in my chest will fly out my mouth.

"Jules," Roan repeats. "The blacksmith's daughter."

My mouth drops open at the sound of my name in his mouth, intimate and precious. I shut it quickly. "We were friends," I say quietly.

"Of course," The smile rolls slowly back across his face.

"Hide-and-seek. The tree on the north lawn."

In an instant, the whole memory crashes over me too—summer, the smell of mown grass, a breathless game, Roan's hand over mine. I nod, unable to speak.

"I saw you at the party. And then, in the halls the other night . . . ?" Roan says the last part delicately, no doubt wary of discussing my broken heart where anyone can hear. My first thought is that I hope he won't think I'm in love with someone else. Heat courses through me at my own foolishness. And yet—

No, no, it doesn't matter, I tell myself. He's marrying the Queen's daughter.

"I knew it." Roan takes a step closer to me, still grinning. "You were so mysterious. Here one day and gone the next."

"I didn't want to leave," I say, willing my voice not to tremble. In another world, I ask: *Did you look for me?*

A whole life, filled with different memories, opens up in my mind—a life in which I didn't leave Everless—then shutters violently closed.

What does Roan remember? What can I say to him, to explain everything while giving away nothing? "My father—He—"

"My brother chased you off, didn't he?" He smiles after he says it, but I can't tell if it's in jest. Before I can speak, Roan waves his hand through the air like he can brush the past away in one movement. "It doesn't matter, now that you're back."

Almost too quickly to notice, his eyes flicker down my body and back up, sending heat through me. "Where have they put you now, Jules?"

"The kitchen." It's a much lower station than the blacksmith, and I feel my cheeks flush with shame.

Roan makes a *tsk* sound between his teeth and moves even closer. I feel the warmth of his breath against my neck. If I were a different girl, I could reach out and touch him.

"I'm sorry I collided with you," he says after a moment. "I was in a hurry—I have an audience with the Queen."

But he doesn't make a move to leave, and I'm startled to see that he's blushing. That, combined with the absence of his usual easy smile, makes him look vulnerable and childlike.

"Well," he says. "I'd better go. I don't want to be late."

"Wait," I blurt out. My voice comes out high, questioning. Roan turns back to me. "Y-your coat, my lord."

Roan looks down and sees the buttons on his coat misaligned, one side hanging lower than the other. He starts redoing the buttons, fumbling in his hurry.

Without thinking, I step forward to help—then realize what I'm doing, and feel my face flame red. But he drops his hands to allow me access. It would be stranger to stop now, so I don't. I feel the heat of his body through his shirt and vest.

"Thank you, Jules," Roan says softly.

I smell a faint, familiar scent of lavender coming off him, and know he must have just been with Ina Gold. The misaligned buttons, the flush in his cheek—my chest tightens. Quickly, I step away, dipping my head. "Yes, my lord." The lump in my throat warps my words a little, but Roan doesn't seem to notice.

Instead, his hand is on my arm. His grip is warm through the fabric of my dress, and so gentle. Liam's interrogation a few minutes ago seems like a distant memory.

"You have a keen eye," he says, a smile playing over his mouth. "I hope we'll cross paths again."

When? I almost ask—but then another idea blooms in my mind.

"We might," I say.

Roan's eyebrows raise—the smile on his face grows. "How's that?"

My hope grows with it. I'd never thought I'd have a direct path to the Queen. Now it's standing right in front of me in the form of Roan Gerling.

"I'd like to interview for the position of the girl who was banished by the Queen. Addie," I say quickly. His smile falters. "I know they're short on girls. I heard—" Roan blanches, so I stop short and try a different tack. "I want to be in Her Majesty's retinue, to serve Ina. That's where I was coming from just now—the library, studying. I know so little of her history . . ." I try to take all the longing that he's ignited in me and channel it into my voice, as if I've wished for nothing more dearly in my seventeen years than to wait on the Queen's daughter hand and foot.

But Roan's smile returns, and the warmth of it washes over me. "The test? Just a formality, Jules. A load of stuffy nonsense, if you ask me." He grins. "The Queen is gone tomorrow, but I'll put in a good word for you with Caro, the Queen's handmaiden. She decides who gets close to Her Majesty, not some ridiculous test," he says, more than a hint of pride in his voice. He takes a step back, tilts his head at me again—a new habit he picked up sometime in the last ten years—like he's searching for an answer to a question. "In fact, why don't you serve breakfast, for myself and Ina, so she can see how lovely you are? I'll send for you when we have a free morning."

"Thank you, my lord," I whisper, my heart racing.

"Jules—it's Roan," he corrects me.

"Lord Roan," I answer, allowing myself a small, crooked smile.

His laugh, long and loud, rings out in the cramped servants' corridor.

"I am delighted to have run into you, Jules." He leans close, brings his mouth nearly to my ear. "More than you know."

13

Roan keeps his promise. Early the next morning, before the sun has turned from bleeding red to yellow, he sends for me. I slowly work the flour out of my hair in the warm water of the washbasin. I take the blue wool dress from under my pillow and put it on, buttoning it to my chin. All in preparation to meet Ina Gold.

As I leave, Bea raises her eyebrows at me and lets out a low whistle. "Who are you dressing for, Jules?"

The other girls slow their movements, listening. "I'm serving Ina Gold this morning," I say, though the words don't seem to come from me at all. Bea brings her hands together in a small, joyful movement, but I don't think I imagine the way the others' eyes widen, how they suddenly busy themselves with making beds that have already been made.

As soon as I reach the kitchen to tell Lora—before I can even speak—she takes me by the elbow and ushers me into the corner. She looks harried, her face flushed and hair frizzing out from beneath her kerchief.

"Jules," she says. Her voice is tense. "You have to come with me, dear."

"But, Lora—" My voice comes out childish. I wince. "Lord Roan has invited me to serve him and the Queen's ward breakfast." Lora steps back and takes me in, my elbow still in her hand. "Lord Roan—"

"Well, Lord Liam has a different job for you this morning. You'll need to take it up with him."

I bite the inside of my cheek, hard. I would never. He's the eldest and he's—well—

Terrible.

Warily, I follow her to the entrance to the food cellars.

I stop at the doorway, stiffening at the wet, heady scent of dirt, vegetables, and iron. The last time I went down here was the day I discovered Papa's crumpled form amid sacks of turnips and potatoes. Was it six days ago? Seven? Lora takes my arm and gently but firmly tugs me along with her down the stairs.

"You're on mava duty today," she says, avoiding my eyes. "The dye stores are running low."

"What?" For a second, my instinctive horror at the cellar is swallowed up in a rush of anger. The Everless's stores of mava are kept down here, far away from the kitchen, so that the

144

fruit's sickly sweet odor—like honey and copper, or wine gone off—won't distract us in the kitchen. To make the dye, someone has to pick through the leathery skin and extract the noxious, abrasive insides with their hands, leaving stains and scars. I've seen the unfortunate victims stumble up from the cellar on occasion, swaying from the dizzying scent.

But that's not why everyone fears it. The pods have been known to harbor tiny, poisonous scorpions, travelers from the southern deserts where mava is grown. Though the stowaways are rare, I remember attending, as a child, the funeral of a cook who died after a single sting.

Shelling mava is a *punishment*, just short of getting your time bled.

And on top of everything, piling onto me like rocks, I now know how the beautiful color is used—as a mark of death upon people who dare to access the vault. People like Papa.

"W-what have I done?" I sputter indignantly.

But of course, I know. I crossed Liam Gerling.

Lora sighs. "It's not my orders, Jules. This comes directly from Lord Liam."

"*Liam*." The word escapes my mouth like venom, at the same time as fear stabs through me—he remembers my name, my face. He must, to have picked me specifically for this task. A wild thought flies through me: Could he have known about Papa's coming to Everless? Papa's hands were stained trying to access the vault. The vault in Liam's care.

Lora nods, interrupting my thoughts. "I don't know how you attracted his notice, but just be thankful he didn't take a day. Though there's not much difference—you'll be down there quite a long time."

So this is my punishment for my *curiosity*. I clench my fists, my nails digging into my palms, as I try to push down the rage and fear. I thought I had nothing left to be afraid of, now that Papa is dead. But if Liam knows me—if he goes out of his way to torment me—how can I ever be safe at Everless?

And how will I ever get closer to the Queen?

As we walk down into darkness, another thought: Roan knows I'm at Everless, too. The memory of our meeting in the hall, his closeness, is a talisman. I cling to it. *More than you know.*

These thoughts dissolve as Lora leads me into the cellar. When she opens the narrow door at the end of the hall, I nearly faint at the pile of mava in the dark room—thousands of purple-black pods the size of chicken hearts are heaped against the wall, reaching to the ceiling, some splitting to spill their gleaming pulp down the pile. The smell is a physical thing, a wall of sickly sweet air with a tang of something bitter beneath, like wine and vinegar.

The motion of the door opening causes a few of the ugly, leathery fruits to roll down the pile. One comes to a stop at our feet. I resist the urge to grind it with my boot. Lora coughs beside me, obviously affected.

"Come up if you start to feel dizzy," she says, after a

moment of regarding the pile. "I'm sorry, my dear." But she closes the door behind her, leaving me with just a single flickering torch.

Once stripped of its protective shell, mava has to be kept in the cold, so the cellar is freezing—my teeth are chattering, my feet numb through my boots from the cold stone floor. Each fruit has a skin as tough as leather, which I have to tear apart without doing too much damage to the pulp within. After five, my fingertips are bleeding.

At first, I think I'm getting used to the smell; but as the buckets Lora has provided me with slowly fill up with fruit, it overpowers me again. My nails snag and tear on the skins. Juice stains my hands the color of wine. Liam couldn't have devised a more perfect torture for me. Every time I look down, I'm reminded of my loss and my guilt. It occurs to me that I could go back to the vault—try it while my hands are already stained—but if what Liam said was true, it could take any amount of my time. Drink up fifty years in a moment and leave me fainting on the floor. Or dead.

Weighing the risk, I return to the kitchen to take up the buckets of shelled mava and for a meal. Lora doesn't allow me to linger in the warmth, instead sending me back downstairs with a hard roll and pad of butter, her mouth set in a harsh line. I know she's holding in her mind the stories of Tam, of Hinton's father, everyone who crosses the Gerlings. My mood blackens.

At some point there's a knock on the door. I look up to see Lora, wringing her hands. The look of worry on her face strikes fear into me.

"Lord Gerling is coming down to speak with you. Make yourself presentable, quickly." She disappears.

Fear is replaced by hope in quick succession. The events of my encounter with Roan in the servants' hallway—the nearness of him, the heat of him—return to me. Maybe he's heard what happened and has come to fix it.

I wipe my forehead with my sleeve, careful not to smear my face in wine-dark stains, and am cleaning my hands on my apron as best I can when another knock sounds.

The door opens, and my stomach drops. It isn't Roan who stands in the doorway—not with the pulled-back hair, the stiff, awkward posture. It's Liam.

His eyes narrow as they take in the towering pile of fruit, me with my stained apron and hands. Anger and disappointment rush through me like a tide, and a dozen curses spring to the tip of my tongue. I glare at him as if the force of my hatred alone might send him away.

He steps inside, leaving the door open behind him. He's wearing a long coat against the chill of the cellar, his hands jammed awkwardly into its pockets.

"Lord Gerling," I say between gritted teeth. He's only two strides from me.

"Jules."

I curse myself for letting my name slip. The hardness I heard a few days ago, when he confronted me near the vault, has faded from his voice. He sounds softer, or . . . tired.

"I wanted to check on you," he says, and then adds: "Your progress, I mean."

"How kind," I mutter. I want to fold in on myself, slump my shoulders and cross my arms over my chest, hide from his too-direct gaze. But I force myself to sit straight, face him head-on. I don't want to show any weakness.

Liam's gaze flickers past me, to the heap of mava still behind me, the filled buckets and discarded skins that litter the floor. "I didn't realize . . . there was this much." He sounds a little chagrined.

"Perhaps you should stop interfering in things you know nothing about," I blurt out.

"I could say the same to you," he shoots back, his eyes suddenly flinty in the dark. Then he blinks. A beat passes, two, and he lets out a breath, visibly tamps down his anger.

He bends down and picks up a whole mava fruit that has rolled from the pile to rest at his feet, then straightens and considers it. "Show me," he says.

"How to . . . shell the mava?" My voice comes out scathing, incredulous, but he just nods. I can feel myself reddening with frustration, and hope the low light camouflages it. Has he come here to assess my skill?

Furiously, I snatch a fruit from the pile. He approaches,

watching with studied interest as I demonstrate the expertise I've acquired in the last few hours—find the seam at the top, where the fruit was picked from the bush, and pry it in two with my nails. Liam takes his fruit and mimics my motions, too roughly, and juice flies, spattering his coat. He frowns.

I push out my breath carefully. If I speak more, either my anger will spill over, or I'll say something revealing, and Liam Gerling already knows too much about me. I take up another handful of mava and set about shelling it, but out of the corner of my eye I can see Liam looking at me. I focus on my work and wait for him to speak.

"About yesterday," Liam says at length. He sounds uncertain. "My tone was uncalled for. You surprised me."

This half apology is a shock, but I stay quiet. I know that I was careless, to let Liam catch me following him. Maybe he thinks that if he's kind to me, I'll give up my secrets—I've seen Ivan play a similar game. If he is playing games, I can too.

"I'm a servant, my lord," I say, making my voice artificially cheery. "Nothing is uncalled for."

"Aren't you afraid?" he asks, his voice measured.

This surprises me. "What do you mean?" For a moment, I forget to make my voice cold.

"I mean—" He pauses, starts over. "Servants are terrified of this. They say the scorpion steals all your time with one sting." He drops a fruit into a bucket. "But, you know, some people on the far coast eat them. They think if they catch one that's stung somebody, they'll gain a lifetime."

I remember this Liam from childhood, always ready to correct someone with some useless fact he found in one of his books and a harsh word. But what was once merely annoying, he's now using as a weapon. This time, I let the anger saturate my voice. "You're the one who assigned me to this, remember?"

"You didn't answer my question." Liam closes a fruit in his hand, then opens his palm to show me. "Aren't you afraid of what may be hiding in here?"

The question settles heavily in the room as his fingers work silently over a fruit. I think of the blood-irons that pass through his hands—hands that are stained as red as wine. Something whispers to me that he's not just talking about the threat of the scorpion.

I blink. "No," I say, as evenly as I can. "Are you?"

Liam smiles at me, teeth white in the dimness. "Sometimes I am."

His words linger around us, stirring something up inside me. What does Liam Gerling have to fear? And more important . . .

"Why are you punishing me?" I want him to admit it—to say it. Liam Gerling gives out information like his family doles out blood-irons: stingily.

"You broke a house rule," he says. "It could have been worse." But it's a lie. I know it is. *The Tale of Elisa the Traveler,* my favorite childhood book. He remembered it—remembered *me*. His hatred of me has burned just as brightly all these years as mine has of him—just like Papa said—though I cannot imagine why. To a man of his station, I am nothing. Just another Everless girl.

"Why are you here, Jules?" he asks now, the darkness of his eyes deepening somehow. It unnerves me slightly, the way I can sink into those eyes, like the thick mud in the heart of the forest—quiet, and deep, and easy to get stuck in forever until you starve.

"To earn time."

"Where is your father? Peter, wasn't it?"

Instantaneously, I'm on my feet, clenching my fists, mava spilling off my lap onto the floor. "You know *his* name too, you bastard," I hiss. I know he's toying with me—baiting me like an animal—but it doesn't matter, though a voice inside my head is screaming at me to care. To stop. "You've never forgotten either of us. Never let us live down the accident, which was—" *Your fault*, I want to say, but swallow down the words, suddenly fearful again. "Why don't you go find somewhere else to be cruel?"

"Careful," Liam says mildly. "This is my home."

"It was mine too. Before you sent us away." I know now that he remembers this, and the accident in the forge. I know it with more certainty than I've known anything else since coming to the Gerling estate, even if he won't admit it.

But does he know that my father is dead?

"Jules, listen," he begins.

"*No*. Just leave me alone, Liam, *please*." My composure is slipping as I think about Papa, about how much I need him and wish he were here with me still. Angry tears prick my eyes. "Why do you hate me so much?"

Liam doesn't answer. He draws in a breath, but before either of us can speak, another set of approaching footsteps echoes down the hall.

I turn away from Liam, press the back of my hand against my eyes until the threat of tears recedes. Liam spins to face the door.

Roan stands there. His eyes widen when he sees his older brother. "Liam?" Then his gaze cuts past Liam, to me. "Jules? I've been asking after you. What . . . what's going on?"

"Nothing," Liam says, a hairbreadth too late. Even speaking to his own brother, his voice is cold and remote. "The Queen's guards required more mava dye for their weapons. So I assigned someone to shell it."

"Mava?" Roan repeats in disbelief. "And you've shut a poor servant down here in the dark to shell it, rather than having the paste imported like a reasonable person?"

Affection rushes through me, though with a sliver of disappointment at hearing him call me a servant—not Jules.

"Then another servant in another province would shell it," Liam says, his voice clipped. "Do you think the paste can be plucked from trees? If it doesn't happen in front of your eyes, does it matter at all?"

Roan frowns and ignores Liam. He takes me in, my stained apron, my flushed face. "Jules, is this why you missed our appointment this morning?"

Liam's eyes flash so noticeably that I swear they change color. I've read about sea creatures whose whole bodies do the same, just before they're consumed by a predator.

He looks from me to his brother, finally opens his mouth— and says nothing.

Roan continues. "Have you been down here all day?"

"Your concern for servant welfare is touching," Liam bites out, suddenly himself again. "But you're an expert at that, aren't you?"

"It's none of your business." Roan's tone has gone cold, so cold that it's hard to tell the boys' voices apart.

Liam steps closer to his brother. He's slightly taller than Roan, but the difference seems to grow in the dark; the torchlight washes out Roan's blue eyes and deepens Liam's black ones, sharpening the angles of his face. "Then you help her shell the mava, if you care so deeply." He shoulders past Roan and strides from the cellar, letting the door slam heavily behind him.

My ears ring with the new silence, which is broken when I hear Roan utter a string of soft curses—those the servants use. I almost laugh. Instead, I let out a shaky breath, and he turns toward me, his brow creased with concern.

"I'm sorry you had to see that," he says, his voice soft and

warm again. "My brother is . . . well, you know, you've seen."
He steps closer and puts a gentle hand on my arm. "Come on.
I'm overriding Liam's orders. We'll get you out of here."

I follow Roan gratefully and wordlessly from the cellar.
The anxiety in my chest eases the farther we get from the cellar
and the overpowering scent of mava, as we see the bright light
of the kitchen growing ahead of us.

I brace myself to receive strange looks from the other
servants, but Roan unexpectedly stops at the base of the stairs,
turning to face me.

I stop too, my body seeming naturally to echo his. "I'm
sorry for causing trouble between you and your brother," I say.

"I'm sorry Liam bothered you. That's why I came," Roan
says quickly.

I blink, hoping he can't see me blush in the dark. I can feel
sweat prickling at my palms.

"Ina still wants to meet you," Roan adds. "But it seems
you'll need to get freshened up first. If you hurry, you won't
miss her fitting."

I nod quickly, in time with my pulse. Possibilities bloom in
my thoughts. This might be my best chance to get close to the
Queen before she returns to the palace. I can't fail today.

But then I pause. "Wait. Fitting?"

"Lady Gold is having her wedding gown fitted today."

Her wedding gown. For her wedding to Roan, the man
standing in front of me right now. The man who holds my gaze

for a moment longer, a slight smile curving his lips.

Despite the stains on my clothes and the fight with Liam and my awful, cramped fingers, I feel seen in a way I scarcely have since arriving at Everless. A strange feeling flowers in me, like I'm standing at the edge of a cliff, looking out to the green-and-blue sea, which I've only ever seen drawn in books, its waves sloshing and beautiful and endless—and from this height, deadly.

14

It takes almost an hour of scrubbing with Lora's harsh soap before the mava even starts to come off me, leaving my skin and face tender and still stained a dull purple in spots. I draw curious looks from the other servants when I emerge into the kitchen.

Waiting there with Lora is the Queen's handmaiden, the one who helped me with the Queen's jewels when they spilled over the floor. But she is so out of place here in the kitchen that it takes me a beat to recognize her. Pretty, dark-haired, with constellations freckled across her skin, she's maybe a few years older than me. She's dressed more elegantly than the rest of us, in a simple but well-made dress of velvet so dark red it's almost black, so long it brushes the floor, though she's marked as a servant by the white cap pinned to her hair. She smiles shyly at me.

"Jules, this is Caro," Lora says, then adds pointedly, "the Queen's handmaiden."

It's an unsubtle reminder to show respect for someone who outranks me. My heart hardens a little even as I hastily drop into a curtsy. "I'm sorry, miss."

"No matter," Caro says softly—whispers, really. Somehow I still hear her over the din of the kitchen, as if I'm hearing the sea's echo inside a large shell. She gestures airily for me to stand. "I'm pleased to meet you, Jules. Roan told me you were interested in the handmaiden position to Her Majesty and Lady Gold. You can sew, can't you?"

"A . . . a little, I suppose," I say, looking between her and Lora. "I did some mending back in"—the word *Crofton* dies on my lips—"my hometown. But nothing near as fine as Lady Gold's wardrobe." A pang goes through me at the thought of Ina Gold's wedding gown.

"You'll do fine, I'm sure. We only help tack it for the seamstresses in any case." Caro reaches out and takes my hand, startling me, and turns to Lora.

"Take as long as you need," Lora says, eyeing me shrewdly. "Lord Liam had assigned her to a task, but—"

"I'm sure the Queen's wishes override Liam Gerling's," Caro says simply. I try not to smile at Caro's clear disdain for the elder Gerling brother. A hush falls over the kitchen, and Lora's head bobs, quick to agree.

Then, the Queen's handmaiden is tugging me away.

In the hall, she links arms with me, and we stroll side by side like old friends as she explains that the Queen distrusts strangers, so most of my time in this position would be spent attending to Lady Gold. She tells me three of Lady Gold's ladies-in-waiting fell ill on the journey to Everless. The lie falls so easily from her, that I wonder if I misheard Roan and Ina at the whispering wall. But Bea, too, said that people had been killed.

"No other girls will be helping us? I expected more—"

Caro slows down her walk almost imperceptibly, quarter-turning to look at me. Her eyes are a light, washed-out green, and something sparkles in them.

"More . . . ?" she asks, but I have no answer. I avert my eyes, fearful I've pressed too far. But she smiles widely again and picks up her gait. "You have no competition, if that's what you're wondering. People are intimidated by real power, Jules. You mustn't forget that."

As Caro tugs me along, I have to focus to maintain a smile whenever she looks at me. I'm not used to being so close to another person; surprisingly, Caro's closeness and cheer warms me.

"You know the estate well," Caro says, the third time I lead her in a turn toward the royal quarters. "Have you been here very long?"

"Just a couple of weeks." I hesitate, but then the bitter realization sinks in—with Papa gone and Liam and Roan both knowing who I am, there's little risk in being myself. "But my father worked here, when I was a child. I grew up at Everless."

"I see." Caro's voice is even softer now; she seems to hear something amiss in my tone. "And why did you come back?"

The image of Papa's face when I last saw him, alone in the dark cold of the root cellar, flashes through my mind, and for a moment I can't breathe. Suddenly, I feel that I have to tell the truth, or I might suffocate with the weight of it.

"He died," I say simply. "Recently." I don't think I can manage any more of an explanation. Caro just slows a little, looks into my eyes, and clasps my arm tighter.

"I'm sorry," she says gently. "And your mother?"

My silence is its own answer.

Caro nods, grasps my arm again. "My parents, too, when I was younger. If you'd like to do this another time . . ."

I shake my head, grateful for the plain empathy in her words. "No. Thank you. I want to get my mind off it."

"I think that's the best thing to do in a time of loss," Caro says. She smiles, the expression full of shared grief and understanding, and it feels as if an anvil has been lifted from my chest.

Genteel noises of soft music and murmured conversations float toward me as we make our way through the upper floors. It makes my skin prickle with nervousness—the quiet between Caro and me is suddenly deafening. What sparkling conversation can I hope to provide Lady Gold, if I bore her handmaiden? I hope she isn't expecting someone else like Caro, collected and perfectly put together.

As if she can feel what I'm thinking, Caro fills the silence by humming a sweet, sad tune as we walk—it's familiar, though I can't place it. She starts to sing: "Your voice is an hour's rose; your soul a loving thief. I'll follow you through the fledgling woods, till your heart is mine to keep."

"That song," I ask. "What is it?"

"A very old one. The Queen's favorite."

The melody is a simple back-and-forth between only a few notes, though the words tell a story of loss, of love—of violence.

Soon, Caro stops at a door on the right and turns to me. Her lips part slightly, and her eyes widen in shock. "Jules, you're crying."

I bring my hand to one cheek, surprised when my fingers come away wet. My face flames. "It's all right," I assure her, and smile. "It was such a beautiful song."

Caro smiles, nods. "The Queen had it written in honor of the Sorceress."

"Is it true? That the Sorceress walked with the Queen?" I ask.

"Caro!" a voice calls from the other side of the door. "Have you found Roan's friend?"

Roan's friend. The words echo in my mind.

My heart beats quickly—one, two, three—and repeats, like the song's melody, while Caro produces a key from her dress and opens the door. I cock my head, confused that Lady Gold should be locked in.

Caro sees my look and leans in close, speaking even more softly than normal. "Lady Gold's guards were lost recently," she tells me. "And she doesn't like to be surrounded by strangers, so she refused to take any Everless guards. It made the Queen furious."

She opens the door and leads me into a sumptuously decorated suite, all lush red carpets and gossamer curtains floating from huge windows. The space is flooded with the winter sun, but it's warm, and suffused with the fragrance of rosewater.

One corner of the room is taken up with a massive, cloud-like bed, covered now in dresses of every color, flung there haphazardly as if tried on and discarded. By the bed, Lady Ina Gold stands in a silk shift and petticoat, her arms and calves bare except for a few simple metal bangles, and her short hair loose. She's holding one dress—as shiny and liquid as molten emeralds—up to the light, examining it with a critical eye. When the door closes behind us she turns to face me and Caro.

Instinctively I cast my eyes down to avoid seeing her half-dressed. "My lady," I hear Caro say in her carrying whisper. "This is Jules Ember."

I look up, my cheeks burning, to meet Ina Gold's eyes. She's my height exactly, my age, but from a different world than me.

The fact that she's never had a care in the world seems to shine through in her face—her body. Her skin glows, free from even the suggestion of a scar or callus.

A stray thought sends a chill down my spine: someday, long after I'm dead and buried, this girl will be queen.

And another: she'll spend all those years with Roan.

Ina smiles with no self-consciousness as she reaches out and clasps my free hand.

"Miss Ember," she says. Her voice is rich, her vowels bell-like, with the strange accent that only the Queen, Caro, and she seem to have. "Thank you for coming. I'm so pleased you could join us. Roan said you were a treasure—I don't know why he didn't tell his mother that in the first place, before we wasted our time . . ."

Unsure how to react, I curtsy clumsily in response, keeping my eyes on the carpet. "Lord Gerling wasn't aware I was at Everless until yesterday, Lady Gold. The pleasure is all mine."

She turns toward the bed, sweeping her arm out over the array of dresses crumpled there. "Caro and I were just debating. It's tradition that a bride wear the colors of her groom's family, the family she'll be joining. But green doesn't suit me. And technically"—she raises her eyebrows—"I outrank Roan, don't I?"

Despite her teasing words, there's an undercurrent of wonder in her voice when she speaks about the wedding—about Roan—that makes me think she's not just boasting. Her face shines like a little child who's woken up to fresh snow.

Already, I know that she is in love with Roan Gerling. And from the way she's smiling, he must love her back. Who wouldn't?

My feelings twist and take a strange shape inside me. It's easy to be jealous of the future queen, who might be marrying a Gerling for politics' sake; it feels different with the girl in front of me, grinning and barefoot and obviously infatuated.

"Caro thinks I should wear green," Lady Gold continues. She tosses the green silk gown on the bed, glorious even in its disheveled state. "But I like this one." She holds up another dress to her body—red, the color of the Queen, with sleeves that drape artfully off her shoulders. "But is it too risqué for Everless?"

"Not at all," I volunteer, surprising myself. "You haven't seen it yet, but the Gerling ladies wear much more scandalous things on lesser occasions."

A trickle of pleasure drops through me as Ina giggles gratefully. Caro looks cross—as if she's lost a bet. "But do you like it, Jules?" Ina asks. "No Everless girl will tell us the truth. They're afraid of upsetting me."

As a little girl at Everless, I was transfixed by the gowns and the jewels that adorned the women, as taken with pretty objects as any girl of better birth. Papa used to call me a little magpie, for the way I collected things—flawed jewels not good enough for Gerling swords, scraps of ribbon, a stray gold earring—and kept them in a bowl on my nightstand. But they were my own stash of tiny treasures. When we were exiled and went to Rodshire, then Crofton, I turned away from such things. I pretended to scorn them.

But now Lady Gold is looking at me as she holds the red dress to her body. Her eyes are on mine, like she actually cares about my answer. I want to reach out and tear the fabric of the skirt to shreds, but I bite my lip and fold my hands in front of me.

"Maybe something gold?" I venture after a few moments. "It's the secondary color of both your families. And after all . . ." I incline my head meaningfully at Ina Gold, half shocked that I've made a joke, and half hoping desperately that either of the other girls will pick it up.

After a moment, Lady Gold does. Her laugh is sudden and infectious, making me smile in spite of myself.

"You know, I hadn't thought of that," she says. She turns to Caro. "Gold. What do you think?"

Caro smiles. "It's a little unconventional," she whispers. "But gold does look rather lovely on you." She tilts her head, considering Ina. "I'll have the seamstresses make one up; in the meantime, let's keep fitting the others, so they have a model to work off of." She gestures with her hands, and, sighing theatrically, Ina lifts the green dress from the bed and shakes the wrinkles out, then neatly steps into it and turns so Caro can do up the buttons in the back.

Once she has, Caro folds the fabric of the dress against Ina's body and instructs me to hold it in place while she deftly inserts pins, never once nicking Lady Gold's skin. Her voice is no less commanding for being in a whisper.

While I stand blushing, trying to balance keeping a respectful distance from Ina Gold and holding a handful of fabric in place across her chest, Caro and Lady Gold gossip about a hedge witch Caro saw recently, who told her that she would soon reunite with her first and truest love. When Ina teasingly asks her who that might be, Caro blushes and changes the subject to some noblewoman who's birthed a child with a striking resemblance to her handsome footman.

"Jules," Lady Gold's voice breaks through my reverie. "You would know. Is Liam always so dour? Or is it only when everyone else is having a good time?"

The sound of Liam's name sends an unpleasant jolt through me, and I almost drop the fold of green fabric in my hand. "I—I don't know Lord Liam well, my lady," I stammer. I remember that they are outsiders at Everless, though it seems to me that you can never be an outsider when the Queen's bells ring to welcome you. No one from here would dare to criticize him. "He's always been . . . distant."

Lady Gold scrunches her face up, making a show of tipping her nose up high in the air. "*I'm Liam Gerling*," she says in an exaggerated, deep version of her own aristocratic accent. "*I shan't talk to anyone at this party. Clearly, my time is better spent sulking in a corner, glaring daggers at anyone who dares to speak to me.*"

As I choke back a laugh—I've never heard anyone make fun of a Gerling so openly—Caro shakes her head. "His poor mother," she whispers. "Lady Verissa has proposed a dozen possible brides, I hear, and he turned them all down."

"Perhaps they changed their minds when they saw what a storm cloud he is," Lady Gold suggests. "And he just says he turned them down, to cover up the embarrassment. I can't imagine anyone wanting to marry him, not for all the time in Sempera."

"Roan got the looks and the personality," Caro says in a teasing whisper.

"Agreed," I say without thinking, then hurriedly look down to hide the heat I can feel rising in my cheeks.

Ina seems not to have noticed—or care—but I feel Caro's eyes on me.

"How long have you known Lord Roan, my lady?" I say quickly. As the words leave my mouth, I catch a glimpse of myself in the mirror behind Ina, all pallor and sharp angles and shadows under my eyes. The contrast between me and Lady Gold couldn't be clearer.

But the princess doesn't look fazed. "Ah," she says. "Well, first, call me Ina. And I met Roan when the Gerlings visited the palace two years ago."

Dimly, I remember that while the Gerlings were gone,

Crofton set up a row of lean-tos in the market plaza with games for children, an abundance of music and singing, and as much candied fruit as we could spare. They stood the entire week the Gerlings were away, as a kind of celebration—a desperate attempt at merriment.

"We . . . got along well," Ina continues. Another of those giggles that simultaneously entrances me and tears at my heart. I know it will hurt me to hear it, but I want to know everything about Roan and Ina.

"We exchanged letters after that," Ina continues, "but had to keep it a secret; the Queen is supposed to choose who I'll marry. Actually, it's thanks to Caro that she chose Roan." Ina gives the handmaiden a grateful glance. "She'd found one of the letters"—Caro gives a small, mischievous smile—"and the Queen suggested that we forge a closer alliance with the Gerlings before the sun had fully risen. Of course, I never knew about any of this until after the engagement was announced. This one underestimates her influence." Ina looks lovingly at Caro, who blushes.

"That's . . . a wonderful story," I whisper, my chest tight.

"Isn't it?" The happiness in Ina's voice is so genuine that I can't resent her, even though my heart hurts for myself. Once Caro and I release her, she takes a step away from us and twirls, the green fabric lifting in a shining circle around her ankles. It's not even a finished dress, but her movement makes it look like the most polished of gowns.

"Ina's whole life is a wonderful story," Caro whispers to me—a softer version of her normal whisper—as Ina crosses the room to examine our handiwork in the full-length mirror. "You've heard about it, surely?"

I nod, trying not to stare at Ina out of the corner of my eye. It seems impossible she was ever anything other than this— glittering, laughing, beautiful, blessed. But everyone in Sempera knows her history: she was one of the hundreds of children whose parents abandoned them on the shores of the palace or surrendered them to an orphanage in the desperate hope that the child would become the Queen's heir, as she declared centuries ago. A five-hundred-year-old promise, fulfilled now by the girl standing in front of me.

Of course, I, like most of the people of Sempera, am more familiar with the story that lurks underneath the shimmering surface of Ina's own: Almost all the children abandoned to the Queen grow up in an orphanage. When they come of age— often earlier, even—those who aren't adopted by families leave for jobs as servants or laborers. Papa had always scorned the Queen's proclamation. It led to horrors in practice—she lived so long that a child was only chosen once every few decades, only to be found wanting or assigned to some other lesser role, or succumbing to sickness—or, I shudder, remembering Lady Sida's insinuations, falling victim to the Queen's whims when she decided she no longer wanted to give up the throne. But that didn't stop parents from leaving children by the hundreds every year, all fueled by the same delusional hope that their child had to be the one.

Ina approaches us with a handful of fabric clutched in her fist, a silent command that we make it disappear. Sticking a pin between my lips, I kneel in front of the future queen.

And Ina was chosen. The news had sent ripples through the kingdom, or so people said. Vaguely, I remember palace servants gossiping about Ina after she'd been chosen. The smooth stone in her mouth when she was born was supposed to be a blessing from the Sorceress. This news reached the Queen, and the Queen's own surname, Gold, was appended, and the girl taken to the palace, as good as Her Majesty's own daughter.

I wonder who her mother and father are. Are they alive today? Do they even know that Ina is the nameless infant they abandoned on the shores? My heart clenches at the next thought.

Maybe that's what happened to me.

Since reading Papa's note, I have tried not to think about what it said . . . that he was not in fact my father at all. But if that's true, and I've never met my mother either, it's possible I, too, was one of those abandoned orphans, taken in by Papa too early for anyone to remember.

Which means that I, too, could have been chosen by the Queen. But I was not.

Something stabs into my finger. I've stuck myself with the pin. I yank my hand away from Ina before blood gets on her dress, and suck the blood off my skin—but something is wrong. Ina is twisting to look at me, but slowly, like she's moving through amber. I have my hands back in place before she turns around. And when she looks at me, she just blinks once and turns away again, as if she's forgotten what caught her attention. Caro stares at Ina with a confused look for a moment, like she's forgotten herself.

I realize what happened, of course. When I pricked myself, time froze—or slowed—like when I fished for the trout in a stream, so many days ago, or when I confronted the Gerling guard in the Crofton market while waiting to be selected as an Everless girl. Nerves flare in me. It hasn't happened since I arrived, or if it has, it was too subtle to notice.

Thankfully, they both seem to dismiss the irregular moment. Ina submits to further alterations, and Caro smiles her mysterious smile. "It's lucky your parents decided to give you to the kingdom, Ina. No other baby has ever been so lucky, or so deserving."

The clock ticks once, twice before Ina smiles graciously. She surely doesn't remember her parents, but it clearly still wounds her—I don't think I imagined the look of hurt that flashed across her face. It's hard to believe that anything can sadden this beautiful, laughing girl, Roan's betrothed, the future queen—but I've learned firsthand how difficult unanswered questions from one's parents can be.

When Caro finally deems the drapes and folds of the dress

perfect, Ina slips carefully out of the fabric and Caro and I fold it to be taken down to the seamstress. As we line the shoulders up, Caro says, "Jules, I'm going to recommend to the Queen that you be appointed as the new handmaiden."

"If you'd like," Ina adds quickly. "I hope you do."

It takes a second for her words to land, but when they do, I have to stop myself from dropping the dress to throw my arms around Caro. "Thank you!" I say breathlessly. "Thank you so much."

"You'll serve me more than the Queen, of course," Ina says. "She prefers Caro to look after her, and only sparingly."

The joy in my heart feels foreign after so much grief. And if I look too closely at it, there's something dark and strange flitting about its edges—it's odd to be thrilled at being one step closer to the woman who Papa warned me against, who may have driven him to his death.

But the joy is too sweet to think about the darkness now. I push it back into the corners of my heart, to let out and deal with when the time comes.

"First," Caro says, "the Queen must approve. We'll take you to her now."

15

The Queen, Caro tells me, prefers to remain in her room, away from the useless gossip of the estate's inhabitants. The guards posted at either side of her door serve as a testament to this. While we approach, they remain still as stone; watching their ashen faces, I fear for a moment that time has stopped again.

Caro passes between the guards without fear or hesitation. Ina follows close behind, fingers fluttering at her waist. I wonder, with a flicker of pointed curiosity, whether she is always this nervous in the presence of the woman who raised her. Inside, the queen of Sempera sits in a high-backed chair carved from deep brown wood. Both Ina and Caro curtsy low, and I do the same, keeping my eyes trained on the thick, gold-and-green carpet below my feet.

Caro speaks first. "My Queen, may we present to you

Jules Ember. Ina and I would like her to join the royal retinue, to serve you." The Queen remains silent. "She served at Everless in her childhood, and knows the estate well. Jules," Caro finishes.

I straighten up, raising my eyes from the ground to find that the Queen is watching me blankly. Boredom and disdain seem to have carved themselves into her features, making her beauty cold, distant—the beauty of a star. Still, her gaze is piercing, her voice even more so.

"Ina, this will please you?" the Queen asks.

"Yes," Ina answers quickly. "Jules was Roan's companion as a child. Nothing would please me more."

A nearly imperceptible look passes between Caro and the Queen—a silent command that leads Caro to clear her throat. "Jules, serving the Queen and her daughter is not like serving a noble family. It comes with certain dangers." I keep my eyes trained on Caro, though my heart has begun to pound violently in my chest. "You will not speak of the Queen to anyone. You will not enter her chambers uninvited. You will not lay a hand on her, even to assist her. If anyone should approach you about her, or suggest violence against her, you will tell me immediately.

"Threats to the Queen are not uncommon, as I'm sure you might have heard," she explains. "With great power comes great violence, both from within and without." Caro's speech sounds taut—rehearsed. I wonder how many times she's delivered it.

"Threats are dispatched without grief or conscience, and with complete discretion," Caro continues quietly. "If you would like to serve us, you must understand this."

I think the seriousness of her tone would strike fear into anyone's heart, much less someone already harboring treasonous thoughts. I scarcely breathe, and hope my face doesn't betray me. Luckily, Caro mistakes my emotion for something else and tries to give me a reassuring smile. I bow my head, suppressing a shiver. "I understand."

"The same, of course, goes for Ina." Now Caro's words seem slower, as if she's laboring over them. "If you serve her, we must be sure that you'll protect her with your life."

I nod. "I will." Caro manages a weak smile.

The Queen considers me, then rises smoothly to her feet, towering over us. "We'll soon see. Step forward, girl," she says.

When I hesitate, Caro lays a hand on my shoulder, an unspoken prompt to move next to Ina. I swallow and take an uneasy step forward, though my knees are still trembling beneath my skirts. Ina glances at me, smiling encouragingly.

"We're going to administer a loyalty test of sorts, Jules," Caro says, stepping to the side of me. "To make sure you have the instinct for the position."

"Anything you need—"

I stop when a movement ahead of me makes me look toward the Queen. She's produced a knife from somewhere. In her hand, the blade gleams. I freeze in terror as she raises it behind her shoulder.

And throws it straight at Ina's chest.

Silver flashes through the air.

Reflex bursts through my limbs. Faster than I can think, I move in front of Ina, sending up a plea to the Sorceress for time to slow, expecting any second to feel sharp metal biting into me.

But I feel nothing except for the double-time beating of my heart. Nothing comes. And nothing comes. For a second, I think I've done it—but when I open my eyes, my heart still loud in my ears, it's Caro who stands with her arm out, fingers wrapped around the knife's handle. She's caught it only inches away from where it would have sunk into my chest. I marvel at her speed. Her chest rises with the effort of catching it, but only slightly.

I breathe out. A loyalty test. My life for Ina's.

The Queen stares down at me, her face unreadable, as Caro returns the knife to her. I don't know whether it's my imagination or the chill of her words, but cold seems to emanate from her and settle into my own skin.

"Well done," she says. "To you as well, Caro. I see you didn't slip up this time." When the Queen turns her gaze to me, Caro's eyes flash with shame. "Remember that if you don't protect Ina with your life, should any risk come to pass, your years will be forfeit."

My mouth is dry as dust, but I swallow again and force myself to reply. "I understand, Your Majesty," I say, stripping all emotion from my voice.

The ruler of Sempera settles back in her chair and nods, and the room seems to let out a breath. I hear Caro's and Ina's soft breathing, a swish of fabric as they move. As the Queen waves a hand to dismiss us, I turn to look at them. As one, they smile back at me, with something like gratitude—or pity—shining in their eyes.

16

The trunk of clothes deposited at the foot of my bed later that night, and the long red dress like Caro's folded on top, is confirmation: I am to be in the Queen's retinue as Ina's new handmaiden. Ina offered to get me my own room near hers, but I didn't want to leave Alia in the dormitories. I find the company of the others comforting, and I feel my father's presence more here than in the silent, unfamiliar hallways that I visited today.

Now I'm closer than ever to the Queen and, I hope, closer to the meaning behind Papa's warning. Which means that I am closer than ever to danger.

I lay one of the dresses out on my bed, and a group of girls hover around it as if it were a hearth fire. Some of their looks are envious, to be sure, but others are almost pitying. Alia reaches out a small hand to stroke the fabric of the skirt. She's due to leave Everless for Crofton in a few days, so I resolve to smuggle one of the dresses away and alter it for a smaller girl, and bring it back for her when I return. *But when will I return?*

Bea notes, not uncheerfully, that the velvet-lined trunk is more luxurious than the servants' beds.

"The green dress was supposed to be Addie's," a younger girl named Selena says, to no one in particular. "Never worn." She's apprenticed to the seamstress—she would know. The others shuffle off, leaving Selena's words to tie a knot in my stomach.

I haven't told anyone what happened when I met the Queen. I'm too afraid—both of the Queen herself, and that no one will believe me. I tell myself that it was just a test of my loyalty, that Ina was never at risk—how could anyone throw a knife at their own daughter, even if they know it will never strike?

My first task as a royal handmaiden, detailed in a note Caro pinned to the inside of the trunk, is to collect ice holly for Roan and Lady Gold's wedding trellis. Though I'm disappointed that I'm not assigned to a task that would let me be near the Queen, I leave early from breakfast to put on one of the dresses and a thick cloak. I tame my hair as best I can and tuck it into my servant's cap, then walk down to the gardens, which are nestled in the innermost courtyard at the heart of Everless.

The Gerlings keep these gardens jealously to themselves

and their guests—I have to show Caro's note to a guard at the door to gain entrance—so though I've glimpsed the garden through windows, I've never before walked along its pristine mosaic pathways. The small, colored tiles of the path are smattered with snow. The flower beds are already bursting with roses and ivy, though winter is still holding strong against the onslaught of spring. I've heard the gardeners sprinkle the soil here with melted blood-iron, to make the flowers grow stronger and earlier and live longer. As grotesquely wasteful as the idea is, I can't deny the beauty of the blood-red roses against the snow.

Footsteps sound from behind me. I glance over my shoulder and am shocked to see Roan walking my way, holding a cloak over his shoulders, his head bare and curls flying around his face in the soft wind. I have the sudden, urgent, intimate need to tell him to put on a hat. He smiles at me and speeds his steps until he's by my side.

"I'd hoped to encounter you again," he says, giving my clothes an approving once-over. "I thought Liam might have thrown you in the dungeons or made you polish his shoes or some other awful thing."

"I'm a royal maid now." I dip my head. "Thank you again for your help."

He chuckles. It should feel wrong to be in the open with him, like this, but as we start to walk down the garden path, our steps feel as natural and light as they did when we were children. I wouldn't be surprised if he broke into a run, daring me to chase him.

I wish the words would come as easy—some nonsense or story, a teasing jab—but they don't. "I've never been here before," I say finally, gesturing around at the flowers. "The garden is lovely."

To my surprise, Roan sighs. "I suppose so. But I can't help but feel that it's false." Casually, he bats a rose with the back of his hand, watching it swing back and forth like the pendulum of a clock. His smile is mischievous—conspiratorial. "I've always preferred wildflowers to cultivated roses."

A memory floats to the surface, of the scent on him the other day—lavender, not rosewater. I nod. "Does the patch of lavender still grow by the south gate? The one we used to make into a fort?"

At first, he furrows his brow in thought, like he's trying to call up the memory. Then a glint appears in his eyes. "There may be some in the greenhouse," he says, nodding toward the other end of the garden. "We can see for ourselves."

"I'm to wait for Caro here," I say quickly, and Roan's face falls.

"Another time, then. How is life as a handmaiden?" He reaches down and grabs my hand as we walk, bringing it up to examine the ruffle of lace at my wrist. Heat floods my face at his touch, and it's all I can do to keep a casual expression—though I swear, he holds my hand a second longer than he has to before letting it fall to my side. "The dress suits you," he says conversationally.

My laugh comes out a little breathless. "It's not hard to surpass that burlap sack we wore in the kitchen."

Roan returns my laugh. "That too. But it's different. I was thinking about when we were children. How you wanted to be a blacksmith like your father, ran around covered in soot from the forge."

Elation and grief war in my chest. It's hard not to marvel at Roan, whose past seems to have been wiped clean of resentment, even memory, like a schoolchild's slate—but his unintentional slight stings.

He doesn't know about Papa, I tell myself, *he couldn't know. And: If Papa had seen how kind Roan was, maybe things would have been different.*

"Tell me something else," I say, anxious to change the subject. "What else do you remember?"

"Well." He grins. "You always were wild. Do you remember how you would make up stories about the forest animals? Or you'd make the rest of us act out old battles?"

At first, I don't remember, the memories buried under so many years of hunger and scrabbling for coin. But as I stare into Roan's blue eyes, unchanged from childhood, snatches of memories appear to me—hiding under the table in the great hall like we were spies; rolling down grassy hills pretending to be chased by wolves . . .

Suddenly, Roan blinks and breaks our gaze, lifting his hand in greeting to someone in the distance. I follow his eyes to see Caro walking toward us. She cocks her head at the sight of the two of us together.

"Lord Roan. Miss Ember," she says, once she's close enough for her whispery voice to reach us. "Good morning."

"Good morning, Caro," Roan returns gaily, but at a too-high pitch. Out of the corner of my eye, I see him raise his hand—as if to touch my arm—and then drop it, like he's thought better of it.

"Thank you again for your kindness in recommending me, Lord Gerling," I tell him, stepping away to put distance between us. "It's an honor to serve the Queen."

His smile is fleeting, just for me. "My pleasure." He nods at me, then at Caro. "And now if you'll excuse me, ladies. I have an appointment with my betrothed."

"One you're late for," Caro adds with a mild smile.

Roan meets my eyes one more time before striding back toward the castle.

Caro loops her arm through mine, like she did when retrieving me for the dress fitting. I smile at her, trying to hide my nervousness. The charge I feel when Roan is nearby is so strong that it's hard to believe everyone can't see it, like light jumping off my skin.

But Caro's answering smile is carefree. "I'm so glad the Queen approved of your appointment. Very few pass the loyalty test. It's more to scare people off than anything else," she says quickly, as if it's embarrassing to speak of. "To be truthful, with the wedding, I spend more time running errands for Ina than speaking with her. And soon . . ." Her voice trails off, and she stares into the distance. "She needs someone she can confide in. Rely on. Ina was saying after you left how much she likes you."

"She'll be married to Ro—Lord Roan soon," I point out. "Things will change then."

Caro smiles, a little sadly. "You're right, Jules. Things will change." She squeezes my arm and glances appreciatively around the garden. "Have you seen ice holly before?"

I shake my head, smiling in spite of myself, and she leads me toward the heart of the garden. As we go deeper in, the straight, orderly walkways turn narrow and meandering, with the flower beds scattered irregularly throughout. A few yards later, Caro stops and crouches down. She reaches carefully into a rosebush, avoiding the thorns, and extricates something small and silvery.

"There it is, just as the gardener described," she says, holding a thin, shining plant in her palm. It seems to glow. I bend closer to see the tiny sprig, beautiful and ornately edged like nothing I've ever seen. The stem is black, the leaves silver-white, and the berry a deep, dark blue. I realize it's the same plant—spindly stem, sharp narrow leaves—that was depicted on the Queen's jewelry box, the one Addie dropped the first day the Queen came to Everless.

"It's the Queen's sigil," Caro says, seeming again to read my thoughts. "They say it induces truth-telling and only grows in spots where the Sorceress has worked her magic."

I start to laugh and swallow it quickly as Caro looks up at me, surprised.

"Don't you believe it?" she asks.

"I'm sorry, my father . . ." I say quickly. "I wasn't raised to believe in Sorceress magic." What I don't tell her—my father scorned the idea at every turn, when I became too old to crawl into his arms and beg for stories. Without Roan near, my childhood rears again into something dark, severed the moment we were forced to flee the Gerling estate.

"But look." Caro reaches down and carefully parts two sections of rosebush, so we can see beneath. Puzzled, I peer in to see the ice holly that grows in its shade. It clusters, like bushes or tiny trees, but only a few inches high. And it follows a strange pattern along the ground—almost like footprints.

I kneel, feeling the sudden urge to touch the plant. The stone path is cold on my skin, even through my dress. My finger brushes the underside of a leaf, and a vivid image breaks into my mind—the ice holly in the same patch of dirt, but growing wildly under flitting sun and shadow. It's as if I'm watching many days pass in rapid succession.

Dizzily, I straighten up. Caro observes me closely but says nothing. She points out the garden's unorganized center. "That's why the garden is like this. The Gerlings shaped it around the ice holly." She leans closer, lowers her voice. "Ice holly is rare now. The Queen demanded that the Gerlings' patch be picked immediately. I suspect that Verissa is furious."

"I see." I'm not convinced of its magic, but the strange image disturbs me for reasons I can't explain. I crouch next to her and let her show me how to avoid the thorns, how to pick the holly without damaging the root.

We place the ice holly in a wicker basket Caro has brought. The plant is so small and delicate that the basket will take all morning to fill, but, especially after the mava, I don't mind a few scratches on my hands to pick the beautiful ice holly and listen to Caro's stream of soft, warm chatter. She reminds me of a bird, with her quick, efficient movements, musical voice, and glittering eyes.

When the basket is a third full, she says, "Roan seems very taken with you." I stiffen at the words, even as they send an illicit thrill through me. She doesn't sound judgmental, just curious—but still, her words make me wary.

I almost say, *I saved him.* But even in my head, the phrase makes me sound like a child, my wishful heart twisting a ten-year-old daydream into reality. Liam pushed Roan toward the fire. Maybe I caught him. Maybe Papa did, and I shaped it into a story of my own, like I used to do with Roan as a child.

"We were friends when we were children," I say eventually. "When my father worked at Everless. I owe him for suggesting me to you. Lord Liam had assigned me to the mava pile the other day, and Roan got me out of it."

"Mava!" Caro's eyes widen in horror. "I did wonder at the marks on your hands. Whatever did you do to deserve that?"

"I might have deserved it, a little," I say offhandedly, trying to downplay what I've said. "I was in a hall I shouldn't have been in, and of course it was near the vault. Liam found me."

"Were you trying to get in?" Caro asks plainly.

I shake my head vigorously. The last thing I need is Caro thinking me a thief. "I wouldn't dare. It was . . . an accident."

"Hmmm." Caro considers me, a little smile turning her lips up at the corners. "An accident, for the girl who knows Everless so well?"

I open my mouth to speak, but quickly close it again— before I betray myself.

Caro raises her eyebrows, then plucks a berry from a sprig of ice holly, rolling it between two fingers. "You don't have to lie to me, Jules." Her voice is almost wistful. "I'm not a brute, nor as unforgiving as the Queen. I won't throw you in chains."

I shake my head, but she keeps looking at me, clearly expecting me to say something.

I let out a slow, careful breath. "I've been thinking . . . there might be something of my father's inside the vault." I don't want to tell her I was following Liam, but this is true too. And I'm almost shocked by how easily the confession rolls off my tongue, as though I had always meant to tell Caro. She said the

187

ice holly caused truth-telling, but that couldn't possibly be true, could it?

"When we moved away from Everless years ago, we left some valuables behind," I add hastily, by way of explanation. Not a complete lie, anyway. "Maybe they ended up there." I shake my head. "It's silly, I—"

"No, don't say that," Caro says. "It's not silly or foolish. Your father is gone, and you want to treasure what little you can of him. But, yes—even under the Queen's orders, now, it wouldn't do to have you getting caught doing something like that. The Gerlings are quite protective of their precious blood-irons—Liam especially." She pauses. "If I can, I'll look for you. What is it you think might be inside?"

"No!" I exclaim, my voice coming out louder than I'd meant it. I add hastily: "Liam told me that any non-Gerling who tries to get in can die. The door's enchanted."

To my surprise, Caro laughs. The sound is musical, louder than her voice; it floats over the garden like bells. "I'm sure it's a simple time toll," she says.

"You really mustn't."

"I'm leaving with the Queen tonight, for a few days," she says, brushing off my protests. "We're visiting a few of the lesser nobles in the north. But when I'm back, I can be discreet, to check for you. Or perhaps we can go together—I'll take the time toll, and you can be ready with a carafe of years. It might be fun," she finishes, a wild glow in her pale eyes.

"Please, no, Caro. It's far too dangerous." I swallow. All at once I feel foolish—and scared. "I . . . I don't even know if it's true. If something of Papa's is really there."

"But it seems important." Caro smiles. "Will you do me a favor in return?"

"Of course," I say immediately, wanting to turn her away from thoughts of breaking into the vault. "Anything."

"If you notice anything about Roan's behavior that seems . . . notable, will you tell me?" Her voice is sweet, her face slightly pinched in concern. The request turns my tongue to sand as I remember the seconds that passed before he dropped my hand from his.

"Yes, gladly. I'm sure that won't be any work at all."

"Thank you," she says, wrapping me in a light embrace. "You're my friend now, Jules. Ina's as well. We have to look out for one another."

In the distance, an estate bell rings. Caro leaps to her feet before I can reply, and thrusts the basket into my hands. "I have to attend the Queen. Can you take this back to the kitchen? They will be preparing the trellis."

My attention is still snagged on the word *friend*—I don't know how it can be, when I've known Caro for less than two days, but it feels true. I want to please her. "What should I do?" I ask her. "Will I be accompanying you and the Queen?" My pulse quickens at the thought.

"No," Caro says quickly. Disappointment surges in me.

"We'll be sorting out a debt owed to the Queen; it'll be tedious. You should stay here and attend to Ina while we're gone. She'd like your company. When she doesn't need you, do what you want. Unless the Queen or I or Ina need you for something, your evenings will usually be free."

I almost gape at her like an imbecile, but close my mouth and nod—as if the thought of a night off isn't a precious gift, as though I don't want to weep with gratitude at the prospect. A flash of happiness goes through me, different from the tainted, vengeful thrill I felt yesterday at my new appointment. This feeling is different, purer. Born of nothing more complicated than the thought of an evening to myself, and of a friend.

17

It's a strange and uncomfortable thing to be back among the kitchen servants but not be one of them. To be honest, even before being chosen as Ina's servant, I felt set apart—I was new to Everless though I was not new at all, a secret walking the halls of the Gerling estate. Then in my fog of grief, the wedding preparations were the furthest thing from my mind and I barely spoke to the people surrounding me every day.

In a back room off the kitchen, a group of servants weave ivy and a thick, silver ribbon into the latticed wood of the trellis. Deni, a young girl with a crown of braids, takes the basket from me and begins to spread the ice holly on a long table; a boy I don't know unspools a thin wire in his hands.

Bea appears beside me. She reaches out to pluck a glittering branch of holly from the table, begins to weave it in with a wire.

"So what's it like?" she says to me. "Working for the Queen?"

Three other girls at the table look up to hear my answer. I am mindful of Caro's words yesterday—I am not to speak of the Queen or what I learn of her. "I haven't seen much of her so far, to be truthful," I tell them. "I hope to—soon."

"Not if you know what's good for you," Ingrid comments. She rolls a berry between her fingertips. Worry gnaws at me as the others murmur in agreement. "She'll turn you out, Jules, like she did Addie."

"She'll turn you into a coin!" Deni blurts out.

"Don't mind them," Bea says, shooting Deni and Ingrid a sharp glance. "Lot o' fearmongers, if you ask me." She turns back to the group. "My father's father served the Queen as a boy, and she saw to his education—"

"Is that why you're here?" Ingrid snorts. Bea furrows her brow, clearly stung, and turns back to the ice holly spread on the table. "I'm sorry, Bea," Ingrid says. "But it's for your own good, both of y—"

"I'll be fine," I cut in, though every fiber of me screams that I won't. I nod to the silvered leaves on the table, ready to be pierced and hung. "You all have more important things to worry about than me."

Ingrid looks like she's about to protest, but a small figure appears in the doorway and waves to me before a word escapes her mouth. I haven't seen Hinton in a long time—at least it seems so. He darts through the girls, to my side. I bend down and hug him, but he seems nervous, stiff and fidgeting in my arms.

"Someone's here to see you, Jules," he says quietly. "Out in the hallway." He grabs my sleeve and tugs me out of the group, toward the door.

To my shock, it's Liam, leaning against the opposite wall with his hands in his coat pockets. He looks in a foul mood, his brows drawn low over his face. He tosses a coin to Hinton, who catches it and vanishes into the kitchen like a rabbit into its den.

"What are you doing here?" I demand. I have less reason to be afraid of Liam, now that Roan and Caro are on my side—but the old fears run through my blood, and I can't silence the alarm bells that crash in me at the sight of him.

He withdraws a slip of paper from his breast pocket and holds it out. "Ina demanded that I deliver this to you."

I smile, thinking of Ina's impression of Liam during the dress fitting—it seems that she can't resist the urge to remind him that despite his birth, she outranks him. I take a measure of petty satisfaction in his discomfort. Liam glowers at me as I take the paper and step back to unfold and read it. The handwriting is pretty, but slightly uneven, as if the writer was rushing to finish.

Jules, I'm planning to take a ride outside of Everless tomorrow and would like you to join me. Please meet me

at the stables at first light so we can make the most of
the day.

Love, Ina.

"For a servant, you've certainly entangled yourself in the workings of Everless," Liam observes as I tuck the note into my dress pocket.

"I'm sure I don't know what you mean."

"You've found favor with Lady Gold," he says. "And with my brother."

The sharp reply I had ready dissolves on my tongue. I keep my eyes on his face, scanning his eyes for what he knows, and find an unreadable determination. I can't imagine Roan confiding in him. The few times I've seen the brothers in the same room, they've seemed in separate universes—Roan the center of attention, all light and laughter, and Liam observing silently from some corner, eyes so dark they seem to devour any light that comes near, causing candles to gasp and stutter, like my heart is doing right now.

"We were children together," I say. "You know that. You were there too." *Though always off to the side, always observing, always silent.* "Roan and I are—" I stop, unable to finish the thought.

Liam's mouth twists. "Friends?" His laugh is cruel. "I think my brother has something different in mind."

My gut twists—not in pain or pleasure at his implication,

but in anger. All these years, and nothing has changed. "Impugning your brother, your future sister-in-law, and me all at once," I say coldly. "Impressive. Are you so proud that you can't stand to be under someone else's direction even for a few minutes?"

He blinks, his face twisting into something like hurt and then quickly back into impassiveness. "I don't care about rank," he says. "I never have."

"Ah, so it's personal." Before he can answer, I turn and stride down the hall toward the dormitory.

There's a pause, then: "You and your father didn't belong here," Liam calls after me, his voice strangely dispassionate.

The blood in me runs cold, as if all the hours, days, and years coursing through me have stopped. I turn to face Liam—his eyes are flint. As I approach, I see the hint of a spark in them.

"What did you say about my father?" My voice is low and—I hope—carries the weight of my anger. After holding my gaze for a few fleeting seconds, he casts his eyes down to the floor without giving an answer. His shoulders slump, the posture of a boy who's just had his hand slapped for stealing sweets.

Then the Everless bells ring out, loud and long and fiercely, it seems, keeping time with the clenching and unclenching of my fists. I turn and retreat down the corridor again, hoping with every step that Liam Gerling doesn't follow.

18

The next morning, in the dormitory, I slip on one of the warmer—and more luxurious—dresses Caro has given me, boots, and a gray cloak. Though my ugly mood from the conversation with Liam still lingers, I can't help but marvel at the softness of the fabric, the weight of the cloak. Through all of Crofton's bitter winters, I've never had anything so warm.

To my shock, Roan is in the servants' hallway, leaning against the wall, a puncture in the rectangle of light streaming in through a high window. I take in a sharp breath. Was he— waiting for me? Had Ina told him about her request?

But he looks just as startled to see me. "Jules," he says, in lieu of good morning. Then he regains his composure. "Ina mentioned you were accompanying her on an errand. Where are you off to?"

Before I can answer, Bea emerges from the dormitories, with her light, slippered step. She sees Roan first, and a smile spreads over her face—then she sees me, and her eyes widen, the smile slipping. By the time I think to say good morning, she has changed course and disappeared down the corridor, like she suddenly remembered something important.

Roan looks after her for a moment before turning back to me. In the harsh, angled light, his dimples become dark spots on his face. I realize that he's waiting for an answer.

"Just a ride," I say lightly. Even Roan doesn't know where Ina and I are going, apparently. Already, I'm sweating from the warmth of the castle, the weight of the dress, and Roan's gaze. "I know the grounds well, after all."

This satisfies him. He breathes in, then lets the breath out, running one hand through his already messy hair. "Of course. I worry that she's getting restless. Thank you for keeping her company, Jules," he says seriously. "Take care of her, and yourself."

Then, Roan waves, and he's off in the same direction as Bea, covering the corridor quickly with his long stride. Without thinking, I start to reach out a hand toward him, like a plant that always reaches to the sun. The word *wait* melts on my tongue.

When he's gone, I walk in the direction of the stables, wondering why, why, why, Ina Gold would not have told her fiancé what this errand was. With every step down the corridor,

I feel my body become a toy, a puppet; the pull of the Gerlings, Ina, the Queen, and their secrets weave through me, pierce my skin, pull at my limbs. All I wanted was to learn the truth about Papa—how did it land me in the middle of this chessboard?

It's a relief to get outside, into the fresh cold air of the courtyard. Snow has fallen during the night, covering the great lawn with a thin, sparkling dusting of white. I wish I could walk, observe the palisades and turrets of Everless from a distance, look out over the lake. But the sun is a hand's width above the horizon by now, so instead I hurry to the stables to meet Ina.

She's already there, also dressed in a traveling dress and gray cloak, a leather bag slung over her shoulder. Catching sight of my bare hands, she takes a pair of gloves out of her cloak and offers them to me. I'm immediately surprised, not just by her generosity but also by the fact that she's dressed like me—like a high-ranking servant.

She is standing by two horses, one dun and one chestnut. The dun one is already saddled; behind her, Tam is strapping the gear to the chestnut's back. My stomach drops like a stone into water, and I feel sweat prickling at my palms. I had expected we would be taking a cart or carriage.

While I can ride—in Crofton, I occasionally found odd jobs carrying messages or making deliveries on horseback—I'm not a natural at it, and the Gerlings' huge, well-fed, spirited horses make me nervous. After a moment I realize I've stopped and am staring rudely, so I hurriedly lower my head and curtsy to Ina.

"No need for that," she says. Despite her plain dress, she looks as beautiful and regal as always. But something about her is hesitant, almost somber. Her short hair is stuck under a plain wool cap, the ends a dark, blunt fringe on her ears. "It's good to have you here, Jules."

Cautiously, I approach the horses, greeting Tam with a nod and a smile. He's looking curiously between me and Lady Gold, asking me with his eyes why I'm standing here, next to the Queen's daughter. I shake my head slightly, mouthing: *I'll explain later.* I see his mouth twist, how stiffly he bows. I add him to the list of people—Lora and Bea and Hinton already—to whom I owe explanations for my rudeness.

"Which horse would you like?" Ina asks politely, as if she's asking if I prefer sugar or milk in my tea. "This is Honey"—she pets the dun horse's nose—"and this is Mava."

"Honey," I say, so quickly that Ina laughs. "I'll have Honey."

"All right, then." She presses the dun horse's reins into my hands, and I blink away nervousness as the creature turns to regard me, its big eyes seeming to measure me up. I remember what Papa told me about horses: don't act nervous, even if you are.

The same thing could be said of royalty.

Somehow, I expect that there will be more preparation, but Ina is ready, and so Tam comes around to my side to boost me up into Honey's saddle. I clamber awkwardly into place, gripping the saddle horn nervously.

Ina sees my tense shoulders, and surprise flashes across her face, followed by embarrassment. I can tell it hasn't occurred to her that I might not know how to ride, and now she's ashamed, wondering how to backpedal. Everything Ina Gold feels is transparent, clear as day on her beautiful face. That she never has to hide her emotions is a luxury—but I can't resent her for it. She's known me for all of two days, but she truly cares whether I'm comfortable.

"I'm fine riding," I say before she can speak—wanting to get out of Everless, to breathe free, if only for a day. I straighten in the saddle and move my hands to the reins, trying not to think about how far off the ground I am. Ina swings up onto her horse all on her own—she's as graceful as a dancer—and pulls her hood up over her head. She leads us out of the stables. Luckily for me, Honey follows Mava out of instinct.

"I want to go to an orphanage between Crofton and Laista," Ina says quietly, once we're out of earshot of Tam. "About an hour's ride away. I haven't exactly told anyone about this little outing. Not Roan or Caro or the Queen. They all think I'm going to be hunted and slaughtered like spotted hare," she says, so cavalierly that I have to laugh. "So I would be grateful if— you know . . ."

Ina turns to me, biting her lip. Lady Ina Gold doesn't seem the sort to keep secrets, much less from her betrothed or the Queen, her surrogate mother, but then, I remember, neither do I.

I nod, and smile.

Ina catches sight of something over my shoulder and closes her mouth. She motions at me to fall in behind her as we come up on the south gate, a smaller set of doors than the great gates she and the Queen came through a week ago, this one meant for servants and deliveries. It's guarded by two freezing-looking guards, who watch us coming without interest but snap to attention when they see Ina's face. They both bow deeply.

"Lady Gold," one stammers, after they straighten up. "Ought—ought you be going outside the walls without an escort?"

Ina doesn't miss a beat, and there's an easy cheerfulness in her voice that wasn't there when we were alone. "I am escorted, in case you think this girl is a ghost," she says, sweeping her hand in my direction. "I'm only going to surprise Roan on his hunt."

Again, I'm surprised by how easily the lie falls from her lips. Her eyes, clear and pure as drops of water, give away nothing. Instinct kicks at me to tell Ina about Roan's visit to the servants' quarters this morning—instead, I tuck the knowledge away, next to my other secrets to keep for later.

Regardless, it works—the guards stand back and let us through. We ride out into the plain beyond Everless's walls; the doors stand open a moment longer, then swing heavily shut. It's amazing how rapidly I feel lighter, as if I hadn't noticed the iron weight sitting on my chest until it was lifted away.

Ina leads us to the main road. It's early enough that travelers are few and far between—we pass a handful of carts ambling toward Everless, loaded up with hay or wood or piles of grain, but no one else seems to be heading away. Ina keeps her hood up, but outside the walls of Everless, nobody looks her way twice. Or rather, people look, but only in the way anyone would upon seeing a girl as beautiful as Ina. None of the farmers and merchants we pass seem to know she's the Queen's daughter, the future ruler of Sempera.

When she pulls Mava to a smaller road that cuts through the forest, I follow, though my fingers grip the reins, making them slick with sweat. I wonder if my father walked through these woods on his last trip to Everless.

"You don't think there would be . . . bleeders in these woods?" Ina glances around fearfully, less dismissive now that we're surrounded by twisting black trunks and shadows. I wonder if she was badly frightened in the raid that killed their servants. To my confused look, she replies, "Have you heard? A hedge witch was murdered yesterday in Ayleston."

A chill runs down my spine. Papa always told me that hedge witches and other so-called lesser sorcerers were charlatans, but not everyone believes that—and someone said to have a special relationship with time might make a pretty target for thieves. I shake my head, clear my throat as well as my mind. "We're safe this close to Everless." Since I am expected to die for her if we're attacked, I hope that it's the truth. "But I don't know this part of the forest well."

"That's all right," Ina says, pulling a folded map out of her dress pocket.

The light grows thicker as the tree branches give way to the sky. I'm uneasy on Honey's back—every time she turns slightly to follow Mava or avoid debris in the path, I grip the saddle with my thighs, afraid of falling. At least the cold has eased some as the sun has risen. And the landscape around us is strangely beautiful; it all sparkles now with snow and melting ice.

As grateful as I am for the change of scenery, I can't push aside the suspicion the Queen's daughter may be hiding something.

"Ina . . ." I trail off. Questioning the Queen's charge still feels more than unnatural—Ina's power hovers in the air like a creature waiting to strike. But I push on. "Why are we going to an orphanage? If you don't mind my asking."

"Oh." Ina laughs a little, though it sounds hollow to me. "You know, I've been so engrossed in this map that I forgot I didn't tell you."

She half turns in her saddle, just as at ease as if she is on a chaise longue at the palace on the shores. Still, she takes a long time to respond, and when she does, her voice is slow and soft. "I want to know who my birth parents are," she says matter-of-factly. "I love the Queen, and am grateful to her, but I want to know who . . . who came before."

She faces forward again, so I no longer see her face. "I thought about asking Roan along, but he's so—so lighthearted. I didn't want him to think about something sad, or to think that I was unhappy." This I understand perfectly, wanting to keep all the darkness and grief of the world from touching Roan. "And if the Queen finds out . . ."

I finish her sentence in my head: *she'll be disappointed.*

She'll accuse me of treason.

She'll have my head.

I wonder which is true, though I don't yet dare to ask. The memory of the Queen's knife flying toward Ina flashes through my mind.

"And Caro?" I ask.

Ina sighs, sounding disappointed. "She knows I go out on rides by myself, but not where I go. She wouldn't approve either. Anyway, she's off on one of her mysterious errands for the Queen."

"What are the errands?" I ask, curious, then blush for my nosiness.

"Nothing important," Ina says dismissively. "You know the Queen is obsessed with the Sorceress. She likes to go to the old places, battle sites and graves and so on, and she always takes Caro with her."

A thought occurs to me. "How did Caro come into the

Queen's favor? Was she . . ." I let my words trail off, though by the way her hand grips the reins, I know Ina understands what I mean to say.

"Was she abandoned, like the others?" Ina finishes softly.

My silence is a nod.

Ina turns her head again and flashes a smile—though the sadness still hangs delicately in her features, like smoke. "She says she's never been curious about her parents, and neither should I. She thinks it was fate that brought her to the palace, to the Queen, so she doesn't care about what came before. She's very loyal, as good as family. If she hadn't come to the Queen at an older age, I wonder . . ."

There's an emotion tangled in Ina's voice—whether it's doubt, guilt, or envy, I can't quite tell. Perhaps it's all three.

She glances at me out of the corner of her eye. "I'm grateful to you for being discreet. It's good to talk to another or—" She pulls Mava to a sudden halt. "I'm so foolish. I didn't mean to bring up family just after your father passed."

"It's fine," I say automatically, though my heart twists a little. It's a good kind of pain, if there is such a thing. To have these words—*parents*, *orphan*—out in the air is strange, but it's better than having them boiling under my skin. Part of me wonders that Ina Gold should be so trusting. But why shouldn't she be? Maybe it's me, with my hidden landscapes of secrets and fears, who's the abnormal one.

Ina blinks, as if she feels it too. "It's such a relief to trust

you, Jules—I feel like I can talk to you. Like you understand."
She smiles, a little bashfully. "Do tell me to stop if I'm not
making sense. I know it's forward of me—"

I shake my head—I do understand, at least in regards to
how she feels about her parentage. My whole being wants
to cling to the idea of Papa. His letter in my breast pocket,
now almost falling apart from being folded and refolded so
many times, is a testament to that. And I want Ina to know
that. I want her to trust me.

Ina kicks Mava forward. Honey follows. Ina and I make a
strange pair—a princess and a servant, one long-time orphaned
and one freshly so, one with the favor of the Queen and one
with the love of a father. It occurs to me that I wouldn't trade
places with her if I was given the chance, wouldn't trade Papa
for the Queen.

The thought sends a fresh bolt of grief through me, and
I cast around for another topic of conversation quickly, before
it overcomes me. "I thought the Queen's orphanage was on the
eastern shore, near the palace," I say. Of course, that would be
a journey of weeks. Ina and I are packed for hours.

"That was the first orphanage," Ina says. "I've almost been
to them all, by now. There are so many, Jules, all over the
kingdom—families still abandon their children on the palace
shores. We could form a whole city by ourselves."

I shake my head, imagining a city of orphans, running wild
with no knowledge of their past.

"I've visited every one I could find, to look through their records," Ina continues. The outpouring of words makes it clear she's thought about this, turned it over in her head many times. "The truth is that I have no idea which one I came from. I cannot ask Her Majesty."

"Of course not," I murmur. Something makes me shiver, and I pull the wool cloak closer to me.

"All I know is that Ina is the name my birth mother gave me." She pauses. "And still, I don't know that for sure." Without being told, I know what Ina is feeling: the ache of longing for a parent's kind touch, a reassuring word, has carved out a hole in my chest. "So I've gone to nearly every orphanage in the kingdom. And I've found nothing."

Now a morbid curiosity has taken hold of me. Are my birth parents alive or dead? Did they leave me on the shores of the palace, to be chosen by the Queen, picked up by an orphanage, or else die breathing the sea-salt air? How did Papa come to claim me as his own?

Does it have anything to do with why he died for me?

We pass through a clearing; though the sun is high now, I shiver again, then let the letter tucked near my heart warm me. Papa must have found me at one of these orphanages, and given me what even Ina Gold, princess of Sempera, lacks: love.

After the gloomy turn in the conversation, we ride the rest of the way in relative quiet. Ina's map takes us down narrower and narrower roads, through plains and woods, until finally in a forest of birch we encounter a huge and ornate but rusted wrought-iron gate. The words carved at the top have been crusted over with snow and ice, but I can still make them out: *Here is a refuge for Sempera's children, so that all may have a home.* The inscription twists at something deeply buried in my heart.

We pause at the gate for a few minutes, unsure whether to call out—all we can see beyond it is more snow and more trees. But before either of us get down from our horses, a child appears at the bars—a little girl with shorn black hair and wide, wide eyes, no older than six or seven. She regards us solemnly, wrapping bare hands around the carved iron. She's wearing a threadbare coat and trousers too big for her, not remotely enough for this cold.

"Are you a fairy?" the child asks.

Ina opens her mouth and falters, then glances at me. Her usual composure seems to have deserted her; she looks anxious and uncertain, her lips chapped where she's bitten them. Except for the brief moment outside the Queen's chambers, I've never seen her nervous—not even when she was parading into Everless for the first time at the Queen's side. But she's nervous now. So I swing down from the saddle, landing heavily in the snow.

The little girl doesn't move as I draw near. At the gate, I crouch down so I'm at her eye level and try to channel the way Lora speaks to me, or the way Papa did when I was little.

"Fairies aren't real, love," I say trying to sound bright and open, though I can't shake the thought of how cold she must be, her fingers entwined in the metal of the gate.

The girl nods and stares past me. Then I realize she's not gazing at me or Ina, but at the horses. I glance over my shoulder and see them through her eyes, Mava's shiny coat and silky mane, the proud arch of Honey's neck. "You can pet them," I tell the girl. "Go on."

She blinks at me, then the barest hint of a smile brightens her face. She grips the metal bars and backs up, hauling the gate along with her. I beckon to Ina—she blinks uncertainly, then dismounts and takes the reins of both horses in hand, leading them through the gate. The girl lifts her hand to brush Mava's side as Ina leads them past, captivated.

Between the trees ahead of us, a building starts to take form—a large, ramshackle building that looks as if someone tried to imitate Everless without possessing either the blood-iron or foresight of the Gerlings. Two wings of black stone wrap around a large, bare courtyard, where dozens of young boys and girls are scattered, racing about and playing in the snow. None of them seem to be older than ten. Their shrieks and yells echo off the trees.

Ina puts a hand on my arm. She's hanging back, looking up at the building with trepidation.

"Will you . . . will you go inside for me?" she asks. "I need to walk."

I blink. "Don't you want to see for yourself?"

"We're nearly the same age . . ." Ina avoids my gaze, staring instead at the children who are now gawking at the horses. "Ask if we can look through the records from the month before the day the Queen found me. That should be enough, I think. But say it's for you—that you're wondering about you." Talking faster and faster with nervousness, she gives me the day of her birth as the Queen remembers it—March the sixth— and I register with surprise that she is only a few days older than me, born on the eleventh.

With a flash of clarity, I also understand why she means me to pose as the one seeking information, because it can't be known that she's out here in the country, trying to learn about her life before the Queen. My gut twists in a combination of disappointment and hurt. I'm still a tool, or a glove to be slipped on and used as needed by those more powerful— even to Ina Gold, the girl who only an hour before said she could trust me, that we understood each other. But I say, "Of course."

Ina leaves to find a stable for the horses, and I continue inside. Up close, I can see that the orphanage building is ill-maintained. Some bricks in the wall look loose, and I find myself standing on a floor of ancient, warped boards. A little fire burns in a hearth. A small, balding older man is seated at a desk across the room, writing in a ledger. When the door closes, he looks up, startled, and takes me in.

"Good afternoon," he says, his voice creaky. "How can I help you, miss?"

"Good afternoon." I clear my throat and recite the words Ina gave me to say—I am a curious orphan working in Laista, hoping to examine the institution's records for any hint of my birth during one winter, seventeen years ago.

The clerk listens attentively, then rises from his seat—I can hear his bones creak—and walks to a bookshelf along the wall, lined with huge, aged ledgers in various states of decrepitude. He floats his finger around them, using no logic that I can follow, and finally pulls one off the top shelf. He places it on a desk with a heavy thud, and I cough on the ensuing cloud of dust.

As he opens the book, I draw closer to read over his shoulder. Each large, yellowed page is filled with rows of names and numbers. The name of the child and his or her birthday, if known; the day and state in which they entered the orphanage; the name of their adopter, if there was one. The last column is only a third as full as the first two. But then I reach a section where all the information is scattered. There are numbers instead of names, and many blanks.

The man sees the confusion on my face. "The woman who ran this orphanage before my husband and I was terrible at record keeping," he explains. "Then, a few decades ago, there were some nasty cases, people who would adopt children just to steal their time. The Queen hanged them all and dismissed the orphanage workers who had let it happen. To keep order, you know." He laughs, but there is no humor in it. "To be safe, our records have gotten quite good over the years. But still—" He frowns, looking closer. "This was the year of those tremors."

"The tremors?" I echo. "In the earth?" We hadn't felt them in Crofton, but the stories kept me awake—in one town near the palace, the ground ripped in two, swallowing buildings and people whole.

The attendant raises his eyebrows. "No—tremors in time." Dimly, I call up a memory of my father dismissing stories about time shattering. "The winter you asked about, we saw all sorts of disturbances. Frozen moments, days that seemed too long. Once, we all lost an hour together. People were frantic. There was panic up and down the coast, looting, and then there was the whole business with Briarsmoor." The man chews on his cheek, staring at some point over my shoulder.

I'm beginning to feel like Papa didn't tell me anything about the world. "What's Briarsmoor?"

"Nothing like education these days." The attendant's voice is mildly chiding, though not aimed at me. "It's a town, Briarsmoor, some miles north of here. It's twelve hours behind the rest of us—if you and I were sitting there now, it'd be the dark of night. Time froze in that town for half a day that winter. And people started saying that all the children who came from there were cursed."

He leans his chin on his hand and tilts his head at me,

waiting for a reaction, but my mind is still grappling with what he's said. It's not unusual for time to trip over itself in places, to slow down or speed up or pause entirely for a moment, the wind and sun hold still while we move about our lives, oblivious that we're out of time's current. But everything always irons itself out. It's unbelievable that anywhere time could drag to half a day behind—and even more so that the lag could last so long.

"The Queen ordered everyone to evacuate," he continues, "but the damage was done."

A half hour later, I've paged through the ledger three times, front to back and back to front to back again. But I've seen no sign of baby Ina, or of me. And indeed, one entire week is absent from the ledger. Is it possible that we were abandoned in the week out of time?

Briarsmoor. The name sparks something like recognition in me—although how could it, if Papa had never mentioned it?

"Jules?" Ina's voice calls from outside, making me start. I thank the man for his help, and return the useless ledger to its shelf. Then I hurry out to find the Queen's daughter.

It's started to snow outside, just a faint dust of white crowning Ina's hood. She sees me and her face falls. "Nothing? No record?"

"No names," I say. "But—"

Before I can tell her about Briarsmoor, Ina's huffed a sigh and turned away from me. "These places and their shoddy

213

record keeping," she says, muffled. The bluster is visible in her frame. Though I don't know her well enough to say for sure, I'd swear she's on the verge of tears. "I've scoured practically every orphanage in the kingdom."

I want to say something to comfort her, but she's already off, walking fast toward the orphanage's half-tipped-over stables. The crowd of wide-eyed children admiring our horses scatter when we come in, disappearing out a back exit before either of us can say a word.

As we saddle up, an idea forms in my head. "The clerk did mention something . . ." I start, making Ina look up sharply. "He said there's a town north of here—"

"I know," Ina interrupts. "Briarsmoor." Her mouth twists like she's just eaten a rotten fruit.

"You've been?"

"No, but I know it," Ina says with finality. "And there's nothing there. It's a ruin."

My heart sinks, but— "There couldn't have been *nothing*," I press. "Maybe no people, but what about books? Papers?"

"I cannot go to Briarsmoor. The Queen forbids it." Her voice is hard as stone, and I wonder if there isn't an old conflict buried there, one still too raw to reveal to me. "She says it's cursed."

"Maybe . . ." I start, but Ina has already made it into her saddle. She glances toward me and then up the road to the north, stiffening. But then something goes out of her. Her

214

shoulders slump, making her look less like a princess, more like any sad girl I might have known in Crofton.

"And what would we do there, even if the Queen didn't discover us?" she says, an uncharacteristic note of roughness in her voice. "No. I'm tired of dead ends and strange towns."

A protest rises in my throat, but I push it back down and clamber onto my horse. It's not my place to contest her.

We ride back to Everless in silence—Ina's in a dark mood, whereas I'm still too consumed by what the clerk told me. Briarsmoor. How can it be—and how could Papa not have mentioned the name or the curious town that dropped out of time?

But there's no end to what my father kept secret from me. Even his death is a mystery.

Another thought hits me with brute force: maybe I am a mystery—a secret—that needs unraveling, too.

The idea takes hold of me, somewhere deep down, and I know that as soon as I can, I will have to find my own way to the town out of time.

With a sack of Gerling hours on my belt, I think.

If there is some truth to the superstition he mentioned— that Briarsmoor babies are cursed—I'm sure that Ina, the kingdom's most blessed child, couldn't have been born there.

But that doesn't mean I wasn't.

Time has always moved strangely around me, clinging for one moment too long, then stuttering to catch up with the world. Maybe Briarsmoor has clung to me all these years.

And I certainly feel cursed. The weight of everything I've lost is like a collection of stones in my chest. My mother and Papa are the heaviest, but there are a thousand other things too, little things, taken from me—our tiny garden in Crofton, Amma's comforting embrace . . . and further back, the blazing warmth of the blacksmith's workshop, Roan's childhood smile. I pull on Honey's reins and fall behind, so Ina won't see the couple of tears that escape and track down my face.

We come into view of Everless just as the sun is starting to set. The estate is a spiky dark silhouette against the orange glow of the sky. Ina stops on the empty road, and I pull to a halt beside her. I peer at her, unsure if something is wrong, but she's just staring at it, this temporary home we both share, a curious mix of wonder and grief on her beautiful face.

"Maybe it's better that I don't know," she says, half to herself. I lean close to hear her. "There are less than three weeks left until the wedding, for Sorceress's sake. Maybe this is a sign I shouldn't be running all over the kingdom looking for answers that probably don't exist . . . I mean, I have everything I need already."

She looks over at me, vulnerable. And though I can't understand why Ina Gold, the daughter of the Queen, should need reassurance from a servant girl, she clearly does. The need is written all over her face.

A hint of irritation seeps into me. Why should Ina need me to comfort her, when she has everything she could ever dream of at her fingertips, when she will sit on the throne one day?

But her eyes remind me of the does I used to see, foraging alone in the Crofton forest. My survival, and Papa's, depended on my being a merciless hunter. Even so, if a doe ever looked me straight in the eye, I could never bring myself to fire.

I take her gloved hand in my own. In spite of everything, I want to help her. I know what it is to be lost. "My father raised me as his, but then confessed that I wasn't, Ina," I tell her. She squeezes my hands so tightly that I wince. "I know what it's like not to know. But—" I pause, letting the truth swirl inside of me. "It's more lonely that he didn't tell me the truth. That he was afraid to, I think, because he thought I wouldn't love him like a father. But he was wrong."

The Queen's daughter takes her hands from mine, covers her own face. Then, in the growing shadow of the estate, she sobs. The sound pierces me—I've said the wrong thing, let my grief carry me away.

"Everyone at Everless loves you," I say. She leans over and quietly nods into my shoulder. "No one talked of anything else before you arrived—just Ina Gold, how beautiful and kind she was, and how lucky Roan was to have her." Saying Roan's name makes the stones in my chest get heavier, but I push past them. "And that's only the beginning. Anyone can see how much the Queen loves you. Caro loves you. Roan"—I pause—"adores you."

A smile, faint but genuine, breaks out over Ina's face. "Thank you, Jules." She gazes back at Everless. "I'm about to marry Roan Gerling. Surely no girl ever had less cause to be ungrateful."

A memory sneaks into the back of my mind—Roan in the narrow hallway where I ran into him the other day, flushed and smelling of perfume. *Lavender, not rosewater*. It's not my business, I shouldn't, but—"Do you love him?" I blurt out.

Surprise flashes across Ina's face. She looks at me, at Everless, and at me again. "Yes," she says. "More than anything."

Ina urges her horse forward, toward Everless, toward Roan, toward her future. My horse follows ploddingly along—a living, breathing shadow of Ina's own. I close my eyes against the sight. *I am escorted, in case you think this girl is a ghost*, she'd said. But right now, I feel like I might be.

After we've left Honey and Mava at the stables with Tam and are approaching the east entrance, Ina whispers to me in the pooling shadows.

"It's not that I'm unhappy, Jules, you must know that," she urges.

"I do," I say. "I understand." It's possible to feel joy and grief at the same time. It's possible to look forward to the horizon while mourning what you've lost.

I realize Ina's stopped. I turn to her—she's wringing her hands. There's something else on her face, longing to escape. "Ina . . . what is it?"

"You have to promise not to tell anyone," she says. "Not Caro, not the other servants."

My heart pounds. "I promise."

"There was a man." Her voice is quiet. "A few years ago, at the summer harvest in an Elsen province, the Queen was addressing the crowd. I was standing among them, so I could watch, too." She swallows. "The man reached me—he took me by the arm. Of course, I yelled for my guard, as I was trained to do. Before he ran off, he told me—" She stops, looks around.

"What? Tell me," I say, unthinking and then shocked at the command. Ina's mouth twitches.

"The Queen means you harm. She'll kill you." Immediately after she says it, Ina looks as though she's swallowed poison. I hear her breathing quicken. "I've thought and thought about it. He reached me—risked his life to do so. Why did he do that? He didn't seem to want to hurt me."

"He sounds mad," I say, my voice a whisper. His words sound less mad, though, than they would have before I saw the Queen's knife flying at Ina's chest. Lady Sida's words float through my head once again. She is mad too, certainly, and yet . . .

Ina nods. "That must be it. That's what I told myself until I got sick of thinking it. For a moment, I thought he might be . . ." She presses her lips together in a tight line. "My father. That the Queen stole me from my parents, like a fairy stealing away with a child in the night." She laughs. Her laugh is short and bitter. "Impossible, I know. Don't tell anyone, Jules, please. It would ruin me."

"Of course," I murmur, but say nothing more, and neither does Ina. But I know that the same thought has woven itself into our minds.

What if he told the truth?

19

The Queen returns to Everless before dawn breaks the next morning. That she prefers to travel at night is a message, tied up in brown paper, desperate to speak.

When I get back to the women's dormitory after watching her carriage pull into Everless, I find a little velvet bag sitting on top of my made bed. Another gift—which means more gossip at my expense. Beside it, a note, in Ina's pretty handwriting: *Thank you for your discretion, Jules.*

I sit down and pick up the bag. The weight of blood-irons inside is like a blow to the stomach. The bag drops from my hand, spilling a glittering month-coin onto my thin coverlet, and around me, women turn to stare, their purposefully averted gazes now drawn by the flash of gold.

I grab it up, feeling sick, and see the other girls quickly turn away. They mistake it for suspicion—as if I think one of them will take it from me. But they're not the reason for the queasy sadness churning through me.

Yesterday—the closeness I felt with Ina, the kinship, the shared secrets—was a soap bubble, growing and glimmering in me, but now it's broken. I thought Ina was . . . well, not my friend, that would be foolish, but something. That I was more than just a servant to be paid off. There's at least a few years inside the bag. My cheeks burn in humiliation. But as I stuff the money furiously beneath my pillow, a snide, calm voice in my head informs me that it's not sweet, oblivious Ina I should be angry at. It's myself—for forgetting who the both of us are, for daring to think that I could mean something to the future queen of Sempera.

Shame mixes into the turmoil inside me. I'm no closer to discovering the secret behind my father's death—his murder, as I've begun to think of it, the time pulled from his blood killing him as surely as a knife to the heart. Have I grown distracted, my head turned by Ina's beautiful gowns, Caro's friendly gossip, Roan's smiles that seem just for me, and forgotten the promise I made by the lakeshore after Papa died?

I didn't stay here at Everless to make friends with Ina Gold. If I'm to spend my days serving the Gerlings, I want Papa's death to mean something. The need for knowledge flares in me, brighter than ever.

I must see her. The Queen.

Over the next few days, I invent reasons to approach her, finding little tasks that will bring me to the long hallway where her rooms are in hopes of catching a glimpse. I tell Caro I'll deliver any messages the Queen needs. I carry her worn clothes, heaps of velvet and silk, to and from the laundry. I make tea in the mornings and evenings, and leave it by her door while the guards stationed there glower at me.

When I go to the Queen's door at sunset one day to deliver her evening tea, the guards are absent. I knock and set the tray down just outside her door. But then I linger longer than I should, standing there in the empty hallway until the tea has surely lost all its warmth, waiting for the Queen to appear. Just when I'm on the brink of giving up and going back to the dormitory, the door opens.

It's a long, confused moment before I realize that the woman who has stepped into the hall is, in fact, the queen of Sempera. She looks more like one of the drunkards who stumble out of Crofton's worst taverns in the early hours of the morning. Her flame-colored hair is knotted and tangled, and her clothes seem to have been put on in the dark—the buttons on her gown are only two-thirds of the way done up, revealing a swath of white skin across her chest. The corners of her mouth are stained with dark red smudges that could be lipstick or blood.

She takes a halting step forward, and I nearly fall backward in my scramble to get away. But my shoulders slam against someone's chest; small but strong hands close around my upper arms, keeping me upright. The scream is halfway out of my throat when Caro yanks me around to face her.

"Shh, Jules," she murmurs, her eyes huge in the dark hall. "It's all right."

She sets me aside like a small child and walks toward the Queen. I stare in confusion as Caro lays her bare hand over the Queen's heart. Our untouchable ruler lets her eyes drift shut and leans into Caro's touch, seeming to draw strength from it. A moment later, she turns and vanishes back into her room without a word. *You will not lay a hand on her, even to assist her*, I think, but it seems Caro is different. Side by side in the dim light, they almost look like mother and daughter, the Queen's eyes reflecting Caro, their posture the same.

Caro turns to me, sighing heavily. "I'm sorry you had to see that, Jules," she says. "Sometimes Her Majesty lets her duties get in the way of her well-being and doesn't rest like she should. She has night terrors."

I've seen nightmares, I think, *my own and others', but never anyone who looked like that, like they'd crawled out of a grave*. But my terror is still stuck in my throat, so all I can do is nod. Caro puts an arm around me, and warmth flows back in. I wonder if that is what the Queen felt a moment ago.

"You must keep this between us, Jules," Caro says softly. Another secret. "If word of her weakness got around . . ."

"Of course," I say hurriedly, regaining my voice. "I serve the Queen."

Caro leans closer. "Jules, you must understand something. You know the Queen—you've seen her—" She stops, stares at me as if to make sure I'm listening. "The Queen will soon die. Blood-irons cannot save her. Nothing can be done. In just a short time, Ina will be married, and Sempera will have a new ruler."

Questions flood my mind. *Will I ever know if my father died for a reason?* Looking for something—anything—to do, I bend down and pick up the cup of tea I've left outside the Queen's door. The cup rattles in its saucer. Caro gently takes them from me.

"Now," Caro says gently, "while the Queen rests, why don't we do something for ourselves?" I stare at her. "Soon Ina won't have a moment to herself, what with getting ready for the wedding. She wanted one last frolic before . . ." Her brow furrows. Despite the forced lightness of her tone, her revelation about the Queen's death hangs in the air. "She's a married woman."

Frolicking and marriage are as far from my thoughts right now as the moon. But I let Caro pull me along, not knowing what else to do. "I've just been to the stables," she tells me, low and excited, as we hurry down the hall. "I've arranged for a carriage to take us to a tavern that I know in Laista. We'll have a party, just the three of us."

The sumptuous carpets quiet our footsteps all the way into the wing that contains Ina's rooms. When we knock on her door, Ina opens it immediately. It takes me a moment to recognize her: she's done up her hair with silver pins and flowers. Her dress is a confection of tulle and lace with a neckline that makes me blush.

"So nice of you to join us, Jules," she says, giggling, as Caro propels me inside. "Have a drink?" She is already holding something by the neck—a green glass bottle of sparkling liquid. She proffers it to me.

The look on my face must be sufficient answer, because Caro tucks a defensive arm around my waist. "Ina, give the poor girl time to adjust," she whispers, turning me away from the princess and toward a massive, open wardrobe, which spills silk and velvet in every color I can think of and then some. "First we need to find her something to wear."

"Oh . . ." My weak protest is swept away when Ina dives in, pulling out one dress after another until her arms are heaped with them.

She motions for me to follow her to the bed, where she lays out the gowns excitedly—they're all bright-colored, skimpy, frivolous, or all three. Ina is already choosing a garment of blue silk that looks alarmingly small in her hands. She passes it to me, and I have a hard time believing this light thing is a dress, much less something I could wear outside the castle in cold weather.

But now Ina's standing with her hand on her hip, with Caro a little behind her, her head cocked to one side and a mischievous glint in her eyes. I have no choice, so I reach up behind my neck to unclasp my dress. I remember Ina waltzing around in her underthings the other day, trying on wedding dresses. But Ina has an effortless beauty I could never match. In front of them, I feel gawky and awkward, all elbows and knees and sharp angles—a body that grew up hungry.

Caro's eyes flicker over me and her forehead creases a little, but she doesn't say anything. Meanwhile, Ina's oblivious, shaking the dress at me. I lift my arms and allow her to pull the dress over my head while Caro comes around behind me, lacing up the back.

Ina tugs me to the vanity. Already scattered over its polished top is a mess of paints and kohl and vials of things I can't name, open and boasting rich browns and blacks and reds for Ina, and coral and rose and bronze for Caro. Their powdery scent wafts into the room. Ina takes up a powder puff, Caro a wooden hairbrush. I close my eyes and let them work.

When I finally look, my face in the mirror fills with surprise. I still look like me, but the shadows beneath my eyes have gone. My hollow cheeks are filled out and glowing. Outlined in kohl, my brown eyes reveal strands of amber that I've never seen before, and Caro has swept my hair up into a deceptively simple-seeming bun at the nape of my neck.

The dull skin and tired eyes have vanished. Realizing those are not a part of me, my heart lifts a little.

"Ina," I say, "you must be magic."

She laughs and squeezes my shoulder.

While they put finishing touches on their own faces, I'm overcome by curiosity, and give in—another small rebellion against Liam Gerling's insistence that I keep to my own path, a servant's life. I take a sip from the green bottle on Ina's nightstand. The liquor tastes of fruit and honey and fizzes on my tongue. By the time Caro and Ina are ready to go, I feel warm inside, ready to smile at anyone who passes, my heavy thoughts a distant memory.

Laughing, we make our way to the stables. Distantly I register how strange this is—sneaking out of Everless in the company of the princess and her handmaiden. When I notice the jewels that adorn Ina's neck, Addie's face flares in my mind like a flame, then quickly dies.

As soon as we duck into the stables, someone clears his throat off to the left. We look over to see a handsome but plain black carriage, a footman I don't recognize lounging in the driver's seat. Ina turns delightedly to Caro, who just smiles mysteriously. Its slight, thin, curved shape reminds me of a crescent moon.

"Ina," I exclaim, "let's hope this outing is more successful than . . ." I intend to remind her of the trip to the orphanage, of course. But she turns to me quickly, her eyes wide, shaking her head slightly. I swallow my words. Caro cocks her head. I remember how closely Ina guards the secret of her curiosity— not even a footman can hear of it.

Everything is easier with Caro's organizing hand. The

footman, a young man about Caro's age, is clearly in on the game. He flashes Ina a toothy grin as we clamber into the carriage. "Feeling restless, Your Highness?" he jokes.

Ina volleys an easy smile back at him and shakes a mocking finger. "I'm going to live in a stuffy palace my whole life." The footman nods tightly, as if he's afraid of incurring the Gerlings' wrath for the slander that so easily falls from Ina's lips. Caro watches her with something like longing on her face. I wonder if Ina knows what's to come—the Queen's death. "I may as well have a little fun now, while I still can."

In the carriage, a tiny oil lamp overhead illuminates velvet seats and paneled walls. Ina casts her gaze out the window. In the dim light, her eyes take on a sudden sadness. Discomfort prickles inside me, too, puncturing the lightness from the drink. While Caro speaks to the footman, I follow Ina's stare, trying to see what she sees—the high walls of Sempera's palace, the gilded throne, the tight, claustrophobic ribbing of a formal dress.

Her past—her birth—flits through it all like a shadow, only to vanish when you bring a light to it.

Caro falls back onto the seat next to me. I tear my eyes from the window and avoid Caro's, afraid that meeting her gaze will reveal what I've just understood about Ina—that it's the orphanage and her traitorous thoughts about the Queen, not this tipsy midnight excursion, that would be scandalous, maybe deadly, if her adoptive mother found out.

The liquor in my veins shields me from the cold as we ride out into the night. All that's gnawed at me since I started at Everless—my fear, my discomfort at not fitting in, and even my constant, desperate desire for justice, for answers—has receded to the back of my mind as I watch the road go by outside the window. Ina's knees brush mine as we're jostled by the ruts in the carriage road; she chats with Caro, no trace of sadness in her features. I suppose she must have learned to snatch moments of privacy as a child learns to steal treats from the pantry.

Soon, the scattered lights of Laista are glowing before us. The carriage deposits us in front of an unmarked door of polished wood, on a narrow but well-kept street. We're in the good part of Laista, on the side of the road closest to Everless. When Papa was the Gerlings' blacksmith, he used to take me to Laista's summer carnival every year, to see strange animals and eat shaved ice flavored with honey. Even after we moved to Crofton, I begged to go again—but Papa refused, saying he would still be able to smell the smoke from Everless.

Though nearly empty, the streets are just as I remember. The clean cobblestone rings out underneath our mares' hooves, and torches light up the street at intervals. Even the snow on the rooftops is clean. It covers the row of buildings like a blanket, unmarred and shining. While Caro pays the driver, Ina points out the wreaths that dot Laista's doorways. My eyes stop on a pane of fogged glass—behind it, a slim, curly-haired figure works her rag around a kettle . . .

She raises one hand to clear the moisture from the window, then peers through the glass, directly at us, before suddenly receding. A spark of familiarity flies through me.

"Ina, Jules!" Caro's already walking away, gesturing for us to follow. When I turn my head again, all trace of the girl is gone. I walk toward Caro's beckoning hand. She leads us inside one of the taller buildings and down a set of stairs, narrow but well kept.

The tavern I worked at was a dingy, hopeless place, filled with men and women with prematurely lined faces and cloudy eyes, burning their time for another mug even as they drank to forget how little life they had left. But this is another world—not luxurious like Everless, but comfortably elegant. Moneyed. I'm reminded that in this world, people drink to enjoy themselves rather than to dull the sting of a hard life.

Something in me—sharp, angry—stirs.

The room is dim and expansive inside; the marble countertops gleam and the wall behind the counter ripples with bottles of every shape and color. Tobacco smoke drifts from the bar, where a handful of people sip from crystal glasses. A handsome young man quickly ushers us to an empty, private table in a back corner. I find myself wondering if that is simply how everyone is treated in places such as this, or if this, too, is Caro's quiet planning at work.

"One bottle of your best red wine and one of madel, please," Caro orders in her carrying whisper. She looks beautiful in this low light, her pale eyes glittering against her skin.

Before I realize any time has passed at all, two bottles appear: one dark green, one red. The waiter places three heavy crystal glasses in front of us.

When I drink a sip of the madel, the drink froths and burns in my throat; the fire shoots to my belly much faster than it did in Caro's chambers. I sputter, and Caro laughs, a light tinkling sound of bells.

"Here," she whispers. "Let me show you." She pours a bit of red wine into her glass, then, carefully, adds a tiny bit of gold madel. The wine fizzes slightly, then settles. Caro extends the cup to me.

Cautiously, I sip. The wine has diluted the madel, making it strange and smoky. It still burns a little going down, but not enough to make my eyes water. As Caro grins and Ina laughs, a bolt of unexpected happiness surges through me. The moment stretches—Ina's laugh turns into a song, and Caro's smile melts over her face—into one shimmering, expanding bubble. Then Caro speaks, bringing the world back to a normal pace.

"Start with that," she says, "and maybe we can work you up to straight madel by the end of the night." She takes a long sip out of her own cup.

Ina giggles as she looks around the room, pure joy lighting her face. She raises her glass. "A cheer," she says. "To three long-orphaned girls who found their home."

I smile back and start to raise my glass, but the expression

232

on Caro's face catches me. For a moment, it's shock, her eyes wide—then it solidifies into something close to anger as she looks between me and Ina.

"Jules," she says, her voice even, but her eyes tight. "I thought your father only just passed."

Hurt stabs through my chest at her bluntness. "He—he did," I stammer. "But I found out that I was adopted a few weeks ago. Not that it matters," I add quickly. "He raised me."

Ina has finally noticed something amiss. She stares at me, her eyes apologetic, then words spill out of her mouth to cover the awkwardness of sharing my secret. "She might be one of those Briarsmoor children, Caro. We should convince the Queen to take us there. For Jules."

"Perhaps," Caro says blankly.

I look down, mortified at Ina's request and embarrassed that Caro thinks I've kept something from her. But in the span of a breath, Caro's face smooths out, her pleasant smile returned.

She gestures around us. "Ina, even if you have the best liquor in the palace next year, I don't think you'll find anything to match this atmosphere."

I hear Ina reply, "Oh, I think Roan's company will make up for that. He doesn't want to stay around his older brother a day longer than he has to, and I like Everless well enough, but it's nothing like Shorehaven."

In the palace next year. I make some vague noise of interest, studying my drink intently and hoping Ina and Caro can't see the wetness that has suddenly sprung to my eyes.

With all the furor and breathlessness pervading Everless over the wedding, it never occurred to me to wonder what would come after.

Ina will leave Everless. *Roan* will leave Everless.

The Queen will disappear, too, and I'll be left with only the mystery of my father's death for company. And Liam's dark glares.

I mumble something about getting us another round of drinks and push back from the table, keeping my face angled away from Caro and Ina. A few moments before, the madel warmed my blood and loosened my limbs. Now I feel a little like I did at the mava pile—surrounded by a thin haze of fog, faces and voices swirling around me but never quite solidifying into sense. I can tell I'm swaying slightly as I walk but can't steady myself.

My thoughts become jagged and sharp-edged: Ina and Roan are moving to the palace; and I'll be alone again, my childhood love gone.

Maybe it wasn't entirely the pursuit of truth giving me strength these past two weeks.

Suddenly, the heat and smoke are pressing in on me. The tavern feels like a furnace. Faces smear into blurs, voices and laughter muddle into one harsh sound. I grip the counter to keep my balance. My head spins.

Air. I need air.

20

Somehow I stumble away from the bar and toward the door—
no one sees the panic in my eyes. When I emerge onto the quiet
street, I gratefully gulp down the night air. It smells of melting
snow. A gentle mist has begun to fall, and droplets swirl in the
small spheres of light cast by the street lanterns. No one else is
out here. I lean against the brick wall to let my heart slow.

Then, my feet start to walk away from the tavern, tracing
the path we followed to come here. I slow to a stop in front of
the squat brick teahouse, staring through the same glass as
earlier. The window is almost opaque with fog except for one
handprint-sized mark where the condensation has been smeared
away. I peer inside. Even through the glass, I recognize the girl.

Addie.

The door opens up to a room of people, a different sort of

scene from the tavern—this one dim and humble and quiet, filled with older townspeople who drink steaming cups of tea or chat quietly in groups of two or three. Addie is behind the counter, an apron pulled over her dress.

"Addie?" I say tentatively.

Her head shoots up; I see her note my cloak, and the Queen's insignia embroidered on it. "You're an Everless girl," she says brusquely. Her name for me drips with scorn, but I don't miss the currents of envy and fury underneath.

"What do you want?" She glances out the window, toward the tavern. "Has the Queen sent you to punish me further?"

"No," I say quickly. "She didn't send me. You don't know me, but . . ." I can't quite meet her eyes, awash with shame. I stayed while she was banished. I took her place. "What happened?"

But her face softens a little. "You helped me pick up the jewels."

"And much good that did you," I mutter.

"It's probably better for me here." Addie glances around, as if checking that no one is listening. After a moment, she says, "I didn't have the chance to explain myself before Ivan hauled me away." She leans forward, her eyes darting across the nearest drinkers before she speaks again, in a hushed whisper. "I touched the Queen when she fell. I was trying to help. But she . . . she was ice-cold. More than cold. She was—" Addie stops, biting her lip. "It felt like my life was being drained away, just by touching her. Like getting your time drawn, but worse."

It's as though a trickle of ice runs down my own spine, when I think of how the Queen appeared to me in the doorway just a few hours ago. How she seemed to draw something from Caro.

"I could have suffered worse than this. Ivan, he tried—" Addie stops, wipes a spot in front of her that's already clean. "I might have died if it weren't for Lord Liam."

My disbelief must show on my face, because Addie continues. "He interviewed me, got me a job here. He's friends with the owner—I think he comes here to get out from under his parents' noses, to do his research without being bothered."

"Research?"

"He's back there now." Addie jerks one thumb over her shoulder, indicating a nondescript back door I hadn't noticed before.

My blood freezes, then heats. Maybe it's just the drink making me brave, but I want to learn something from him, once and for all. What could he possibly need to hide out in a teahouse in Laista for?

He looks up when I march through the door. The desk before him is strewn with books and papers. He's dressed simply: a long wool coat over a white shirt and breeches. But the plainest clothes in the world couldn't disguise his hungry eyes, his forward-leaning posture. A thousand thoughts and calculations race through my mind. Cutting through everything are my father's words: *If you ever see Liam Gerling, run.*

Though every muscle in my body is crying for me to flee, I walk toward Liam and sit down across from him, pushing my cloak back from my shoulders. He stares at me. His pupils grow huge in the dim light.

"Lord Gerling," I say, making my voice as frostily calm as I can. "Why does it seem that everywhere I am, you are there, too?"

At my words, his jaw hardens. "This town belongs to my family," he says. "I can go where I please. But I can't say the same about you, Jules." My name in his voice makes goose bumps break out along my arms. "Shouldn't you be at Everless?"

"Your future sister invited me here," I snap back. "So if you don't want me in *your town*, take it up with her."

Liam shakes his head, wraps his hands around his shoulders like he's cold. It makes me very aware of how I'm dressed, Ina's silk clinging to me and leaving my arms bare. The warm feeling from the madel evaporates, and suddenly I feel chilly and vulnerable.

"It's not about what I want," Liam says, his voice so low I unconsciously lean closer to hear. There's a note of urgency there, some undercurrent I don't understand. "You're out here in the town, alone. Do you always race openhearted into danger like this?"

"The only danger here is people like you—your family. You," I say, my voice poisonous, "are the reason we are all

238

unsafe." I can't hold back a snort. "You of all people should know that Everless is much more dangerous than Laista."

"Yet you're still there." Liam stares at me for a moment, his brow furrowed, as if I'm some thorny exam question he's trying to untangle. Then his face unfolds and he smiles as he runs his hands through his hair, tipping his head back like a plea to the Sorceress. It's a strange mix of amusement and desperation, and so unexpected that I hardly remember where I am, with whom I'm speaking.

"You're not wrong about Everless being dangerous," he continues, looking back at me. "Especially for someone so close to the Queen."

"So you think the Queen is dangerous," I say.

"I didn't say that," he replies deliberately. "But you'd do well not to say it, either, no matter who you're friends with." He leans forward, his eyes suddenly pleading. "Listen to what I'm telling you."

"Why shouldn't I say it?" I challenge him, feeling the heat of madel in my veins. I tilt my head upward, speak as if to a crowd. "If she's safe, if she's good—"

"Stop it." Liam remains still. "Jules—"

"I'm done listening to greedy time thieves."

"I'm not the one you should fear," he says, a hint of pleading in his voice.

"You—" My voice falters but I swallow the lump of fear in my throat, maintain his gaze. "You tried to kill Roan. You pushed him into the forge when we were children. Of course I'm afraid of you."

His cheek twitches, as if I've slapped him, but he recovers quickly.

"Your memory fails you," Liam says. "Ask him yourself—he'll tell you he remembers nothing."

For a moment, doubt pierces me, but I push it away. I know to trust myself more than Liam Gerling. Papa's memory gives me strength. I want to shock Liam, to put him off-balance as he's done to me, so I continue, "The Queen is dying. Did you know that?"

This gets to him—he leans back forcefully, as if he's received a blow. "The queen of Sempera is not dying." His voice is soft but sure, and his eyes cloud over in thought as if he's forgotten me entirely. "It's not that simple. Trust me, Jules."

"Why?" I spit. His lie and his request mix in the air and fill my lungs. "Why would I trust you?"

"If you're not careful, you will be hurt, Jules. Leave Everless. Go tonight. Stop looking for secrets from your past." He takes a breath. "Pehr wasn't your father, but he would have wanted the same."

Shock freezes my chest. "How do you know that? And why . . ." I whisper, my voice ragged.

"It doesn't matter. What matters is that with only a little effort and luck, anyone can find out anything."

"Tell me," I demand, infuriated that Liam, sitting in front

of me, seems to know more about me than I know about myself, as if my life is another coin to be counted and locked away.

Liam leans forward on the desk. I notice how he taps the notebook in front of him with one finger in a simple, persistent rhythm—an unconscious movement. My eyes follow. Immediately, I recognize its slim spine and brown leather cover. His personal notebook, the one he was writing in that day I followed him from the library.

He knew I was an orphan, it seems, perhaps before I knew myself. What else might he know, have written down in that notebook?

"I'll escort you back." Liam pushes his chair back from the table. "Stay here while I pay my tab," he says brusquely to me, before striding out into the main bar area.

My anger rises at his presumption. But then, behind where he was sitting, I spot a narrow door in the back. From the small window set into it, I can see the light of streetlamps.

Triumph thrills in my veins. I am done doing what Liam Gerling—or any Gerling—tells me. Before I can think better of it, or consider the consequences, I snatch up the brown notebook and slip out the back door.

I hurry around the building and down the street to the tavern, my head ducked in case Liam glances out the front window. My heart is pounding, making my head spin. When I reach the tavern, I lean against the brick exterior and open the journal, rifling through the pages, catching a glimpse here and there of numbers, dates, and notes. It's in what must be Liam's hand, neat and blocky, but one page catches my eye. The words themselves are familiar—strange, simple stories, but achingly familiar.

One night, Fox and Snake wanted to play a game of sticks. But the man in the tower said no. Fox was so angry, she crushed her soup bowl to powder, and Snake made it burst into flames . . .

I devour the page. The words melt into one another and over me, hot and searing, like wax dripping from a candle. When I realize that, for some reason, I'm crying, I don't wipe away the tears.

"I'll free us," Snake said. "All you have to do is trust me . . ."

Stories. These are my stories, my games, from childhood. What could Liam possibly want with them? Am I to lose everything I've ever had at his hands?

Then Ina's voice is at my back, shouting my name. I look up to see her and Caro emerging from the tavern.

Quickly, I slip the book into an inner pocket of my cloak. Ina and Caro are hurrying toward me, looking concerned. Ina sees the tears on my face and takes my hands in hers.

But Caro is looking warily at something over my shoulder.

I follow her gaze to see Liam stalking toward us through the snow. My heart sinks—he must have realized his notebook was gone, and that I lied. I start polishing another lie in my head, not wanting Ina and Caro to know what I've done.

But he just stops a few feet away from us and bows low. "Lady Gold. I didn't expect to meet you here."

"Liam," Ina greets him. She sounds wary. "What brings you here?"

"I saw Jules outside, and just wanted to catch up with an old friend," Liam says coolly. He's speaking to Ina, but his eyes don't leave mine. "I've been thinking about the stories you used to tell, Jules. Do you remember?"

Fox crushed her bowl to powder; Snake made it burst into flames. A little girl's nonsense. What does any of it matter to him? My hands curl into fists at my sides. From the gleam in his eyes, I know that he knows about the journal tucked into my cloak. We are having two parallel conversations, one that includes Ina and Caro and one that is just between us. "Childish things," I say.

Liam shrugs elegantly. "They were good stories. You ought to try to remember them."

Caro's eyes narrow as she looks from me to him. "As nice as this is," she says politely, "we still have one more stop tonight, Lord Gerling. I'm sure you don't begrudge Lady Gold a little frivolity before her wedding." She moves subtly so she's in front of me, half shielding me from Liam's gaze, and I feel a rush of gratitude for her.

"Not at all," Liam says, his voice somehow gracious and cutting at the same time. "I'm sure my brother is doing the same. I'll let you be on your way."

Ina makes a face after Liam as he strides off, and I have to bite back a relieved laugh. I turn to mouth *thank you* to Caro. But she is staring at me, her head cocked a little, like I'm a puzzle she's trying to solve.

"I'm freezing," Ina says. When neither of us respond, she threads her arm through mine and tugs on Caro's sleeve. "Let's go." She has the gleam in her eyes that I've come to understand means she's conceived some madcap idea—it's the same look she had in the stables before we went to the orphanage, and in her room this evening when she told me of her plans for this last hurrah before her wedding. She squints at me.

"Jules," she says, "why were you crying?"

"Just thinking of my father," I tell her. "I needed some air."

"Well." She pauses, her voice hesitant. Then, she plunges on. "Caro's had this thought—she knows this place—well, you tell her," she finishes, turning to Caro. Ina's swaying slightly, still holding on to my arm. Tipsy, I imagine, with madel.

Caro smiles her secret smile and tucks an arm around Ina's waist. "Ina let slip that she's curious about her birth parents," she informs me in her soft voice. And I had an idea—

I've heard stories about a hedge witch around here who can do blood regressions."

"Blood regressions?" I echo. My heart is sinking. The realization of Ina and Roan's impending departure, the glimpse of Addie pouring tea, and most of all the encounter with Liam have wrecked me. I feel grossly out of place in this elegant, smoky town, and I long to run; I want to be back at Everless or nowhere at all, to throw the Queen's door open and demand that she spill her secrets.

Somewhere in the haze of the street lanterns, Caro is still speaking, explaining blood regressions—an old countryside ritual, where a hedge witch trances you into falling back through your own time and letting your buried memories float to the surface. I don't understand—nor can I bring myself to care. I'm bone-tired, and just now appreciating how foolish I was to come here with Caro and Ina, foolish to think I could be like them, with their pretty dresses and strange larks.

But of course I am not in charge, of course arguing would be even worse, and so I don't protest when Ina links her arms through both of ours and heads off.

I've long lost track of the passing hours, but I can tell by the low-hanging moon, the dark windows, and the exhaustion creeping into my bones that it must be well past midnight as Caro leads us down a side street and toward a small, ramshackle old storefront tucked between pubs. I stopped drinking before Ina and Caro, and so though they seem comfortable in their cloaks, I'm shivering as we knock, watching the thin crack of light that shows between the door and the ground.

I've never been out so late, and resentment toward Caro and Ina is growing. And I can't help glancing nervously over my shoulder every few moments. Looking for Liam Gerling.

But the streets remain empty, a slight wind whistling off the sleeping buildings. It seems wrong to knock on a door in the dead of night, but Caro's assured us that the hedge witch operates at all hours. As long as you can pay, she says.

After what seems a long time, the door opens to reveal a small, hunched old woman with gray hair down to her waist. She wears a tattered, patched gown that looks a little like that of Everless's Lady Sida, out of style by a hundred years or so— but looking at Caro's supposed lesser sorcerer, I can tell right away that she is more like me than the Gerling matriarch. Her age is the ordinary kind, her face burnished with sun and lined with the weight of years, though she's powdered herself pale and painted her lips a bloody red.

The artifice seems clear to me, but Ina, beside me, looks a little intimidated. She takes a small step forward. "We'd like to do a blood regression."

The woman takes us in, her eyes lingering on our fine clothes, our buttons and lace, then staying a moment longer on Ina's beautiful face. Finally she steps aside and motions for us to come in. "Follow me," she says.

Ina clutches at Caro's arm and, despite my dark mood, I feel the corners of my mouth twitch. Perhaps I should be frightened, too, but the woman's affected accent—a coarse Laista clashing with a put-on aristocratic trill—makes me want to laugh. I catch Caro's eye, after she scans the bundles of leaves that line the walls with a raised eyebrow.

The witch leads us down a dim hallway into a small, dark room crowded with personal belongings and odd knickknacks— stacks of old leather books in the corners; oil paintings leaning against the walls; small, strange metal contraptions suspended by wire from the ceiling—a copper bird with an hour-coin in its beak, a figurine of a woman whose body is an hourglass. Ina reaches out and touches her metal hand. The sand collected in her torso trickles down through her waist. The room is lit only by a series of candles set in strategic places; every strange shape and sharp angle is magnified, stretching over the walls in gray shadows.

The air is heavy with a sickly sweet incense that makes my stomach rock, and a table in the middle of the room is draped in gauze. Everything is too perfect, arranged—a portrait of a village hedge witch's chambers.

The three of us hang back in the doorway, waiting to be told what to do as the hedge witch glides to the table. Ina steps forward, but then hesitates and glances back at us. "Will one of you go first?" she asks, giving us her most winning smile.

I exchange glances with Caro, who's frowning a little, her eyes wide. I sigh. If both of my friends are afraid of this charlatan, I'll go first, if only to get us back to Everless faster. Perhaps my turn will prove this is all a farce. I step forward.

The woman gestures, a little impatiently, for me to sit down on a cushion by the table. I look from Caro to Ina—Caro's brow is creased as she studies the witch; Ina shrugs a *why not?* at me. Hesitantly, I take a seat as the old woman drops herself across from me. She produces a small bottle filled with a cloudy dark liquid, and my stomach sinks. I've had more than enough of mystery liquors for one night.

"It's a potion of corrupted time," she says, as if that explains anything. "The time entering your blood will trick your body into believing that you are young again, and allow memories that have sunk deep into your mind to rise to the surface."

I want to get back to Everless, so I uncork the bottle and nearly gag as I recognize the smell of mava wafting up from the purple-black liquid inside. The hedge witch notices and frowns. "It's an alchemical mixture," she explains, for a moment forgetting to sound mysterious. "It must be strong, to take you away from the present time."

I pause before bringing the bottle closer to my face, taking as small a sip as I can. It tastes like mava juice that's gone off, perhaps mixed with honey to mask the spoiling.

As I force another swallow down, the woman takes a dusty tome from one of the piles around her. She settles it on the table, opens it to a bookmarked page, and starts to read. Her voice, almost too low for me to hear, speaks in a language that sounds like old Semperan but isn't, not quite—I can hear the echoes of words I recognize, *time* and *blood* and *return*, but they are submerged in something different, lilting, more ancient.

Don't use my blood, a young woman's voice snaps.

My eyes flutter open. I look around to see Ina and Caro staring at me—Caro with interest, Ina like she's about to burst out laughing. With a chill, I realize the voice was only in my head.

"Close your eyes," the witch tells me again, a strange appraising look in her eye. "Think back to the earliest thing you can remember, and then think of before that."

With my eyes closed to the clutter and tawdriness of the room, the old woman's voice is actually soothing. The rhythmic quality of her chant makes it easy to recall a stream of images—Ina's bright face and Addie's gaunt one; the carved door of the vault promising so many secrets; Roan standing close to me in the servant corridors; Liam looming over me, his glittering black eyes.

I let my mind drift back and back, and my life unspools in reverse behind my eyes, the images getting blurrier and more disjointed the further I go. And I am tired, so tired, and the madel has made me sluggish and slow. My blood flows like honey through my veins, but I move further. My heart squeezes painfully as images flash of me and Papa and our life in Crofton, our little garden in the summer, his drawing of my mother on the wall. The old years at Everless, the glow of the blacksmith fires, Roan as a child with his feet dangling over the branch of the oak tree, the smell of his burning flesh and my hands, dragging him backward.

Heart racing, I claw back to my first memory—something I've never been sure whether real or imagined—being held securely in my mother's arms, her face as luminous and steady as the moon, blood-flecked. "My little snake," she croons. "Sweet love."

I hear her voice. I have never remembered it before. Her voice singing me a sweet, familiar song. My mind lurches.

The part of me that is still here in the reading room with Caro and Ina Gold and the witch, still seventeen, expects to wake here . . . but I don't wake. My mother's face wavers and dissolves before me, though the song doesn't. I see green, green grass through a window, gleaming in the sun.

Then, the song curdles into a scream.

I'm screaming too, and the air turns to blood all around me. After what seems like forever, the woman's scream stops.

"Take her," I hear her pant, somewhere above me. "Take her, now."

Wait—

The scene changes. I am in a man's arms, and we are running, running over the grass, through a town square I cannot name. The man—whose face is a blur above me, but whose presence gives me comfort—stops for just a moment at a great gray statue, looming a foot taller than he is against a pale sky. The statue is strange, a young woman holding a handful of pebbles in her cupped hands, as if receiving an offering—or giving one. The traditional pose of the Sorceress, depicting the moment when she holds the Alchemist's supposed gift and knows he's betrayed her. The man shifts to cradling me in one arm. He reaches out and plucks a pebble from the statue's immobile fingers.

Suddenly, darkness falls over the vision, and new images swim through it—unfamiliar images, that are of no place I know, no place that exists in Sempera I've seen. There are round structures made of heaped fur on a field of ice, a set of stone steps rising from a steaming, deep green forest, and what I think must be Sempera's great palace by the sea, but half torn down and burning.

A young woman on a dark plain, her face in shadow, raises her palms toward me. For a moment, she is like the statue come to life. Wind whips her dark hair into a frenzy around her face, the same wind I can feel battering at me as I run toward her. There is a knife in my hand, and there is something I need from the girl, something that will have to be bought with blood.

It's only when I get closer that I realize my enemy has a knife too. She throws it, and it pierces the air, flying straight toward my heart . . .

21

I wake, gasping for air.

The perfume of the hedge witch's home is cloying, but I drag it in, like I've been pulled up from deep water. The old woman across the table gapes at me. The blood has fled from Ina's face, and Caro looks at me as if I'm a stranger. I see the whites all around the edges of her eyes.

Something drips into my lap—the bottle of potion, which I must have upended in my trance. A dark, scented stain is spreading over the tabletop.

My voice comes out raw. "What happened?"

The witch doesn't respond. Seeming to recover herself a little, she reaches out and rights the bottle, stopping the liquid from glugging out over the table.

Ina is the one to break the silence. "You were talking," she says, eyes wide. "We . . . we couldn't understand all of it. Some didn't sound like Semperan."

A chill runs down my spine, and I push myself away from the table. "I'm sorry for making a mess."

"It's all right." The old woman looks paler than before. After a long moment, she just nods and peels the stained cloth from the table. "Would either of you like to try?" she asks, looking at Caro and Ina, forgetting to put on the accent. She sounds like any old woman from the wrong part of town, voice scratchy and a little scared.

Caro shakes her head right away, but Ina looks at me, at the hedge witch, and back at me. I can see the desire in her wide eyes and trembling hands, the same as at the gates to the orphanage the other day. Maybe Ina can sense that we share this, this consuming, fatal desire to know ourselves, where we came from—even if the story turns out to be an ugly one.

Slowly, she nods. She comes over and takes my place at the table, across from the witch.

My legs still feel wobbly and uncertain beneath me, but I retreat to Caro's side, where she's leaning against the wall to watch, her arms crossed over her chest, the flickering candlelight making her eyes seem even bigger and darker. While Ina drinks from the bottle and the old woman reads from the book, I lean close to Caro's ear.

"Do you think it's real?" I ask softly. I'm not sure what I want anymore—to think that what I just saw was a figment of my imagination or the truth.

Caro's eyes flick to me, her brows drawing together. "If you weren't putting it on?" she whispers.

I shake my head vigorously.

"The drink might be drugged, and it was a hallucination." She looks at Ina. "We'll soon find out."

That hadn't occurred to me, and my skin crawls at the thought—and Caro's terse words. We turn toward the table at the same time, where Ina has drunk from the green bottle.

But from the expression on the princess's face—she's frowning, her forehead creased in concentration—and her hands folded primly in her lap, it's clear she experiences nothing. Caro watches intently, her gaze shifting between Ina and the old woman. The woman is watching too, periodically looking up to glance at Ina. The cadence of her voice rises and falls with the text, but Ina doesn't seem to do anything out of the ordinary.

After a while, the woman lets the words peter out. Ina opens her eyes, looking both disappointed and relieved.

"Nothing, Ina?" Caro asks.

Ina looks down at her hands. "Nothing."

For a moment, we all stand there in silence. The mood in the room is different now—even Caro and Ina seem to regard this as no longer a game. Then Caro gives herself a little shake and reaches for her belt. She withdraws three day-coins and hands them to the hedge witch. Outside the window, the sky has begun to lighten a little over Laista's streets.

As we make our way out, the witch catches me by the arm, her bony fingers digging into my flesh. "Can you stay a moment and help me clean up that stain, dear?" Her eyes bore into mine, bloodshot and urgent.

Caro and Ina have stopped, looking back at me. I motion them toward the door. "I'll be out in a minute."

When the door closes behind them, I turn back to the hedge witch, the old woman. I have an odd, terrible feeling I know what she's going to say. But I ask anyway: "What is it?"

She drops my arm—and when she speaks, she's dropped, too, all traces of the affectation she put on for Caro and Ina. Her words to me are plain and direct, in the accent I've grown up hearing. "You've surely guessed this already: it's all a show what I do, girl. There's nothing special about that book, that poem I read." She fingers the coins Caro gave her like good-luck charms.

My stomach plummets. I'd suspected as much, but it's something else to hear it, to know for sure. "What about the drink?"

"Mava and honey and a little madel," she says. "That's all."
I feel dizzy. "So, back there, that was . . ."
"I don't know," she says. "But it wasn't my doing."

Back at Everless, we cling to one another, still swaying a little as we make our way to Ina's room, intending to collapse on her giant bed. My head is spinning with the visions from the hedge witch's house, and her words after. Liam's notebook, pressed into my skin beneath my cloak, seems trivial now.

But after Ina unlocks the door to her room, she stops short in the doorway. I slam into her back, and my blood turns to ice water as I look over her shoulder and see the Queen waiting there in the dark. Her frame stands tall, straight. Her hair, arranged in a simple braid down her back, is nothing like the knotted mess I saw earlier.

The Queen is resplendent and terrifying.

"Your Majesty," Ina squeaks, and even she seems to tremble in terror at the apparition. "What are you doing here?"

"That is an impertinent question." The Queen's eyes seem to look straight through Ina, searing into me instead. Beside me, Caro looks as though she's going to be sick. "Come with me," she intones. "All of you."

Helplessly, we follow the Queen into a sparsely decorated side chamber, just a table and a few chairs where Ina can take meals when she doesn't feel like going down to the dining hall. But when the Queen sits in one of the chairs and levels her gaze up at us, she looks as regal and terrifying as if she were on the throne in the seaside palace. She directs her fiery gaze at Ina first.

"To atone for your nonsense, you and Lord Roan will travel with me to the statue of the Sorceress in Tilden tomorrow, and beg her forgiveness." I shudder, reminded of the statue in my vision. "And you two"—I shrink back as her eyes land on me like two beams of fire—"you'll not leave Everless tomorrow. I'll deal with you when I return."

Caro and Ina are bowing their heads, so I follow suit. "Yes, Your Majesty," Caro says in her softest whisper.

"We'll do better," Ina adds. I can feel her tremble.

When the Queen has left us, we undress quietly, wash our faces, and change into nightgowns. Shame has burned away the last vestiges of drunkenness, leaving me hollow and wrung out and, looking at Caro and Ina, I can tell from their sallow faces and sunken eyes that they feel the same way.

Ina, between Caro and me, falls asleep almost as soon as her head hits the pillow, but I hear Caro's shallow, wakeful breathing on the other side of the bed for what seems like a long time. I still have the notebook hidden beneath my nightgown and, despite my exhaustion, I'm aching to take it out and read more of the strange stories within. But for some reason the words on the page feel secret, too close even for Caro.

"I'm sorry I didn't tell you the truth about my father," I say, soft as I can. She doesn't answer right away, but her breathing changes slightly, so I know she hears.

"It's all right," she answers eventually. "It's your secret to share. I shouldn't have been so upset by it." She trails into silence, and I almost think she's fallen asleep, but then she speaks again.

"I'm sorry to get you wrapped up in this," she says. *In what*, I want to ask, but don't. "The guards will be relaxed

257

tomorrow, with the Queen gone," she continues. "We'll go to the vault and look for your father's things."

"I've told you," I protest softly. "We really mustn't. I should never have said anything about it."

"We'll discuss it tomorrow, then. We have a long day ahead of us," she says, her voice heavy with sleep. She reaches across Ina's body, interlaces her fingers with mine. "Tomorrow, Jules."

She turns over and pulls the blankets up. As soon as I'm sure of her deep breathing, I slide out the notebook and hold it in the scant moonlight that pours over the bed through a small window, trying to make out Liam's words. But the first few pages I turn to are Everless business, figures and charts and mundane notes on the amount of taxes brought in or debts paid, and I feel my eyelids sliding earthward. Every few pages, I catch a snippet of something—a fox, a snake—before sleep closes in on me.

I wake to the sound of bells. It takes me a moment to remember where I am—alone in Ina's huge bed, with late-morning sunlight pouring in through the window. The notes of the bells are sweet, but the melody sends a low thrum of alarm through me.

I sit upright, take in a sharp breath.

I'd heard it before—not in the past weeks, but as a child. It's the group of tones played to summon the servants together for punishments.

I leap out of bed, ignoring the dull pain that clamors inside my skull, and strip off the nightdress. Quickly, I find the servants' clothes I abandoned here last night, and stuff Liam's notebook, which was tucked partway under my pillow, into my apron pocket.

In the refectory, an uneasy mood hangs over the servants. Although we fill the room, there is little chatter. I fall in with a group of kitchen servants in our kerchiefs and aprons, and for the first time wish I was still one of them.

My heart sinks as soon as I see who stands at the front of the room. Of course, there is Ivan, looking out over the gathering crowd with a leering smirk on his face. He's in uniform, a dark green cloak swinging down over a leather tunic. Two more Everless guards flank him. And behind them is Liam Gerling, looking grim.

A few feet in front of me, Lora looks anxious—when I glance down, I can see her worrying at the hem of the apron she still wears.

When everyone seems accounted for, Ivan steps forward. "Good afternoon," he calls, his jovial voice, as ever, making my skin crawl. "It's my unfortunate duty this afternoon to announce a punishment of one of your own. One who was found to be tampering with, no less, the ancient vault of the Gerlings, the family who feeds and shelters you all."

My body goes rigid. The vault. Ivan looks over us with a threatening scowl, but his voice is languid. He's enjoying himself—savoring the terror in the room. I notice a handful of guards in royal maroon—but they are outnumbered and stand back from Ivan and the Everless guards. They have their arms crossed, and look unhappy.

Before I can think what this means, Ivan steps aside, and a door behind him opens. The two guards who enter haul in a crying girl by the arm, a girl with freckled skin and pale green eyes . . .

No.

"Caro Elysia was found in the hall outside the vault, tampering with the door," Ivan says, reading off something in his hand. "As punishment for violating this most important of places, as an officer of the family Gerling, I impose the maximum penalty of forty years—to be withdrawn from the blood immediately." He looks over his shoulder at Liam. And Liam—acting as representative of the Gerlings, I realize—gives a tight nod. An assent.

Caro struggles weakly against the guards holding her, tears streaming down her face. A soft *no* escapes my lips.

Forty years? Even from Ivan, it's barbaric.

And it's my fault.

I push my way through the crowd of servants. They stare and whisper as I pass, but I don't let it slow my feet. I was the one who wanted to see inside the vault, and Caro is going to lose forty years of her life for it. She was only trying to help me regain something of my father's. Because she cares.

"Wait!" Without knowing what I'm doing, I lunge forward as Ivan passes and catch at his cloak.

He looks at me, eyebrows raised in mild amusement, like I'm a pet that has done a new trick. "What do you want?"

"You . . . you can't take forty years," I say breathlessly, miserably. "It's too much at once." Horrible memories flood my mind of Papa coming home from the time lender in Crofton, pale and sick and staggering after having a few months withdrawn. Could a person survive losing that much time, if she even has that much?

And that's when the real weight of it sinks in. Because what are the chances that a servant girl has forty years at all?

This punishment may kill her.

Ivan plucks his cloak away from my hands. "That's not my concern," he drawls. "If you're so worried, you can get yourself down to the time lender and withdraw some of your own time to give this thief."

A hand appears on his shoulder. He turns, and I see that Liam has come up behind him, silent as a ghost.

"Move on, Ivan," he growls, looking furious for some reason. "Do your job."

Ivan scowls but obeys, striding off and gesturing to the guards holding Caro to follow him. The four of them disappear through the door they came in, and the last I see of them is a glimpse, in profile, of Caro's tear-smeared face.

As the other servants start to file out, muttering sadly and shaking their heads, Liam reaches out as if to steady me. I stumble back. "Don't touch me." His earlier nod replays in my mind—such a tiny motion, but carrying such a weight of death and pain. "Where's Roan?" Surely he would stop this.

Liam freezes, something folding in his face. Finally, he says, "I'm sorry, Jules," and follows Ivan from the room.

I stand numbly, watching the closed door where they vanished. Every beat of my heart feels like a knife in me, twisting.

Ivan didn't mean what he said about going to the time lender. It was a cruel joke. But now that the idea is there—

Surely Ina can save her; any one of her elegant gowns or glittering jewels must be worth many years. But Ina is away, along with the Queen, because of our foolishness. There may not be any time left to wait for her. Between the pouch on my belt and the stash under my mattress in the dormitory, I have almost three years of blood-iron to my name. I could run there now, and bring it to Caro. But it's not enough. Not nearly enough—and if she has less than forty years to begin with, it won't even save her.

No. I know nothing else will stop the twisting knife, ease the guilt burrowing into my heart.

I have to find the time lender.

22

Bursting from one of the castle's side doors, I sprint across the lawn toward the south gate, where the road will lead me back to Laista. Fear drags at my feet, and my thin indoor shoes immediately soak through with snow. But I know if I stop running, if I even slow down, the fear will overcome me. *You don't have to do this*, something in me whispers.

Caro will die, another voice says, *and it will be your fault.*

I run.

I reach the time lender's shop, a thin, simple wooden building tucked into an alley lined with the ugly back sides of Laista's storefronts, all willfully blind to its business. A crude sign by the entrance marks it—an hourglass symbol burned into an unpainted square of wood. The dark, narrow alley is heaped with dirty snow and smatterings of old blood. Laista's time lender—Wick, I learn from the guard posted at the door—is busy today. He smiles grimly as he lets me pass.

In the dimness, few people look up at me as I take my place in line. Unlike the rest of Laista's citizens, the likes of whom I drank with the night before, the people in line are gray, shivering. Ahead of me, the table is heaped haphazardly with a burnished knife and silver bowls, and a simple kiln smolders farther back. The cheap balsa wood inside it gives off a sour, acrid scent as it burns. The man moving behind the table must be Wick. Lank hair and ragged, bloodstained apron aside, he looks young and healthy compared to the people using his services, his eyes pale from the consumption of blood-iron. My skin crawls, but it's not as if I have another choice.

After a time that seems like forever and also entirely too soon, it's my turn to step up to the table. The older woman ahead of me hobbles away, cradling her bandaged hand. I approach the table and sit down on the rickety stool. Wick ignores me as he shakes a few stray droplets of blood onto the tabletop and wipes his knife clean with a rag.

For a moment, I think I'm going to vomit all over the instruments of bloodletting. I've seen enough of this in Crofton, but now, watching Wick hold his blade over the leaping flame of an oil lamp to prepare it for my skin, I know why Papa made sure that I'd never had it drawn myself.

When Wick takes my arm and lays it out on the table. I clamp my lips shut, bite the inside of my cheek. Caro risked everything for me. To try and bring me something—anything—of my father's. Some tiny piece of a memory. One small act of justice.

It's my fault what happened to her. My duty to save her.

I expect Wick to say something, try to comfort me before he cuts, but Wick is all business. "How much?" he asks.

"What?"

"How much time d'you want to withdraw?" he repeats impatiently.

My voice cracks when I say, "Forty years."

Wick's face draws together in a moment of shock, then disapproval. "You're joking," he says. "How old are you?"

"Seventeen." My whole life stretches out in my mind, seventeen years filled with memories and pain and everything that makes me who I am. For the span of a breath, I don't think of Everless or the Queen or darkness or anything but small, pearled moments of pure joy: Roan's hand held tight by mine and a child's shriek of laugher, Amma's smile as she sends Jacob away, the smell of charcoal as my father tames my hair with his fingers and a length of ribbon.

I'll have those, always—but what moments am I about to bleed, and how many—if any—will I have left?

"I'll have to measure the time in your blood first," Wick tells me, apparently seeing the determination on my face. "I don't want anyone dropping dead at my table."

I nod mutely. My heart is beating fast, making my pulse hammer away in my wrist and throat, try as I might to quiet it.

As if my blood is afraid to leave me. But Wick just shakes his head wearily and lowers the knife.

"Don't look," he tells me.

I look—how can I not?—and gasp and shudder as he pricks my finger with the knife tip, catching the drop of blood in a glass vial. He turns, and I watch in horrified fascination as he fiddles with the mess of instruments on the makeshift tabletop. He has a contraption consisting of a little glass dish held with wire over a candle, and presently he lights the candle and tips the drop of blood into the dish. Finally, he sprinkles a pinch of green powder into the blood; we both watch as it hisses and smokes. He checks a watch at his waist, I wonder how much of this is for show, and how much is real alchemy.

The mixed blood and powder in the dish ignites, and burns with a small, steady flame like at the head of a match. Wick studies it with a businesslike air, glancing briskly between the flame and his stopwatch. But as the seconds tick on, he slowly lowers the timepiece, and a deep frown furrows his face. Though I've never seen timeletting before, I know from his expression that something is wrong.

"What is it?" My voice rises as I try to interpret the look on his face.

He shakes his head. "Give me your hand," he says.

Reluctantly, I extend my hand, and he squeezes another drop of blood from the tip of my finger. He repeats the process, mixing my blood with the powder in a new spot on the dish and setting it alight, all with the same result. He watches with confusion as the two flames burn and burn.

"What's happening?" My voice is brittle with fear and frustration. "What's wrong?"

Wick purses his lips, considering. At length, he says, "It's supposed to burn out. That'll tell us about how much time you have left—for instance, if it had burned out quickly, you might have less than a year."

I was meant to have a long life. It's a small comfort. "So I would have lived a long time. I can afford forty years." Perhaps I can earn the years back, or some of them.

"No one can afford forty years," Wick snaps, still staring at the candle flame.

Out of the corner of my eye, I notice an old man in line peering curiously at us. I shiver, anxious to be back within the walls of Everless.

"This isn't right." He raises the pocket watch, taps a nail against its glass face. "It should have stopped by now, even if you lived to be a hundred . . . Maybe something's wrong with my powder." He pulls out a second set of instruments and before I realize what he's doing, nicks his own finger with the knife. He doesn't bother with the vial, just flicks the drop of blood into the dish, sprinkles the powder in, and lights the candle. The blood ignites.

While Wick and I watch, I find myself counting—*one, two, three, four, five, six*—and the flame dies halfway through seven. Wick blinks.

"See," he says without feeling. "I reckon fifteen years."

I don't know how to react to this—Wick's seeming carelessness about the time of his own death—but my eyes are drawn back to my own blood, still burning. Now Wick is watching me with suspicion and distrust on his face, his mouth flat and arms crossed over his chest. Around us, I see, the few other people in the store have gone still, watching.

"I don't understand," I say weakly. Does he think me a Gerling, my blood running with hundreds of years? "I'm not— I'm from Crofton. I've never taken time, not once."

Wick raises his eyebrows, but as the seconds pass, something in my face seems to soften him. "Maybe something is wrong with my instruments," he says doubtfully.

"But can you still withdraw time?" I press desperately. Have the forty years been taken from Caro's blood already? "It's for my friend. She needs it."

"I can try," Wick says after a moment. He studies his instruments—an array of knives and needles that makes my stomach contract queasily—and chooses a short knife that seems to be made of blue glass. Next he picks up a small, tarnished-looking tin cup and wipes both objects down with a cloth.

"Hold out your hand," he instructs, and I obey, suddenly thankful that I haven't eaten this morning. My stomach is heaving.

Wick holds my wrist down with one practiced hand, and

with the other, makes a long shallow cut along the skin of my palm. The pain hits me a second after the blooming blood, a thin line of fire. Wick holds the cup beneath my hand and catches the rivulet of blood inside.

As red splashes against the glass, my strength begins to go out of me—far more than the small amount of blood in the cup would seem to suggest. I feel like I'm aging even as I sit on this stool, watching dazedly as my blood fills up the cup.

When it's full, Wick tilts my hand up, stopping the flow, and sets the cup aside before wrapping a bandage expertly and neatly around my hand. I realize I'm gripping the table with my other hand to stay upright. My head is spinning, and I remain on the stool as Wick goes about his procedure, afraid to rise.

I've witnessed the process of blood minting but now it seems to take eons. I fall into a kind of haze, watching as he pours my blood into the cup on the scale, bright as rubies even in this dim store. He adds a careful spoonful of a different powder, this one dark and glittering like obsidian. As soon as the powder comes into contact with my blood, the contents of the whole cup ignite with a flash of white flame. A blast of heat hits my face, along with the smell of copper.

The flame burns bright for several long moments and then dies down. When it's extinguished, Wick takes the cup and tilts it so I can see. Through darkness at the edges of my vision, I stare at the bright liquid in the bottom of the cup. It shimmers like oil, shines like mercury—if mercury was red-gold. When

Wick moves the cup, it rolls around slow as honey. Pure time. My time.

"Now I'll make it into coin," Wick says, his tone a little kinder after seeing my distress. He picks another item, a heavy lead block on which I can see inverted versions of the Queen's insignia, the symbol appearing on every blood-iron in Sempera. On his desk are molds for every kind of blood-iron, from tiny, flimsy hour-coins the size of my thumbnail to the one he's holding: molds for year-coins, each circle's diameter almost as wide as my fist.

Wick carefully pours a bit of my time into the mold, and I watch, dizzily fascinated, as the coin takes shape before my eyes, the metal cooling and slowing even as he pours. The block has ten molds; Wick fills each of them with molten time. Twice, he has to stop to remelt my cooling time over the flame. "Come back later and I'll take another ten," he says gruffly. "Don't want to do it all at once."

By the time he's finished, the first of the coins have cooled completely, until they look exactly like the blood-irons I see every day. My stomach turns as I consider the fact that for every coin I've ever spent, handled, even touched, someone had to suffer as I'm suffering now. Someone had to sit and watch as their life was bled out of them, to be transformed into coin to buy that night's thin strip of dried meat or a pint of beer or a thatched roof over one's head.

When all the coins have cooled, Wick turns the block over

and shakes it a little so that the new blood-irons tumble down to the wooden table with heavy clinks. I reach out to take one in hand, eyeing it with equal fascination and revulsion. This time has flowed through my veins for seventeen years. And now it's outside of my body, and I am diminished. The metal is hot against my skin. If it weren't so horrifying, it would be almost beautiful.

"How are you feeling?" Wick asks, but I'm already pushing back from the table. I can't—I don't have the time, I think grimly, to sit in this shop and ponder the unfairness of life. Even now, Caro's years might be draining from her. She could be dying, if she's not already dead. Because of me. *For* me. Going to the vault for me was more than an act of bravery—or foolishness—on Caro's part. Something deep inside me knows, it was an act of true kindness. No one has cared for me like that other than Papa. And Papa's gone.

I have to get these blood-irons to her.

I stand as Wick bags up the coins in a cloth and hands the package to me. They are still warm through the fabric.

He puts a hand on my shoulder. "Easy there," he says. "You just lost a lot of time. You could pass out or worse if you overexert yourself."

The sudden movement has made me dizzy, the close walls momentarily melting in my vision. But I have to go. "I'm fine," I manage, my voice coming out a little slurred. "I'll be fine." I shrug his hand off and stand to go, realizing as I do that he may be right, that the distance to the door seems like a mile. But I can't sit and recover. I have to go. For Caro.

Dimly, I feel a rough pallet of lumber under my back and a gentle, steady swaying, up and down, up and down. For a moment, I think I'm at sea, and reach my arm out to skim the water with my fingers—but then, the blurred smear of a face appears above me, and a pair of arms props me upright. I realize it's only a merchant's cart dropping me at the gates of Everless.

I blink against the gray light, remembering I've never seen the sea. With the time drained out of me—just ten years now, but thirty more to come—I most likely never will.

I walk, as fast as my unsteady legs will let me, to Caro's room.

Having ten years drained from one's blood is a little like being drunk, but without the pleasant warmth of madel. When I stumble and reach out to the wall for support, I'm racked with shivers. The servants' quarters feel strange and threatening, twisting and claustrophobic. I can sense people passing me, fellow servants going about their day, but I can't make out their faces. They give me a wide berth, maybe thinking me drunk. Against the torchlight illuminating the corridor, their shadows rear like monsters, warped limbs and sharp teeth, all reaching out to me.

I fall, and someone catches me. A hope blooms in my throat; I give it voice. "Roan?"

"No, love." The voice is soft, gentle, laced with sugar. Bea. I slump against her. "You're too good for that snake," she says, her voice distant. *Snake.* I'm overtaken by the feeling of falling backward through time, just like in the hedge witch's shop. The rotten smell of sulfur fills my nose, and I'm somewhere else, somewhere dark and cramped. Cold. The smell of sulfur again, sending a wave of nausea over me. But it's mixed with the scent of lavender—*Bea's hair, Bea's hair,* I tell myself, trying to remember where I am. I reach for her, my mind and sense scrambling for purchase. "Now tell me what you've done . . ."

Whose voice is that? *Bea's,* I tell myself, *it's Bea calling me.*

What have you done? Underneath Bea's high, panicked voice is a different one—deeper, angry, like someone is speaking over her shoulder to me.

I feel fingers turn my wrist. A sharp intake of breath. "Jules, you haven't—you've done this for Caro, haven't you? Jules!"

Caro. The name brings Bea and Everless into focus. I straighten up, still gripping Bea's forearms. She stares at me, her eyes wide with concern. "Jules, you need rest. Come to the dormitories—"

"No." The harshness of it makes Bea's mouth a thin line. She steps back from me. "I have to get to Caro," I say, instead of *sorry.*

Bea begins to speak, but I turn in the direction of the Queen's suites. She doesn't follow.

Somehow I get to the corridor that runs behind the suites

of the Gerlings and their guests. By now I know which of the heavy oak doors leads to Caro's chamber. I wipe the sweat from my face and do my best to stand up straight as I approach, holding my head high and clutching the bag of blood-irons tightly below my cloak. I press the door with my palms. Pain shoots through me, but the door swings open.

The mood in Caro's bedroom is somber. The curtains are drawn, shutting out the afternoon light and turning Caro's cozy room into a place of strange shadows, which dance thanks to the small fire crackling in the hearth. Briefly, I wonder who would have arranged this for the scorned handmaiden—but then I see Caro in her bed, asleep and shivering with each breath, an empty chair at her side. I collapse into it. Caro shifts in her sleep but doesn't wake.

I'd wondered whether they'd taken her time so soon, immediately after she was sentenced, but, looking at her drawn features, the answer is plain. Part of me hoped that there would be more time—that Caro, with her prized place at Lady Gold's side, would have a trial, a chance to prove her innocence. Or the Queen would have intervened on her behalf. But I should have known that that was not how Captain Ivan's justice works.

She's young, I tell myself, trying to stay calm. Had she ever said how many years she had left? She must have had far more than forty years before they took this time. Of course, Ivan wouldn't have checked how much time was in her blood, as Wick did with me. Nor would Ivan have cared that *no one can afford forty years*, as Wick advised me. My head spins with the thought; Caro could be in mortal danger even now. It's not unheard of for young people to withdraw time, thinking they surely have plenty left, only to drop dead a year or a month or a day later.

I take the pouch of blood-iron and put it on Caro's nightstand. "This is for you," I tell her, as if she can hear my gratitude and guilt for caring so much about me. "Ten years."

Caro, of course, doesn't move or react. She's scarcely breathing, and my skin prickles. What if she is dying?

I've never consumed time before, but I know well enough how the process is supposed to work. So I cross the room to Caro's shelves, and return with a small bottle of wine. I pour the wine into a kettle and heat it over the fire. After a few minutes, when a heady, aromatic steam is rising from the kettle, I remove it from the flame and bring it to the nightstand. I take the simple wooden cup that waits there and stack three of my fresh-minted year-coins from my purse inside the cup, then watch in fascination as I pour a measure of steaming wine over them.

There's a hiss where hot liquid and metal meet, and smoke rises from the cup, smelling like sugar and ash. I stir the mixture with a spoon and then set it aside and gently shake Caro's shoulder.

She comes awake gradually, blinking and shivering despite the room being both dark and warm. Her eyes focus slowly on me. "Jules," she says, sounding more exhausted than surprised as she lifts herself up to a sitting position. "You're here."

"I'm sorry, Caro," I say miserably. I take up the steaming cup of wine and blood-iron and offer it to her. "Drink."

Caro accepts the cup, her movements slow and punctuated by winces. I'm still dizzy from my loss of time, my body as tender as a bruise, and I can't imagine how she must be feeling, having lost four times as much. Her hands aren't bandaged, like mine—Ivan must have pulled it from her arms. My stomach makes a fist. Her wrists are covered by her thick velvet dress, so I can't see the marks. "Thank you, Jules," she says, her voice a hoarse whisper, and drinks.

The effect is immediate. Points of color appear in Caro's white cheeks, and her grip on the cup tightens as she swallows the mixture of wine and time. Even her posture seems to change, her back becoming straighter in the bed. She sighs, the sound of her breath stronger than it was before, and moves to put the empty cup back on the nightstand.

Before her hand reaches the table, Caro stops abruptly. The room is thick with heat—her arm hangs crooked in midair, and her fingers uncurl from the cup until it falls, cracking against the floorboards. Caro gasps in pain and brings her hand to her throat.

I lean forward, pulse spiking in my blood. "Caro, what's wrong?" Had I melted the blood-irons enough? Did I administer them wrongly somehow?

Caro opens and closes her mouth, but nothing comes out. She doesn't seem to be able to breathe; her face twists in pain and she goes rigid, then begins thrashing in the sheets, spluttering and choking. The sounds are harsh and urgent, gasps that are cut off uselessly before the air can reach her lungs. Her face has turned bright scarlet, and her eyes are bulging in her skull.

She's choking.

"Caro," I hear myself shout. Panic swelling my throat, I cup her head with one hand and force her jaw open with the other. Something glints in the back of her throat.

Shaking with fear, I push Caro's head to the side and reach into her mouth with two fingers, but with her struggling, I can't reach the object, can't dislodge it. Caro spasms, her face turning redder and redder, and I hear myself begging the Sorceress for Caro's life and internally screaming to hurry, please hurry. My own heart is pounding so hard I think it will splinter my ribs and burst out through my chest.

Caro's eyes roll up in her head, and she goes slack in my arms.

The world falls silent.

She has passed out. My own breath comes in gasps. The rest of the room is quiet—a quiet so thick that it settles into me like stone.

I look up and almost scream.

Nothing looks immediately wrong about the room, but something about it has turned to terror. The gauzy curtains don't wave in the wind, but stick in their billowed-out shapes as if they're made of ice. From the rose in a vase on Caro's vanity, one falling petal is frozen in midair, halfway to the ground.

And Caro's not moving—not in the slightest. Her body is still as a statue—no movement of her chest as she breathes, not even a blink. The wrongness of it makes the hair stand up on my arms. I don't know if she's alive or dead. As I look down at her, I notice a droplet of sweat gleaming on her cheek. It's stretched, poised to drip from the ridge of her cheekbone down to the floor. But it doesn't fall. And doesn't fall. It's only when I brush it away with my hand that it drops, hitting the floor with a plink audible in this dead silence.

Certainty takes hold of me, cold and terrifying.

Something is wrong with time.

In the silence and the stillness, I feel more alone than I've ever been, with my friend lying as still as death in my arms. She doesn't stir when a sob, formerly held back by adrenaline, bursts from my chest.

When I release Caro and sink to my knees beside her bed, she slumps back into the pillows, her face bright red but utterly still. The floorboards creak under my weight, the mattress rises back into place when I take my weight off it, but everything else in the room remains as motionless as if it has all become suddenly encased in glass. It's dizzying, nightmarish; and my tears come hot and fast. I've felt time slow before, but never this full stop, this eerie space where I alone can move. What if I'm stuck, like the town of Briarsmoor?

Fear clears my mind. Taking a deep breath to master myself, I get to my feet and bend over Caro. I grip her shoulder and hip carefully and turn her onto her side. Then I climb up beside her and, remembering some instructions from Lora on choking victims, strike her between the shoulder blades with the heel of my hand.

Nothing changes. I steel myself and hit again, harder. And again, until my recently bandaged hand screams and aches and begins to bleed.

On the fourth blow, something gives. A blur of gold bursts from Caro's lips—I gasp with shock and relief—and the thing hits the floorboards with a heavy thud before rolling under the wardrobe. Though my eyes are blurred with sweat and tears, it looks thicker and heavier than a year-coin.

A strange, strangled sound comes from beside me—the second half of a sob. I turn my head to see Caro draw in a ragged, painful-sounding breath.

"Thank the Sorceress," I say, and bend over her. She's breathing hard, her chest heaving, and there's blood on her lips—but her face is going slowly from red to pink, and I can feel her pulse where I grip her shoulder, strong and alive. I look to where the gold thing fell on the floor. "You were choking."

Caro's crying quiets. She stares at me, her eyes ringed with red. It's more than surprise, I realize as she follows my gaze to the floor—it's suspicion.

No, something else—betrayal.

I don't understand. Does she think I meant to hurt her?

Finally tearing her eyes away from mine, Caro leans over and tries to grab the object, but she's too weak. I bend down, thankful to be free of her eyes on mine. But the relief in me twists back toward dread at the thought of what I will find beneath the wardrobe.

It's not a coin. I kneel down to the floor, both to look closer and to hide my face from Caro. On the floor, trailing blood and spit but immaculately clean itself, is a gold sphere the size of a walnut. It's new blood-iron—that's obvious from the sheen of the metal—but it's as if the three coins that I had dissolved in the wine have reformed into this sphere.

Slowly, something takes hold of me again: the feeling that I'm trapped on the board of a game I can't begin to understand. The thing sickens me and calls to me at the same time. I reach out for it.

The metal, when I close my hand around it, isn't hot but gently warm, as if it's been sitting in the sun. It's smooth and seems almost to be humming, as if there's something alive inside. It's heavy and—

I gasp as I my fingers sink into its surface, as if the metal is melting under my touch. I drop it and scramble back.

"Hold on to it." The voice is a whisper, barely audible, but unmistakable.

I look up at Caro, who's weakly pulling herself to the edge of the bed. Her face is still flushed and shining with sweat, but she's staring down at the ball of metal with wide, alert eyes.

"See what happens," she adds, meeting my eyes again. There's a flicker of something there, some emotion I can't identify, but in a moment she's cast her eyes down and is looking at the gold sphere again. I want to protest, go and hide until I can puzzle out what in the name of the Sorceress is happening, but Caro is waiting expectantly. And she's alive, for now, which is all that should matter.

Reluctantly, I reach out and touch one fingertip to the gold sphere.

For a moment, nothing happens. Then the surface begins to shift, my finger sinking in, as if it's melting without heat. As it softens, the half-liquid metal starts to move up my finger. I shiver, but force myself not to pull away as the gold crawls up to reach my knuckle, my palm. I can hear both of our ragged breaths as the strands of gold creep up and disappear beneath the bandage Wick recently wound around my hand. It feels like warm water, trickling upward.

Soon the sphere is entirely gone, and strands of liquid metal run up my skin like veins.

"Take off the bandage," Caro says softly. Something in her voice makes me obey; I unwind the bloodstained cloth. It falls away to reveal the cut the time lender made, still fresh and angry red, and a tiny rivulet of gold—of blood-iron—of my time slipping into it, back beneath my skin where it belongs.

23

In the early hours of the night, Caro—still fever-hot, sweat sticking strands of her dark hair to her face—demands that I tell her *how*. Her voice is rough, her throat scratched from the shard of my time that stuck there. I tell her the truth over and over: that I don't know, that I have no idea what made the time in my blood rebel against her and return to me. I've never seen or heard of anything like it. I put my seven remaining year-coins on Caro's dresser, afraid to try feeding her again, and afraid to have them near me.

When I try to leave, to find blood-iron that behaves the way blood-iron is supposed to, Caro begs me to stay. After hours of this, she finally falls asleep in my arms, clinging to me with the ferocity of a child. Did my blood-iron make her worse? She's pale, but her pulse beats steadily. Exhausted from the day, and knowing that Ina will return soon to help us, I let my eyes close.

When the dreams come this time, I welcome them.

In the darkness, I beckon to the girl with her face in shadow, already knowing that I must defeat her or die myself. She comes toward me with her hands raised. A terrifying world comes into focus around me: we face off on a dark plain, the grass around us is scorched black, with no other sign of life as far as I can see.

The girl approaches me, and flames spring up where her feet have fallen. A cloak snaps behind her, as black as ink, its hood hiding her face.

I am going to die, I think in the dream.

The girl stops two arm lengths away. She holds her hands out toward me, as if entreating me. Her wild, mocking laugh rises above the wind.

"*My friend*," I hear her say, the sweet high voice seeming to emanate from all around me. "*Don't you trust me?*"

The image dissolves, and I'm sitting on my bed, in our cottage in Crofton, looking down at my mother's statue of the Sorceress. I'm cradling the carved stone in my palm. The relief is so strong it stings—but this time, I know I am dreaming. The stillness in the room frightens me more than the vision of the girl. All I can do is stare down at the statue, and stare, and stare.

Then, the statue moves.

It opens its mouth and laughs.

It brings its hand up, the one holding the knife.

I jolt awake in Caro's bed, the collar of my dress soaked in sweat and tears. Familiarity stabs through me suddenly. The girl's pose flashes in my mind—leaning slightly forward, her hands cupped in front of her. It aligns with what I saw in the vision at the hedge witch's, of being held as an infant while the man carrying me stopped before a statue of the Sorceress, plucked a stone from her hands.

And then the same woman, but alive, not stone.

Then, in my mother's statue, turned to stone again.

I shiver, bringing my arms around me for warmth. Is this what my father was trying to hide from me—that I have some connection to the Sorceress herself?

Beside me, Caro stirs. I realize that in my dreams, I've kicked our blankets off, exposing her upper torso. When I bring the fabric up to cover her, I realize her hands are cold. As I tuck them in, I notice for the first time how pale they are . . .

My mind slows to a stop. She was caught near the vault only yesterday—and after my time in the mava cellar, it took days before my hands were completely clean.

I stare at her hands, and begin to shiver, a wave of confusion and fear threatening to drown me.

Gently, so as not to wake her, I roll back her sleeves—and stop. There is no mark from timeletting. No cut. No bandage.

She lied. Or someone did. Whatever happened to Caro

is not what I've been told.

The lie is dark, opaque, unreadable, like a river so burdened with silt you can't see the bottom. It courses through me, thick as my own time turned to liquid metal in my veins.

A line from Liam's notebook, or my dreams, or my past, filters into my awareness, as though it has slept all along in my veins and finally made its way to my heart.

"Snake," said Fox. "What have you done?"

There must be some mistake.

I ease off the mattress, careful not to shift it and wake Caro. I exit the room as quietly as I can, my breath tight in my throat.

Strengthened by the new-old time in my blood, I wind through the barely lit corridors. Just a few torches are lit, casting the empty halls in an eerie half-light, and the only sound is the snapping of the flames and my own uncertain footsteps.

My head begins to spin with thoughts, hard and blinding as gems in light.

Caro's deception.

Papa's secrets, his well-meaning lies.

The shock of the so-called hedge witch when her fraudulent spell worked on me.

The way that time has misbehaved around me all my life.

The dreams I keep having of the girl who would kill me, and all the other dreams of running from a shadowy figure, rising up now through the years, that Papa—and eventually, I—dismissed as the nightmares of an anxious child. Even the snatches of words and images from my favorite childhood stories, the ones about Fox and Snake—the ones Liam recorded in his little book . . .

All of these things are tied together in shifting and complicated ways, yet still nothing is clear. The revelation of how much Papa hid from me—how much he lied to me over my whole life—is like looking down, expecting to find stone beneath my feet, and seeing nothing but air.

I need to get inside the vault. I need to see what Caro lied about, and what Papa died for.

I turn a door handle, and another line shoots out of my memory, coating my whole body in gooseflesh.

"Fox," said Snake, curling slowly around her friend's heart. "It's time we face the truth."

24

In the dark, surrounded by mirrors and portraits of dead Gerlings, the distance from here to the vault seems to stretch out before me, the halls unspooling faster than I can walk, no matter how I quicken my pace. Tree branches scratch at the windows, and distant wind howls, as if winter itself is clawing at Everless's stone walls, trying to find a crack by which it can reach in and drag me out.

Caro didn't enter the vault. She didn't have her time drained at all.

It's still night. I pass the dormitories, where I hear the women—those who have the earliest chores, such as tending the fires in the Gerling hearths so the nobles never feel the pinch of morning air—getting out of bed and dressing. The sounds come to me as if from miles away. My mind and heart are racing, the adrenaline of the dream coursing through my body as if I were still asleep, though my eyes are wide-open.

I hurry toward the wing that contains the vault, sticking to the servants' corridors when I can, keeping my head down and my eyes on the floor when I cannot. I've no idea where Liam Gerling lurks, if he's awake.

When I reach the door to the vault at last, the hall is empty and silent, specks of dust floating in the light that floods in through the tall windows from the lawn. I stand before the door and look up, its shining mass reminding me how little power I have. The door bears an inlay of bronze panels in a long strip down the middle, carved with strange shapes—birds and snakes and jewels spilling from cups; but these transform farther down the panel into the shapes of people, women dancing in silk gowns, clasping hands. If I step back and squint, the entire effect is of a face with a jewel in the shape of a heart falling from its lips. It makes me think of Ina, and I wonder what she will think when she returns from her journey with the Queen and Roan, to learn of Caro's punishment . . . and everything that followed.

Cautiously, I put my hands on the wood. It feels as solid as stone beneath my palms. When I give a push, nothing happens, not even a creak. My hands come away clean.

I bend down and see that a series of tiny gears are woven throughout the carvings, trailing down the door like buttons. I follow them upward, until I realize that running alongside them is a thin, red-stained channel, hardly deep enough to fit a wire. A trickle of cold goes down my spine.

Liam told me that the door took blood to open, took time, and you never knew how much. Before today, I never would have taken such a risk. But now I don't even hesitate before raising my fingers to the panel, carefully exploring its design.

The walls of the little channel are stained reddish-brown, not with age. At the top is a little handle in the shape of a scorpion tail emerging from a fruit, sharp-edged as a razor. Its purpose is clear. Just a blood payment, but a payment no one but a Gerling could risk. Cruel, elegant. Just like the Gerlings.

I trace the channel with my fingertip. Is any of this Papa's blood? Anger, fear, grief—they course through me together, and I double over with nausea. I lean my head against the door, allow myself to let the emotion escape in one choked sob. Papa would have known how the door worked—and he knew how close to death he was—but he thought it was worth the risk.

Before I can talk myself out of it, I reach up and press my finger onto the scorpion's blade. Heat blooms, and I feel the peculiarly unpleasant sensation of time being drained from my blood. For a moment, I'm dizzy, but less so than when Wick took ten years.

Then something behind the door clicks. When I push on the wood, it opens without resistance, and my hands come away purple. For a moment, I'm in awe of the mechanism and its creator—before the awe curdles to anger. I step into darkness, leaving the door cracked just the slightest bit so I'm not locked in.

Gradually, my eyes adjust to reveal a narrow stone staircase lit by torches, just like the one leading to Lady Sida's chambers. I climb and climb until the top of the stairs opens up into darkness. Doubling back, I take one of the torches from its sconce, holding it high over my head.

For a long moment, I don't comprehend what I see. A room of dark stone, windowless, with a shining, tiled floor. Its walls curve with the tower, only maybe twenty paces in diameter, though it stretches into shadow over my head.

And it's not tiles on the floor. The ground beneath my feet is blanketed with blood-irons of every size and color, mixed in with other treasures—cups of gold and silver, pearls and rings, raw jewels tossed on the ground like refuse. Rusted-looking ceremonial swords hang on the wall, blades dulled with age. But money means almost nothing to me now that Papa's gone. I don't have the urge to bend down and pile month- and year-coins into my skirt, as once I might have. I scan the room for something, anything that calls out to me, anything that reminds me of Papa, and why he'd come here, what he'd die for—and I come up with nothing.

Disappointment gathers in my throat, thick and bitter and suffocating.

But then something catches my eye on one of the shelves— an ancient-looking book. I draw closer, kicking blood-irons out of my way. There's no reason for a book to be here, sitting among several hundred lifetimes of coins and treasure. My heart pounding, I open the cover, and a familiar scent washes over me—straw and metal and woodsmoke. The inside page bears no type, just words scribbled in an unfamiliar slanting handwriting: *Antonia Ivera.*

I don't know the name, but it tugs at something deep inside me.

Next to it, small bits of torn paper peek out from the binding. Transfixed, I take my mother's portrait out of my pocket— where I always keep it—and fit it perfectly into the space.

And then, I know. My father died for this book.

Surrounding the words—surrounding the text on every page, I realize as I flip through—are little drawings, doodles of spirals and trees and forest animals. And I do know where those came from.

Me.

The memories are flooding back: of sitting in my father's lap—before any darkness touched our lives, before the accident—while he read of the snake and the fox in his deep, lilting voice, and of stealing the book away to my cot to make my mark on the pages, which for some reason my father never seemed to mind. Holding this book is like having a piece of Papa back again—and even myself, another Jules who had never told a lie, known hunger, missed her parents, or struck a terrible bargain.

I turn back to the first page to read the stories, but as I read down the lines—still in Antonia Ivera's handwriting—the ink seems to flood off the page and rise up around me. Darkness floods my vision. I can't pinpoint the moment when reality gives way to dreams, but after my experience with the hedge witch I know what to expect, and though I'm frightened, I force myself not to close off. I hold still, my mind wide-open, and let the visions—memories—cascade through me.

Before my eyes is the girl, but much younger, dark hair hiding her face. She's sitting against a wall, half lit by candlelight, her arms wrapped around her knees. Heavy iron chains link her wrists. She drops her head in her hands.

"We're never going to get out of here, are we?" Her voice is as familiar to me as my own heartbeat.

When I turn to face her, the chains on my own limbs clink and drag. But I reach out to her. Touch her shoulder. *We will*, I tell her. *I have an idea.*

And I do. It glitters beneath the surface of my mind, there but indistinct, like stones at the bottom of a rushing river.

Then, the light of a candle. Under my arm is a book, at my fingers a spindly quill. Vaguely, I feel my arm ache, and notice a splatter of blood on the corner of the cream-colored page. Though the book's leather is newer—still warm, almost, from the animal's hide—I know it's the same book that I hold in my hands, trembling in the Gerling vault. The connection grounds me; I look down at my own hand furiously scribbling as if at a distance. The nib begins to spell out a familiar name: *Briarsmoor*.

Briarsmoor. It's the only word that makes sense. I cling to it.

Then I'm running, running through an ancient forest, branches tearing at my face and roots seeming to reach up and grasp at my ankles. Behind me, the baying of hounds, the shouting of hunters, the girl's wrath and hunger, eternal, inescapable. Ahead of me, I can picture the town, the sweeping green lawn, the statue of the Sorceress in the square. Everyone I love is there. *Briarsmoor*, a voice whispers in my ear. If I can get there, I can save them, I can save myself.

The terror in my heart is threaded through with stinging grief, with betrayal. Every footfall, every heartbeat, every gasping breath sounds the same: *my friend, my friend, my friend, my friend. What have you done?*

Then another noise reaches me, something from outside the world of visions. My eyes flutter open, still heavy with visions, and it takes me a moment to remember why I'm lying on my side on a blanket of blood-iron, a jewel pressing painfully into my cheek.

But then the sound of footsteps on stone snaps me back to alertness. I scramble into a sitting position as torchlight brightens the stairwell, and I see men's shadows against the wall. I hear voices. Everless guards.

I left the door open for anyone to see. What a foolish thing to do, a foolish way to die.

As they appear in the doorway, I throw my hands up, my panicked mind insisting, like a child, that if I can't see them they can't see me. Silence falls, and I flinch, waiting for the shouts that will mean my doom, for hands to fall on me and drag me away.

But they don't come. I lower my hands to see a man looking out over the doorway, torch raised high, his hand on the pommel of his sword. But he's—still. He doesn't breathe or blink; not even the flame topping his torch flickers. Behind him, the pattern of brightness and shadow cast on the wall is eerily stationary—as if someone has painted the stone with firelight and shade.

I don't stop to think about what I'm seeing. Instead, I creep over the carpet of riches and ease around the man, my body tight with tension. I weave around the other three guards behind him on the stairs, careful not to accidentally brush any of them, and then practically throw myself down the stairs and out into the hallway. Noise erupts behind me.

It's only when I'm out on the lawn, halfway to the stables, that I realize I've left the book behind.

25

The wind pries its way beneath my cloak, chilling me to the bone. The mare beneath me gallops hard, pebbles flying up from under her hooves as we charge down the empty road. My whole body aches—I should have stopped to consume the blood-iron that I couldn't give to Caro—but my need to get out of Everless overpowered everything else. It wasn't easy to even haul myself onto the horse's back, or to stay upright as I lied to the guards at the gate, but urgency and terror gave me a wild kind of energy.

Now the adrenaline is sliding away and I'm so exhausted I worry I will fall asleep right here on the mare's bare back, despite the jolting ride and the freezing air sparking along my arms and neck. But somehow I know where to guide her, and it seems like only a few minutes pass before the horse comes to a violent halt.

Empty fields stretch out on both sides of the road, untouched snow gleaming in the moonlight. A hundred yards ahead sits a cluster of derelict-looking houses and buildings, scattered haphazardly on either side of the road. But they are strange—they shimmer slightly in the light of the moon and snow as if it were summer and steam were rising between us and the village. The houses seem to glow, though the streets look empty and the windows dim.

No matter how I nudge, the horse won't go any farther. She's prancing nervously, stamping at the frozen earth and tossing her head. And I understand why—the sight of Briarsmoor ahead of us seems wrong. I realize I'm grinding my teeth, resisting the urge to turn and run.

I'll have to walk the rest of the way. I try to swallow my fear as I tie the horse to a post along the side of the road and face Briarsmoor, hitching my bag up my shoulder. With one last worried glance behind me, I walk.

Now the journey to the town seems to drag, and the strange shimmer hanging around Briarsmoor only intensifies as I approach. By the time I reach it, the distortion is such that the buildings behind it are only vaguely lit shapes against the night, as if I am on the outside looking into a fogged window. My heart pounds in terror. Everything about this seems wrong, but there is no going back now, so I reach out toward the boundary between Briarsmoor and the outside world. Warmth spreads through my hand where I touch it, but nothing else happens, so I step through.

And blink in the sudden sunlight, inhaling sharply.

My head spins as I take in the sight around me. A moment ago, the night sky stretched above me, scattered with stars; now the sky is the thin grayish blue of a clear winter day, a pale sun casting the hint of warmth on my cheeks.

The stories are true.

At first I can't see anything, then my eyes slowly adjust. The glare fades, and I see the remains of a town: a road pockmarked with missing cobblestones, a collection of falling-down houses, dark windows edged with broken glass. I turn around to see the same boundary hanging between me and the rest of Sempera like a curtain of fine gauze. Beyond, all I can see is the faint line of the dark, snow-covered horizon, intersected by a long gray-white cut that is the road.

Goose bumps break out over my body. The orphanage clerk's talk about the town twelve hours behind the rest of the world was one thing, but seeing this place in the flesh is another thing entirely. Wind whistles through the empty houses.

Unsure of what to do next, I start a slow walk around the edge of the town. I don't know exactly what I'm looking for— the statue, a bookstore, any sign of life. But everything looks bereft of humanity, beaten down by years of abandonment. Trees burst through broken windows. Roofs sag beneath their blankets of snow. I almost trip over what looks like the remains of a chair, broken and molding.

When I look down, I know that mementos like this are everywhere, half hidden by snow—the carcasses of furniture, broken plates and bowls, toys and books all unrecognizably swollen with dampness and age. I remember what the orphanage clerk said about looting in the wake of the time crisis, and my stomach clenches at the thought of such chaos.

A flicker of motion in the sky makes me raise my head. I look up and see a thin column of smoke, rising into the blue from somewhere deeper in the town, and my breath seizes in my chest. What kind of person would inhabit such a place?

Well, you're here, a dry inner voice reminds me. Surely all manner of explorers and scavengers have descended upon Briarsmoor since it was abandoned. It may be nothing. And even if it isn't—I won't learn anything about my past by skulking around the edge of town. And though I've scanned everywhere, I can't see a statue that resembles the one from my dreams.

So I square my shoulders and walk toward the smoke.

Eventually I come upon a small house that seems slightly less in disrepair than its neighbors. Pale smoke rises from the chimney. A small path in the snow has been cleared out to the front door. Not daring to give myself time to hesitate, I go up and knock.

There's a long, long pause. Then I hear the sound of footsteps—slow, light, hesitant. The door opens.

I don't know who I expected, but the woman standing in the doorway looks just like anyone in Crofton or any other town: long brown hair in a braid down her back, weather-beaten face and hands, a homespun dress hanging off her thin figure. She seems about Papa's age, maybe a little younger.

"Who are you?" she says. She looks only momentarily surprised to see a stranger on her doorstep before she slips into a familiar smile. "Good afternoon."

"A-ah—" I stutter before finding my voice. "Jules. Jules Ember. I'm looking for—information. I think my family used to live here."

A beat passes, the woman staring intently into my face. Then she says, "Come in."

Clutching my bag to my chest, I follow her inside. A weak fire burns in the hearth, a kettle boiling over it. Furs are piled against one wall, and dried meat and herbs hang from the ceiling. How long has this woman been living alone in this abandoned town?

"My name is Rinn," she tells me as she sits down at a rough wooden table, gesturing that I should do the same. "I live here. I have always."

It doesn't sound like she's mixing up her words—there's no confusion or stutter in her voice. Instead, it sounds like something is plucking her words from the air and scrambling them before they reach my ears.

"Hello," I say gently. "I thought the Queen ordered the

town evacuated."

Rinn smiles. "But in all the confusion, who will notice if one woman stays behind?" she replies. "As long as the fire doesn't catch." She says it like the flames might leap out of their confines, wild and hungry, at any moment. And for all I know, they might.

There's a sinking feeling in my stomach. "What about your family?"

"My son will die." Rinn's voice is matter-of-fact, but I hear the current of grief running underneath it. "He is sickly, and . . . it will be too much for him. Another woman stays with me. But she died of fever."

"I'm so sorry." I swallow my horror at the thought of such aloneness. I stare at her, trying to understand the world as she sees it—her strange language, strung between what was and what will be. Perhaps time has shattered around her, too, like it has the town. "And you've been here by yourself ever since? How have you survived?"

Rinn shrugs one shoulder. "Hunting, planting, preserving. And people come along like you. So I am not so alone. Tea?"

Startled, I nod, and Rinn rises to busy herself around the kettle. "Are you coming to the festival today?" she calls over her shoulder.

My heart sinks. There is no festival today—there can't be. This is a ghost town, a place stuck forever in time. She hands me a mug and I sip at it, waiting to speak, not wanting to tear

300

away her illusion. "If I can. But I came here for another reason. I was born here," I tell her slowly. "I'm looking—" I pause, stumbling over the truth. "I'm separated from my parents. I don't remember them at all." I dig down in my memory to the vision I had of Briarsmoor, the blood and the screaming woman and the man who took me away. "I remember a lawn and a statue of the Sorceress, holding a handful of stones like this." I demonstrate cupping my hands over the table, then let them drop, suddenly embarrassed. "I'm sorry; I know that's a strange thing to remember."

Rinn's gaze on me grows more intent. "I know whose house that is—the Morses, a merchant and his wife and their family. Naomi Morse."

Disappointment surges in me, followed by frustration—who is Antonia Ivera?

Rinn continues, "She and her husband and sister and their children all live in an old manor west of here, near the edge of town." She tilts her head, staring at me like she's desperate to recognize my face. "I am Naomi's midwife."

My stomach twists at her language—the implication that they're still alive. I hold the sides of my chair as my heart beats a little faster, trying not to get my hopes up. It could just be another twist of her mind's grasp on time. "Could you tell me where the manor is? I think— I'd love to go look around."

Rinn blinks. "My dear," she says after a moment. "The house is burning."

My stomach sinks. "Burning?" I echo.

Rinn reaches out and puts a brown hand over mine, her eyes suddenly wide and wild. "We must go," she says, "we must—"

"Rinn." I put my hands on her shoulders. "No house is on fire."

"Jules, you said?" Rinn's calmer now. "Naomi Morse, well . . . they're saying she's a witch. A real one."

"So they burned her house?" My throat is constricted, making it difficult to get the words out. "They killed her?"

She shakes her head. "Naomi's dying," she says. "I see it. A mercy, I'd think—her sister, her husband, their children—they all die in the fire. We will all die in the end, but the fire won't take me. She will." Her voice slips into a whisper.

I grip my mug, fingers strangling the hardened clay. "Who will? Who's she?"

She stares at me, then blinks. "The house is coming down. We have to get out."

Her eyes have gone distant, glassy, like she's fallen back into the past for an instant. Then tears fill her eyes. She bows her head, old-yet-fresh grief clouding her face—and I feel it too, to my surprise. I remember the screams, the blurry faces gathered around the bed in my vision. If my guess is correct, Naomi Morse was my mother, the faces my aunt and cousins. And all of them long dead.

"Did you know my— Naomi's husband?" I ask hoarsely,

stopping myself just in time from saying *my real father*. Papa is my real father, even if not by birth.

"Ezra is strange," she says at length. "Shows up on the road one day, with a traveling cloak and a bag of brand-new blood-irons. He will never tell anyone where he came from, to my knowledge—I'm not even sure if Naomi knows." She takes a sip of her tea, her smile tinged with sadness. "There are rumors about him."

"What kind of rumors?" My fingers ache from clenching the mug, but I can't make myself let go.

"That he's obsessed with time, and dark magic. He'll visit a tavern or a friend's home, and . . . the night will seem to go on longer than normal. People say that he slips tainted blood-irons into their tea. It will happen to me more than once, when Ezra and Naomi come over. We eat and laugh for what seems like hours, but when they leave the house, I'll look at the clock to see that only an hour or two has passed." She laughs to herself. "He makes people uneasy—he has all sorts of strange idols. He speaks ill of the Sorceress."

Chills are running through me, and my whole body is alight with recognition. "And the baby?" I ask breathlessly, forgetting to be tactful.

Rinn's face falls, the happy memories of Ezra and Naomi's dinner visits punctured by the ugliness of what came after. "A girl born with a stone in her mouth," she says at length. Ina's face flashes in my mind. "An omen. The people are frightened, think the baby is the cause of everything . . ." She looks down at her hands.

My breath is coming fast, and I feel dizzy, like I'm hanging over the edge of a cliff. Ina was born with a stone in her mouth. Everyone knows that. But if the house in my dreams was my house, if Naomi was my mother . . .

"A few of us, Naomi's friends, will go to the house—what's left of it—after the fire. We want to bury the Morses before everyone leaves." She pauses. "The Queen . . ." she says. "The Queen wants her."

"Who?" I breathe.

"The baby," Rinn says. A slow, sad smile creeps over her face. "But Naomi's brother won't let her." She looks up at me, her eyes round with fear. "We have to give him time to run."

"Who?" I ask. "Naomi's brother?"

Rinn nods. "The blacksmith."

My breath stops. "Pehr?"

"That was it, he—"

I don't have time to dwell on this revelation, because Rinn's face crumples to pain and she cries out, her hand shooting to her heart. I drop the mug and rush to her. At this distance, so close I can smell the chamomile on her breath, I notice that the fabric of her dress is stained.

She clutches me. "The other one, take the other one," she gasps.

"What other one, Rinn?"

"The twin. But—but— It's too late. She's taking her away . . ."

Her voice trails off, and Rinn releases her fingers from my hands. I look down to see a red spot blooming above her heart. Slowly, carefully, I peel the thick wool of her dress away from her chest.

Her flesh has been split in two, and the mark is ringed with the dark purple color I know so well—mava, the Queen's mark of death. Blood spills from the wound, fresh and plentiful as the day it was given.

After she stills, I hold her body for a long moment, too horror-struck to move. Her blood warms my lap, seeps into the cracks of the floorboards around us. Finally, I'm able to lower her onto the ground. I stand up, shaking, intending to find a sheet to cover her with—and then run from this town and never, ever return.

I've only just turned my back when a sound from behind makes a scream lodge in my throat. I whirl around to see Rinn sitting upright, looking at me with a puzzled expression on her face. Her dress is clean and whole, though mine is still wet with her blood.

"Hello," she says. "Who are you?"

26

When I step back over the boundary between the town of Briarsmoor and the rest of the world, dark falls in an instant—a clear, chilly winter afternoon dissolving into a cold night just on the edge of a cold dawn. For a moment, I sway on my feet, the sudden change making me dizzy. Human beings weren't supposed to move through time like this, and a wave of nausea passes over me. But as my eyes adjust to the dark, I make out the shape of the mare still waiting for me, tied to a fence down the road.

The horse whickers gratefully when I turn her around and urge her back toward Everless, the way we came. I wish I could share in her simple, high-stepping happiness.

Rinn's words echo in my head. Her blood stains my dress, blood she's been spilling over and over for seventeen years.

After I regained my voice, I pleaded with her to come with me, thinking that I could pull her from the snag in time that she seemed to be caught in—but as soon as she reached the threshold of her house, her eyes became misty with confusion. When I tried to pull her outside, she started to scream, and only stopped when I let go of her wrists and walked away.

Dying and dying and dying, over and over again. I was a fool to think I could save her from such powerful magic. Grief tears at my heart for Rinn, for this town. For a family I've never known, now ashes.

But above all else, my thoughts are consumed by the truth slowly but surely taking shape before me. My mind continually circles back to Ezra Morse—the man who slowed time when he was happy. And when his wife gave birth, time stopped entirely, just as it did around me, when Caro was in danger yesterday.

Pehr—Papa—was my uncle. The Morses must have been my birth parents, my birth father a stranger who appeared in Briarsmoor out of nowhere. A man scornful of the Sorceress, who nevertheless had a statue of her near his home, and was rumored to experiment with magic. If I was the baby who was saved, was I the baby who stopped time? And Ina Gold . . .

My sister? My twin?

Impossible. And Roan . . .

My sister is marrying Roan Gerling. My sister will be crowned queen. My sister who doesn't know who I am, about

307

the night of blood and magic and death that bore us.

The riddle of it all pounds through my mind: Papa died to keep me from the Queen. He warned me the very day he died not to let the Queen see me.

But why? And what does it have to do with the Sorceress, who keeps appearing in my dreams, her palms open as I run toward her, knife in hand . . .

What does the Queen have to do with any of the stories Rinn told me? Why would she have wanted a child born in Briarsmoor—a child whose birth stopped time?

Unless the Queen . . . *is* the Sorceress.

The thought stings, blindingly hot then cold. I tell myself it's the air, only the air whipping against my face.

For some reason, the Queen wanted the child who could stop time.

I was saved. Wrenched away from Ina, who was left to be taken by the Queen.

Does this mean that I am the only one with a hidden power coursing through my blood?

If the Queen *is* the Sorceress, I've walked right into her path, and left havoc and destruction in my wake. But what would she want with me anyhow? The Queen may be cold and cruel, but she has never harmed my sister. If the Queen thought that Ina was the child born with the stone, is she still to discover her mistake?

And, of course, there is the equally pressing question

making my head burn in pain from the enormity of it: Who am I? Why would my birth have stopped time? Why did my time harden and lodge in Caro's throat, unable to be taken in by anyone else but me?

And finally, another, far more sickening thought clouds out all the rest like a plume of black, stifling smoke, so heavy it makes my eyes tear and run. I think back to the stories I wrote as a child, how Fox and Snake's innocent games slowly darkened and changed until Snake was curling around Fox's heart, stealing the life from her. What if the Queen is not the one to be feared at all?

What if the person to be feared is me?

Papa is buried in an anonymous grave somewhere in the woods. He would still be alive if I had never gone to Everless. He would still be alive if seventeen years ago, he had allowed me to die in Briarsmoor with Naomi Morse.

I stare down at my shaking, blood-and-mava-stained hands, the mare thundering over the ground below me. I can't go back there. I must leave. I must go far, far away from here. But how can I travel without money—and where will I go?

Quickly, the plan forms in my mind. I'll return to Everless, but only long enough to gather my belongings and clothes that are not covered in blood. I wish I could get the book too, but I expect the Gerlings will have posted a guard outside the vault, so I put that thought out of my mind. I'll have to leave without it, slip away and escape through the servants' entrance.

With any luck, I'll be far away before I'm even missed among the servants.

The thought of not saying goodbye to my friends at the estate—Lora and Hinton, who propped me up in the depths of my grief, and Ina—*my sister*—is like a knife between my ribs. Caro's face flits through my mind, too—but so do her unmarked hands, clean of the stain of the vault. Her arms, free of bloodletting incisions. Ivan lied for her. She lied to me.

Maybe once I'm away from Everless, I can untangle the mystery to be free of it, so I can someday return.

Fantasy.

I urge the horse forward.

The trip back to Everless passes in a blur, and soon I'm through the gates, hurrying along the servants' corridors, and into the dormitory, which is mercifully empty, everyone in the midst of their daily chores and activities. It doesn't take long to gather my things, and I stand for a moment over my narrow bed—hard and unwelcoming and yet, for a brief time, my home. In the quiet of the dorms, I change my dress, shoving the bloodstained one in the hearth, and slip the soft pair of gloves Ina gave me over my still-stained hands. And then I'm hurrying through the back entrance. I do my best to shut everything out except for my next goal: this doorway, that staircase, the door leading outside. It's only someone calling my name—the voice male, velvety, familiar—that infiltrates the fog in my mind, and I stop in my tracks. I turn around.

For the first time since leaving the dormitory, I notice my surroundings: I've walked straight into the beautiful royal gardens, no less stunning for being locked in snow and ice. Except for the walking paths that wind through the garden, the blanket of snow on the ground is immaculate, blindingly white. And in the midst of it all is Roan Gerling in his green hunting cloak, his cheeks flushed, snowflakes caught in his hair and eyelashes.

I have scarcely seen Roan in days. But seeing him now before me, all rich color against the white and black and gray of the garden, brings my feelings rushing back in a wave. He holds an elegant bronze-handled rifle casually in one hand, and with his other sweeps his hair out of his face.

"Jules," he says again, his smile far more dazzling than the weak morning sun above us. "Where have you been?"

I almost laugh, thinking of the tavern, the time lender's alley, the vault, the abandoned town. I have an urge to tell him everything, his eyes the color of the summer sky promising comfort and understanding. After all, he's known me longer than anyone else here. But I bite my tongue at the last moment. "I've been busy with chores, Lord Gerling," I say, avoiding his eyes. "And besides, you've been away. With Lady Gold." The words are cold in my throat. As I say them, I realize that Ina and the Queen must have returned to Everless as well if Roan is here. I should leave now, before we cross paths. I'm not sure if I could look into Ina's face without blurting out the truth about us. And the Queen . . .

But my thoughts dissipate when Roan tilts his head, his usual smile absent. His gaze turns serious. He steps closer, and in spite of myself, my grip tightens on my bag.

"Jules." My name in Roan's mouth is softer now, his gaze heavy on me. "Are you all right?"

In a flash, I see him as a child, reaching down from his perch in the oak tree to help me up beside him. My words rise in an unstoppable rush. "Do you love her?"

Roan stops where he is, one hand half extended toward me. His brow creases. "What?"

Shame and fear crash down on me, leaving me small, hollowed out. But I'm leaving, I'll never see Roan Gerling again after today, so—"Ina," I say again. "Do you love her?"

Roan blinks. Swallows. He takes a step closer to me, close enough that I can smell the scent of pine that clings to his skin. No trace of either lavender or rosewater today. He takes a deep breath that has the hint of a shudder in it.

"No," he says finally. "I don't."

I'm frozen, stunned. I can't move, not even when Roan reaches out and closes my hand in his.

"You're here," he says haltingly. "You're here, and I missed you, and I . . . I can't see Ina anymore, not like I used to. Not when I know you're at Everless." He steps even closer. I can feel the heat of him, his breath stirring my hair.

"Roan . . ." I'm not sure what I'm going to say—tell him it's all right, or that he's a coward for knowing this and marrying Ina anyway, or ask him to let me go, or to come closer.

Roan, the boy who smells of different perfumes, depending on the day.

Roan, the boy who once chased me, head tipped back in laughter, through fields of wildflowers. The boy who grew up to love nothing more than Everless, its pudding and roasted birds, its flutes of sparkling liquor, its garden parties in the middle of winter.

Words tumble in my gut, a tangle of confused memory and feeling.

It turns out not to matter, because Roan has already made the decision. He leans down, closing the distance between us and, before I can move, before I can even think, his lips find mine.

I gasp against his mouth. For a moment, I'm frozen, stiff—then a private war erupts across every cell in my body, starting from my chest and moving outward, until every part of me is screaming simultaneously to pull away and to press closer. And the latter side is winning, rapidly. Roan threads his fingers through my hair, tilting my face back to meet his; and in response, as if of their own accord, my arms come up around his waist, and I pull him against me. The desire—not just for Roan himself but to be wanted, to be loved the way I loved him when I was young, to belong, for some wholeness in my childhood to be restored, to be *true*—rushes through me, carrying away all the dark discoveries of the night.

Roan trails a hand down my cheek, cups the side of my neck, his touch sending off waves of chills all over my body. Someone's pulse is fluttering where his hand rests on my neck—I can't tell if it's his or mine. Everything is riotous, hands and breath and lips. It's only when we pause to draw breath that I realize that everything has fallen silent.

I hadn't really heard the sounds of the garden until they vanished—now, their absence rings much louder than the sounds themselves. The world is silent around us.

No.

Roan has felt me stiffen. He pulls back, looks questioningly into my eyes, a slight smile on his mouth. Then the absence of sound seems to register for him too. He glances around, and his brow furrows.

I can tell exactly what he's thinking, because I see now what's happened. Nothing *looks* wrong—but complete stillness is more conspicuous to the eye than gentle motion, and I see the confusion on Roan's face as he realizes the tree branches aren't swaying, that two birds bathing in a nearby fountain have frozen midsplash, that the thin clouds aren't scudding across the sky, but hanging in place like in a painting.

I've frozen time again. And this time, another person is here with me. Roan looks down at me, and I watch the expression in his blue eyes turn slowly from confusion to fear. Hurt stabs through me.

The stretched-out instant doesn't last long. The silence is split by the bang of a slamming door—someone from outside the stillness I had cast over the garden—and a shouted oath. "There she is!" a man yells.

The sounds of the garden, returning, are immediately drowned out by heavy, running footsteps. I step away from Roan, and we both turn to see three Everless guards sprinting toward us. I'm too shocked to move, as the fastest of them seizes me by the arm.

"What—what's the meaning of this?" Roan sounds weakly. He looks pale, badly shaken. Then his eyes widen. "Liam!"

I whip back around to see Liam striding into the garden, a black cloak swirling behind him, all ice and sharp angles where Roan is color and life.

"Step back, Roan," Liam says coolly, as if he's not surprised at all to see his brother here next to me. "Miss Ember's arrest doesn't concern you."

My breath catches in my throat, while Roan takes a step forward, his hands curling into fists at his sides. "Arrest? What could possibly warrant that?"

But the words die in the air around us as a guard pulls off my gloves—exposing my hands, stained a deep, wine-dark red. He has his answer.

Liam cuts his eyes toward me, and my heart turns to ice. He is all malice, his mouth a cruel slash and his eyes bottomlessly

315

dark, unreadable. He gestures fluidly to his guards. "Take her away."

Roan stands motionless as the guards drag me from the gardens, two of them gripping my forearms with bruising strength. I stare at him, willing him to say something, to stop this, but he doesn't. He just watches them pull me away. Disappointment makes my mouth taste bitter—disappointment not so much at Roan as at myself, for pouring so many dreams into the hands of a boy who can't even open his mouth to save me.

Liam walks apace with the guards, his stride easy and his eyes forward.

"Don't scream," he says to me.

I grit my teeth in rage as we emerge from the gardens into an empty courtyard, where a nondescript, windowless carriage is waiting, its back doors hanging open.

Unceremoniously, the guards heave me up and inside, and I land heavily on my back. I scramble upright, grabbing at the wall for balance, but it's too late—the doors are already closing, locking me in darkness. The last thing I see before the daylight disappears is Liam pulling his hood up to hide his face.

27

We ride for what seems like hours, until the frantic racing of my mind congeals into a slow dread. When I left Briarsmoor, I was so close to the truth that I could feel it buzzing in my bones. Now it seems that I will never learn it—that I'll end up like Papa, bled of my time and dying alone in the cold.

At some point, I notice that the steady rattling of the carriage over the road has given way to a slower, bumpier pace—like we're moving over grass. And then the carriage shudders to a halt. All at once, the doors fly open and light floods in, dazzling me. I scramble into a sitting position, shading my eyes until the figure in the doorway resolves into Liam, standing with one foot propped up on the edge of the carriage. Behind him is what looks like an open field, with no road in sight.

Acidic hatred shoots through me even as the terror roars back. Has he taken me out to the middle of nowhere to kill me?

Liam regards me for a long moment without speaking. Loathing for him throbs through me, pushing at the inside of my skin. I imagine it breaking away from me, an amorphous mass of black smoke, and wrapping itself around Liam's throat.

But I know if I tried to enact the scene, the sword hanging loosely at Liam's side would find my heart in seconds.

"Look out here," Liam says. He steps aside so I can see out the back of the carriage, and points at something. At first, I think he's showing me his three guards, who are standing at intervals a little away from us—out of hearing range, but well within shooting if I try to run.

Then my gaze travels further. In the direction of Liam's finger is a wide smudge of gray on the horizon, a series of small dark shapes, some puffing threads of smoke into the sky. A city, one much bigger than Crofton or Laista. I level my gaze at Liam.

"It's Ambergris," he says. "A dock city on Hunt's Bay. Have you been there before?"

I cross my arms over my chest.

"I'll take that as a no," Liam says after a moment. "Anyway, there are over a hundred thousand people there. You'll be able to disappear." There's no malice in his voice—it's low, clear, direct, as if he's trying to persuade me of something. "Create a new name, a new life."

Liam reaches down to retrieve something at his feet. He

straightens and drops a package on the carriage floor between us—and to my surprise, I see it's a small but heavy purse of blood-iron. "You cannot stay at Everless," he says.

"I know," I spit. The beginnings of furious, confused tears brew in my throat. "But tell me. If you've got proof now that I broke into the vault, why not just have me bled? If you hate me so much, why get rid of me this way?"

This seems to take Liam aback, if only for a moment. He blinks, raises one hand to fiddle nervously with the clasp of his cloak.

"I don't hate you, Jules," he says, voice uneven. "But don't you understand? You're in danger."

"Because of you!" I nearly scream. "You lied. Don't pretend you don't know what I'm talking about. If you'd told the truth about pushing Roan into the fire, we wouldn't have had to run. You blamed my father and tormented us, even though he'd poured his health into serving your family. It was our home, and you banished us." My voice is picking up strength as more and more words tumble out. "It's your fault we ended up the way we did. Your fault he's dead."

Liam looks like he's been slapped, but then something changes in his expression. "Jules," he says, low and hard. And I think of his notebook, his records of my childhood stories.

"You know something about me, don't you?" I say, before he can even speak. Even as I make the accusation, a realization starts to dawn, slowly and painfully, inside my heart.

The accident.

"You used to call me a witch," I whisper, half to myself.

The flames had leaped from the open furnace, toward Roan. They were going to kill him.

Maybe I willed the fire to stop, just like the air in the garden when Roan kissed me. I had stopped time.

"You saw me stop time," I whisper, needing to form the thought aloud for it to make sense.

It takes him a long time to speak. When he does, it's soft. "No. More than that. I saw you turn it back. I pushed Roan, and the molten metal from the pot spilled over him—and you grabbed him and pulled him back. But he wasn't burned." He casts his eyes to the ground, as if embarrassed. "You saved him. I never meant to hurt him, I swear. But if you'd stayed, if someone else found out what you could do . . ."

My panic gradually ebbs away, leaving nothing but bitterness in my mouth. I should calm the anger in my heart and focus on the mystery of my father's death, but what Liam's saying—I stagger under the weight of it.

Papa's hatred for Everless and the Gerlings ran deeper than sense. Unless he was exaggerating, trying to build a wall of silence between me and the dangerous truth.

Liam cuts into my thoughts. "Your father didn't trust me. He knew you weren't safe at Everless." Liam smiles bitterly. "I can imagine what he told you about me, to keep you away. I saw it on your face when I met you outside the vault. I don't blame him. I was terrible, then. I would have done anything to find out what I wanted to know. But that night changed me. You changed me." He looks down. "I'm sorry, Jules. For every piece of suffering I've caused you. But I was trying to protect you."

To protect me. Is it possible? In all the chaos of new information, I can't say one way or another whether his words are yet another lie, or the purest form of truth I've ever known. There's something in his hand, which he gingerly puts down on the ground between us. I hesitate, but when I realize it's Papa's wandering handwriting that covers the paper, I snatch it up. But the world around me seems to slow when I realize that it's a letter for Liam.

"It's true that I came looking for you"—he stops as I shoot him a dangerous look—"but only to help." Liam's voice is so quiet he seems to be speaking half to himself. He stares into my face, his jaw working. "After you left, I wrote to you to make sure you were safe, sending the courier to every village around, but I suspect you never got the letters. Finally, after my disastrous visit, that's when he told me you were dead." His smile and his voice is weak—tired. "I suppose he wanted me to stop looking. When you came to Everless again, I thought that the best way to keep you safe would be to get you to leave the estate—leave Everless forever—by making you miserable there." His voice strengthens some. "I am not your enemy, Jules," he says—slowly, choosing his words carefully. "But you do have enemies. Many."

I desperately want to clap my hands over my ears and block out what he's saying, but I can't. I have the urge to strike him, but I don't. Something deep in me knows that Liam is not lying now. Maybe it's his face, wiped clean of its usual sneer, or his hands, hanging at his sides, his posture open and vulnerable.

"Roan didn't remember what happened in Pehr's workshop. Because of you, it didn't even happen for him to remember," he said. "But what you did today was different. My brother is foolish, not stupid. That's one more person who will know."

"Roan would never . . ." But I stop, thinking of the fear in his voice, the hollowness of his words.

"You were always like that—so trusting," Liam says. He sits down on the lip of the carriage, swinging his legs up and leaning against the wall, so he's sitting across the doorway. Some part of me registers that he is blocking the exit, but my urge to flee has dissipated. I feel rooted to the spot, starving for the truth.

I swallow. *He kept me away on purpose. He knows who I am. What I am.*

The dreams of the statue.

"Am I . . ." It doesn't make any sense. It can't. And yet I have no other way to see it. "You think I'm connected to the Sorceress somehow?" I ask him.

Liam doesn't react for a moment. Then, to my shock, he grins, a wide, earnest smile breaking across his face like sun through storm clouds. It only lasts a moment, but smiling, he looks like Roan. No—he looks like someone all his own.

And then he is shaking his head. "Not exactly," he says. "But maybe."

Confusion and frustration war within me. "I don't understand. You said—"

"When I went away to study," he cuts in, "I couldn't stop thinking about your stories of the snake and the fox, and of what I'd seen in the forge. The moment where you . . ." *Turned back time.* He doesn't say it. Instead he just clears his throat. "It got me obsessed with the history of blood time. I spent several years studying the old myths," he goes on. "Not just at the academy—I went all over Sempera, I found every book and scholar and ancient story I could, but eventually, I had to let it go. My teachers thought I was chasing fairy tales, wasting my talent. People started to talk."

Even as the truth he's sharing transfixes me, his lack of humility—and the rehearsed sound of his speech—still makes me want to roll my eyes. I suppress the urge.

"But even as I turned my focus to my other studies," he goes on, "I kept thinking about the Sorceress and the Alchemist, and the stories people tell about them. There were mixed accounts—impressions of the Sorceress herself that contradicted what I had been raised to believe. You know the standard version, I suppose."

I dig deep for the tales read to the servant children in those

323

early mornings at the Everless library, so many years ago. "They say the Alchemist stole the Sorceress's immortality, binding it to metal, so they could get free of the evil lord. Later, he claimed to know how to give it back, but it was just a trick—a ploy to steal the Sorceress's heart."

"And the twelve stones . . ." Liam prompts.

"He told the Sorceress that she had only to swallow twelve stones. But the Sorceress didn't trust him. She killed him by making him swallow the stones, after which he drowned." I almost feel silly reciting the tale, but there's a deadly urgency in Liam's face that dispels any feeling that this is a game.

"Yes. But where the accounts differ," he says, "is that most of them present the Alchemist as a thief, a trickster, a liar who spurned the Sorceress and died with her heart. *But*. What other accounts say is that the Sorceress and the Alchemist are both still around, her chasing him for her heart back. I wondered—if the Alchemist had survived, *how?*"

I stare at him, helplessly confused. "Magic?"

"The twelve stones. There is one theory of the stones that I just couldn't let go of. The theory that each stone represents—"

"A life," I say, a vague memory stirring in me.

"Exactly. Twelve." Liam leans forward a little. "What if the Alchemist *didn't* lie about his claim? He had found a way to give the Sorceress her immortality back—just in a different way? To be born, live a normal life, die . . . But then be born again, the same soul in a new body, with all the wisdom of his previous lives."

Terrible knowledge gathers in me, taking form.

"Shedding lives, over and over, like a—"

"Like a snake," I say, finishing his sentence.

"But she forced it back on him." Liam talks faster, his face flushed with cold or excitement. "But if that were true, if the Alchemist has twelve lives, why have we heard so little of him since?"

"So what are you saying? That the whole myth is a lie?" Memories of Briarsmoor rush back at me again. Ezra Morse, my birth father, who spoke of the Sorceress with anger. Who seemed to be obsessed with time.

"More that it's incomplete," Liam says. "What if the Alchemist doesn't want to be found? What if he knew the Sorceress would kill him, if she found him?"

I nod slowly, thinking of the Queen, icily cold—indeed, *heartless*—and older than anyone in all of Sempera.

He clears his throat. "Look. I know what it's like to do things that others judge harshly." At this, his eyes gleam and I know he is trying to say something very big, something important, but I don't know if I'm ready to hear it. He runs a hand through his hair. "What if the Alchemist was just misunderstood—if he wanted to stay hidden? That might explain why we haven't heard from him in centuries. But it still doesn't explain one thing."

"Which is?" The sun is beginning to set and a chill is seeping into my bones. I shiver.

"You, Jules. It doesn't explain you." He puts his hands on my shoulders and I instinctively tense, only to feel surprised by the warmth of his touch.

In spite of everything, he beams. "The stories you used to tell . . . I wrote them down as best I could, when I realized what they meant." Liam looks at me meaningfully. "For years, I couldn't piece it together and I had given it up. Until one day, in a class about mathematics and philosophy, a professor was lecturing about the elegance and simplicity of the laws of math and logic. He said, *The shortest distance between two objects is always a straight line.*"

A long silence stretches between us.

"I had spent so much time trying to find a connection between you and the Alchemist. Don't you see how elegantly simple the real answer is?"

I take a deep breath. "Was my father the Alchemist?"

Even as I say it, something in me whispers: *no.* And then Liam laughs breathlessly.

"*You* are the Alchemist, Jules," he says.

I must look like a fish that's just been caught, my mouth gaping open. What he's saying makes no sense at all. And at the same time, his words spear through me with the precision of truth, of memory, of history. My bones sing in answer to my own name. "But . . . my father," I say, scrabbling for purchase with my words.

"Jules," Liam says, his voice strangely gentle. "Lesser magicians can meddle with time, slow it down or speed it up, but only the Alchemist can stop it entirely. And there are other things, sources, I wish I had time to show you . . ." He takes a breath. "About your father . . . there are people who carry on knowledge of the Alchemist—your past lives, your things, scraps of your memory—like they're protecting you. Maybe he was one of them. But only you are the Alchemist." He smiles again, and I feel like I'm floating out of my body, witnessing this conversation from above.

"But—" I manage, then falter. There are a thousand reasons this is impossible, and I seize upon the first one I can think of. "I don't remember anything about . . . past lives."

Liam's eyes search mine, as though he's looking for something already inside of me. As I stare back into his dark eyes, I think of the dreams. The stories.

The book.

"Snake and Fox," I say aloud slowly. My mind has filled with a kind of fog, and it's hiding from me the enormity of what Liam is telling me. I know if it cleared, terror would overtake me, so for now I'm grateful for the calm. "I'm the snake," I say. "And the fox . . ."

Liam's eyes dart to the sides, like someone might hear us. "Who steals time in Sempera?"

"Your family," I say, without thinking or hesitating.

Liam's eyes turn to steel before they soften again. "Yes, but we are not the only ones."

"The Queen." My words are soft, with wonder or fear—I can't tell. It's the same thought I had after leaving Briarsmoor. The Queen is the Sorceress.

Liam nods. "She's been stealing the time of everyone in Sempera for centuries."

"And the Sorceress wants me." Not Ina, me. She was looking for me. In Briarsmoor. But . . . "Why?"

"You have her heart. Jules, if she gets hold of you, she'll kill you. And if she kills you, she'll have her power back, and then . . ." *The Alchemist stole the Sorceress's heart.* "You contain her power. With your blood mixing with hers through all those lives . . ." After a pause, he continues. "Maybe no one knows how much power is in your heart, Jules. Not even the Queen."

My breath vanishes from my lungs. My huge, dark suspicion wasn't wrong. That's why Papa didn't want the Queen to get near me.

Liam looks away. In the gathering twilight, he suddenly looks very tired, the small lines at the corners of his eyes deepening. "So go," he whispers. "And don't come back to Everless, not ever."

And then, before I can fully register everything that has happened, he has turned and is striding away across the field.

28

As I watch Liam go, a single thought crystallizes in my mind.

No.

The full weight of what he's told me hangs in my head, dizzying, threatening to overwhelm me—but at this moment, something else is much more important than the incredible stories of the Alchemist and the Sorceress.

Ina Gold.

The Queen thinks Ina, and not me, is the Alchemist. That's why she adopted her all those years ago. And if Liam is right, the Queen must have some plan to destroy Ina and take her power back—she's only waiting for something . . . something I don't quite understand yet. But whatever it is, I need to warn Ina, need to save her—*my sister*—before someone else suffers in my name.

Instinctively, I fling out my hands, palms toward Liam's retreating figure. All I can think is that if he gets on his horse and rides away, he'll lock the gates of Everless behind him.

The need to stop him is hot and desperate in my chest, and it's as though I can almost see the seconds that pass like physical threads—as though I can grasp them.

Power, ancient and primal and dizzying, rushes up inside me.

It's not like when Caro choked, or when I kissed Roan. Then, stopping time felt like something had gone off, like the world around me was infected—wrong. Now the world stills because I *will* it to. The cold wind dies abruptly around me, and every other noise stops too, even the distant wash of the ocean that I hadn't realized was present until it was gone. Beyond, I can see the blurred shapes of Liam and his guards as they make to mount their horses. *Stop them.*

My blood leaps in my veins as time obeys me, the freeze racing out from my feet, the grass stilling. It's like a soap bubble swelling to encompass the field. In the space of a few heartbeats, it's spread across the twenty yards separating me from the guards, and overtaken them.

An instant later, it takes Liam. I see him clearly as it swallows him. He's looking back toward me, one hand poised on the reins of his horse, and his eyes are wide with terror.

He saw. He saw what I did, before it froze him. But I can't

stop to worry about this. I run for the horses, the crunch of my boots on the ground and my own ragged breath the only two sounds in the universe. Panting, I stop in front of the younger guard and his horse, a small, solid-looking brown mare. With a gentle touch to her cheek, I will her to wake.

She comes to life beneath my hand and rears up, snorting. I jump back, raising my hands. Of course, it seems to her as if a strange human has blinked into existence before her. "It's okay," I say in my calmest tone, my heart pounding. "It's okay."

The mare stamps and whinnies, but allows me to approach and extricate her reins from the guard's still hands. I stroke her cheek, like Tam showed me, and soon she quiets. She shifts nervously when I clamber into the saddle, but obeys when I squeeze my legs and lead her away from the group.

From my vantage point on her back, I can see that our little party has left its mark in the snowy field—divots of horseshoes and long, deep tracks from the carriage wheels, a trail pointing toward the coming dusk. I'll have to hope that it leads me to a road to take me back to Everless. And that my bubble of time will hold even after I've left its boundaries, at least for long enough to give me a decent head start against the guards and Liam.

I can't help but twist around in the saddle to look at Liam once more. He stands, his eyes fixed on the place where he saw me last. I used to think he looked like a statue, with his carved features and cold gaze. But now, though his chest doesn't move and his eyelids don't flutter, he looks anything but. A riot of emotions is suspended on his face, in his parted lips and wide eyes. Shock and fear and anger—but also something like admiration. Like longing.

The road back to Everless seems to fly beneath us, the guard's mare galloping as if we've been riding together for years. Maybe she can feel the power surging through my blood—or more likely, just the urgency in my heart, the kind that all animals seem to be able to sense. I ride south, and the sun is well up by the time I come upon the edges of Laista, the jagged shape of Everless cutting into the sky.

The gates stand open, and a steady stream of carts bearing flowers, wine, and bolts of fabric are already trickling in. I overtake them, my horse dodging neatly between the wagons, and burst through the gates.

The two guards stationed there twist toward me in surprise, gaping at my servant's dress and handsome horse, but I'm already past them, racing toward the courtyard. Everything around me seems to be moving slowly, as if the air has turned to tar for everyone except me. I don't know if time is warping around me or if it's simply the adrenaline rushing through my body, panic converted into motion.

In the courtyard, I vault off the horse and leave her near the stables. I enter the castle through a side door and find myself in the servants' corridors. Even this early in the morning they're crowded, wedding chores added to the normal chores to create a steady stream of servants going this way and that.

I'm afraid of being stopped if I appear too strange, so although my whole body itches to run to Ina's chambers, I walk quickly instead, keeping my head down and my hands pressed to my sides. At first I don't see the face of the person who grabs my arm. Startled, I look up, and my throat constricts as my vision fills with a pale, handsome face framed by dark curls. Liam. He's found me, already, impossibly. But—

"Jules," Roan breathes, pulling me toward the side of the hall. It seems like a year has passed since the moment when he kissed me in the courtyard, but his nearness brings it all back— the thrill, the shame, the confusion and panic. But I try to ignore the sudden pounding of my pulse. What happened between us is the least important thing in the world today.

"I've been searching for you. So has everyone. Where have you been?" he exclaims, once we're in an alcove and out of sight. His hands rest possessively on my upper arms. "What happened? Where did Liam—?"

"I can't explain right now," I say, forcing myself to step back from him. "Roan, where is Ina?"

"Ina?" Roan frowns, seriousness creeping on to his face.

"Is she safe?" *My sister. My sister.* What does the Queen want with her? What does she have planned?

"Safe? I just left her," Roan protests, but his face goes slack. "Why wouldn't she—?"

333

"I can't explain right now," I say hurriedly. "But she's in danger, Roan."

Suspicion spikes through me—does he know that the danger is the Queen, Ina's adoptive mother, her only family? "Roan, please believe me. Get her out of her room and go to yours. Stay with her until I tell you it's safe."

Roan stares at me mutely, his expression fearful.

"Please, Roan," I beg, my voice cracking. "Ina is my friend. Nothing else matters now. If you care for her at all, go stay with her and lock the door. Just until I come. Please."

Roan slowly drops his hands from my arms.

"All right," he says at last. "I'll stay with her. But after that, you'll come fetch us and explain all this?"

"I will," I breathe, so relieved I could cry. "I promise I will. Now go. Lock the door and don't let anyone in, no matter what they say." I turn away from him and head down the hall, forcing myself not to look back.

As soon as my feet move, I know where I'm going.

To the Queen.

29

I have my hands out when I round the corner of the hall where the Queen's suite is, ready to stop time to get past the three guards who are always stationed by her door after dark. But instead I halt in my tracks, faced with an empty hall.

Maybe the Queen is off somewhere—I can wait here and confront her when she returns. I cross the hall to her door and try it, just in case. To my shock, the knob turns under my touch, and the door opens. I hesitate, a small voice inside whispering to me that something is wrong.

The Queen's chamber is dim and glittering, draped in gold fabric and illuminated with the low light of candles. The huge window is covered over with blood-red drapes, and all I can make out are shades of light and shadows as my eyes adjust. The room is vast, easily twice as big as Ina's, and the walls are covered in alternating panes of bookshelves and mirrors. I had expected to find Ivan in here, or more guards—but the room is empty, save for one.

The queen of Sempera is standing at a magnificent vanity in one corner, her back turned to me, a single candle on the vanity lighting her face in the mirror. She's wearing an indigo dressing robe, and her dark red hair is loose around her shoulders, cascading down her back. She doesn't react to the sound of the door closing.

"Your Majesty?" I call softly, running over in my head the story I've come up with. Ina is sick and has sent me to ask that the Queen come to her chambers. It's far-fetched, but I don't need her to believe me for long. If I can just stop her in time, I can tell Ina the truth, and we can decide what to do together.

Still, the Queen doesn't turn around as I pad closer.

It seems to take an eternity to cross the cavernous room. There's something eerie about it—the size and the rich cloth draped everywhere muffle some sounds and amplify others, so it's silent except for my heartbeat, which seems somehow to fill the whole room. "Your Majesty," I say again, louder, when I'm halfway there.

Still the Queen doesn't react. She stands at her mirror with the same erect bearing and lifted chin I can imagine her using when sitting on her throne by the ocean, or giving speeches to an adoring crowd—but she's utterly still, except for the motion of her arm and hand as she carefully applies an outline of kohl to her eyes, then a coat of red to her lips. Of all the things I expected, this silence unnerves me, chews at my resolve.

Now I can see my face in the mirror behind the Queen. Our faces float together in the glass, hers pale as snow and standing out in the dimness, mine sun-browned and small and scared behind her. The rush of power and will that propelled me from the field with Liam has evaporated completely. I don't feel like the Alchemist. I feel like a little girl who has walked knowingly into the mouth of a beast.

The Queen sets down her paints and turns around.

I have never been so close to her before. I can see the paleness of her eyes, the fine lines that fan at the corners. What is it like to move around the world in a body and mind that has seen five centuries? I am facing a mountain, a goddess. An old enemy, though I see nothing familiar in her.

"Jules," she says. And then, "Antonia."

The name sends a momentary surge of rightness through me. Yes. I am Antonia. The author of the book my father died to retrieve, to keep the secret of me safe. I suddenly know it deep in my bones. Another incarnation of the Alchemist, I realize. Perhaps the very first. But the feeling evaporates quickly. The knowledge doesn't make me any safer.

The weight of the Queen's gaze makes me want to flinch, to run. It's like a physical force, a ray of heat trained on my eyes. But I force myself to stand straight, keep my head up.

The Queen laughs, a low, rolling laugh like distant thunder. "We meet and meet and meet."

"It's me you want. Not Ina," I say. "Whatever you're planning, you can let her go now."

That laugh again. I fight not to cower.

"You needn't fear for Ina," the Queen says. "I've no need for her now." Her voice is strange, too soft. "It was sweet of you, though, to task Roan Gerling to guard her, when you love him so yourself."

"I— What?" I choke, fear and confusion crowding together in my throat. How does she know what I said to Roan?

The Queen steps forward and lays a hand on my chest, directly over my pounding heart. Her fingers are ice-cold through the thin fabric of my dress. The cold spreads through my body with wicked speed, and the strength of silver wire.

"You are right. Ina Gold does not have the heart I need." Now the Queen's voice is splitting into two voices, one her own, one girlish and conspiratorial. The two-toned sound makes my stomach turn.

The heart.

As her words fade, I feel myself going numb—when I try to make a fist, my fingers only stiffen in a silent rebellion.

Then my legs buckle, and I go down.

I hit the ground on my knees. Every last bit of strength evaporates from my body, all my muscles and bones turned to water. I remember Addie's words about touching the Queen, the look on her face as frightened as a doe's: *like getting your time drawn.*

I can barely even raise my head, much less defend myself. I hear a door open behind me, and someone else walks into the room.

"No," the Queen repeats, and now her voice is coming from all around, before and behind me, emanating from the walls, the earth itself. "Ina is not the one I need. She never was."

Then a small, cool hand touches my chin, raises my head. I keep my eyes shut, not wanting to see the flash of the knife as it opens my throat or pierces my heart. Not wanting to know how I've failed Ina—failed everyone. If Liam was right, and the Sorceress is evil, I, in my foolishness, have just signed the world over to her.

But—

"Open your eyes, Jules," someone says. Not the Queen.

I obey.

Caro is kneeling before me, cradling my cheek, smiling. Behind her, the Queen stands, her eyes fixed in the middle distance.

"Caro!" I gasp in relief. "The Queen, she's—"

"She is nothing," Caro cuts in.

For the first time since I've known her, she isn't whispering. Her voice is high and clear and familiar as my own heartbeat. She's wearing a black velvet dress, not her servant's uniform, and her hair is unbound.

339

She doesn't look a bit ill or feverish.

She reaches behind herself without looking and touches the Queen's dangling hand. And all at once, the Queen collapses. She falls as quickly and silently as a puppet whose strings have been cut.

My scream finally bursts free, but there's no one to come, and nothing to be done: the Queen sprawls on her side, a heap of velvet and silk and bones. The violence of it makes me shake.

Caro inhales. It's as if something missing has suddenly flowed back into her. Even kneeling in front of me, she looks taller. Regal. Powerful.

I don't say anything, but a tear trickles down my face and over Caro's fingers. She releases me and dries her hand on her skirt. Behind her, the Queen's eyes are closed, the rise and fall of her chest barely perceptible.

"I oughtn't say she was nothing," Caro says, tsking at herself. "The Queen was a friend, once. We were young together. I could see potential in her, even then."

She grins at some long-distant memory, or hallucination. "And then came the invasion. Soon she was leading the Semperan army to victory. After the battle was over, she was named queen. And me at her side, in the shadows, the whole time."

Goose bumps have broken out up and down my arms. Caro is reciting a history lesson—every Semperan child knows how the Queen ascended to power.

But Caro, in her madness, is talking about the five-centuries-ago war like a fond memory, complete with a wistful note in her voice and a faraway look in her eyes. She must be mad. Has to be. Because if she's not, I have been so terribly, terribly mistaken.

"At first, I considered becoming queen," she says thoughtfully. "Without me, the army never would have won—I assassinated enemies, I found out their secrets. But *Jules*"—she draws out my name like a curse—"you wouldn't believe how becoming queen makes you a target." She stares down at me like the idea is the greatest injustice in the world. "I eventually understood that power has nothing to do with position. Especially if you're weak," she hisses, casting a glance at the Queen's crumpled form. "This was the better way. A queen couldn't have done the things I've done—gone the places I've gone, unseen and unnoticed, the way servants are. And it isn't as if I lacked for power. Not when she"—Caro sweeps her hand back at the unconscious Queen—"let me in." She pauses and looks at me meaningfully, like it's my turn to speak.

"What do you mean," I croak, "let you in?"

"You could have learned to do it too, if you had more time. Whisper in someone's ear and make their mind your own." She considers me. "I've had time, Jules, which somewhat makes up for the power you stole from me."

An awful understanding is starting to sink into me—something huge and dark that I've failed to grasp, something

I've missed all along. But my whole body rebels against it, struggling against the realization. I can't put it into words.

Caro laughs softly at the look on my face. "Don't look so shocked, Jules," she chides. "The Queen would be long dead today if not for me—or at least, she'd be a sack of bones like the old hag in the west tower. We helped each other; I gave her life, and she gave me power. But she was never you." She glances back at the Queen's prone form, sighs. "And I tire of the shadows. Of servanthood. Of blood-iron. I've drunk hundreds of years' worth of blood-iron, and I hate the way it tastes."

"*Hundreds of years.*" I swallow. "How could no one have noticed? How could no one see that you didn't age?"

"No one notices, Jules. No one cares about a servant girl. You of all people should know that." Caro flashes her teeth in a smile. "And if they did, they were easy to take care of."

Sickness settles in my stomach as I realize she's right. I can easily imagine nobles of any time failing to note that a particular servant girl is forever unlined, slender, bright-eyed.

I stare at her, horrified and immobile, as she laughs to herself. The sun in the covered window is starting to set, making the room even dimmer than it was when I came in. The details of her face are fading to contours only, sharp cheekbones and white teeth and impossibly dark eyes. I have seen that face before, amid fire and lightning and shadows.

"How did you know?" I rasp.

"Your blood-iron, of course," Caro says, beginning to pace

in front of me like a wild cat. "I had suspected before then— when I realized you'd lied about your parentage, and what happened with the hedge witch—but I knew for sure when I saw your time go back into you. I've seen it before, when you were Eryn, and May, and Cecily, and . . . well."

"But Ivan had you arrested, he dragged you in front of everyone, he . . ." I trail off, already realizing the truth even before she grins in satisfaction. Of course—she had Ivan under her thumb the whole time. The entire story of the vault was a ruse, to entrap me. To test me. "You *knew* I'd bleed time to try to save your life."

"It seems I know you better than you know yourself."

A true friend.

An unthinkable enemy.

"You really are the Sorceress," I whisper, putting my worst fears into words, still hoping she'll laugh in my face, tell me I'm wrong, that I'm mad. But she doesn't.

"I should be hurt, you know," she says instead. "That you never remember me as well as I remember you. Though I will admit, it took me a little while to be sure this time. You've always been a shifty one, Antonia. In each of your lives. But worse, you've always had help." She spits the last word like an oath.

I can barely spare a thought for Papa, Lora, Liam, everyone who's helped me before she reaches out for me, takes my face in her hands. She has never stopped smiling at me, real affection in her eyes. And hunger, a fierce, ancient hunger like nothing I have ever seen.

"What do you want?" I gasp.

"I want to be timeless again," she says. "Centuries I've been aging. Slower than most, yes, but still. I want to be as I was, no fear of aging or death, without having to drink peasant blood like a damned wolf." Her eyes bore into mine, still that terrible combination of love and hunger, and something darker and deeper enters her voice. "I want what you stole from me so long ago."

All the levity is gone from her voice now. She lets go of me and suddenly my body is my own again. I scramble upright on weak legs, grasping a bedpost for support. My chest feels crushed from the inside, like a breath held too long.

Caro takes a step back, looking around the opulent room with an expression of mild disgust. "Things will be as they were before you bound time to iron," she hisses. "You took away my immortality. You doomed us both. I will make things right, but we cannot both live."

When I flinch, she laughs. "For almost five hundred years, my power has been locked in your heart. I used to think I could release it by killing you. It took dispatching you four or five times before I realized that wasn't enough." She taps her own chest with one finger. "I had to break your heart first."

"Then you're out of luck," I hiss. I take a step backward, reaching subtly behind me in hopes of finding something on the nightstand I can use as a weapon, but my fingers meet with nothing. "My father is dead. My mother is dead. I've watched friends starve—my heart's already broken."

But Caro is shaking her head impatiently. "No," she says. "You do not know brokenness. Not until the person you love most in the world dies in your arms." The smile she gives me now is twisted and terrifying. "Now, if you don't mind company," she says as though I have any choice, "there's someone I think you'll be happy to see."

She moves to the door, her stride buoyant, and opens it. Ivan is there in the doorway, along with Roan Gerling, his hands bound.

30

At first, I don't understand what I'm seeing—Roan pale and wide-eyed, with his shoulders bent awkwardly and his hands tied in front of him. He takes another two steps into the Queen's suite, Ivan pushing him forward. The traitorous captain is holding a knife, its tip hovering a finger's width away from the base of Roan's spine. Ivan keeps his eyes determinedly forward, but Roan sees the Queen's broken form on the floor, and his mouth drops open.

I want to scream at Roan to run, to fight, but find that I cannot speak—I'm not sure whether it's Caro's magic or the fear of her that seals my mouth shut. Caro's lips curl into a pleased smile. Ivan glances at her, and answers her smile with his own.

How long did it take her, I wonder, to get him under her

control? What else has he done for her? Under his smile, in his eyes, I see a glint of fear, though the knife in his hand doesn't waver. He fears Caro. That frightens me as much as seeing the Queen collapse like a rag doll.

"Thank you for your assistance, Captain," Caro purrs. "Remember—five minutes."

Ivan blinks, lingering. Her strange command fills me with a dread I've never known.

For an instant, Caro's face transforms into an expression of pure wrath, her eyes flying wide and her lips peeling back to bare her teeth. "*Go*," she snarls, "and leave the knife." Ivan takes a step back. He glances at Roan briefly, then turns to leave the room. Before the door shuts, Ivan twists around and tosses the blade. It arcs through the air, a flash of silver, then skitters to Caro's feet. I freeze.

She picks it up and turns to Roan. "On your knees." Her face is pleasant again, but a current of menace runs below the surface of her voice. Roan obeys, his face utterly afraid, like an animal brought to slaughter. I imagine it's the same look in my own eyes.

You do not know brokenness. Not until the person you love most in the world dies in your arms.

All at once, I know what Caro's planning. Forgetting all caution, I dash across the room and throw myself between Roan's frozen form and Caro. Facing her with my hands up, I have an eerie sense that I'm acting out one of my nightmares.

She laughs.

"You won't get away with it," I tell her, trying to keep my voice even. "He's a Gerling. Practically a prince."

"What's a prince to a goddess?" Caro says. "In fact," she says, turning from me and bending down to the Queen, who's still crumpled on the floor, "what's a queen to a goddess?"

Caro reaches out, making a fist in the fabric of the Queen's gown, and pulls the taller woman upright with unnatural, easy strength.

A terrible rasping sound emits from the Queen's throat—I hadn't been sure she was even still alive. Her head rocks back, and dark red blood trickles from one nostril. She opens her eyes and sees Caro.

The Queen lunges, lurching forward off-balance, her hands claws at the end of wildly swinging arms.

Caro is ready. As I watch in horror, she sidesteps the Queen and embraces her from behind, wrapping one arm around the Queen's waist. With her other hand she plunges her knife into the Queen's chest—one motion and it's over—and then shoves the gasping woman toward me.

My own scream fills the room. I stumble back, but there's nowhere to go. The Queen is on top of me, falling, and I automatically raise my arms to catch her. I snatch a glimpse of her wide, pale eyes, her chest drenched with blood—blood that's spilling onto me, my face, my hands. My scream sounds separate from me, like it's coming from someone else. All I can process is the warmth of the blood and the broken weight of the Queen in my arms, and the sight of her pale eyes as the life drains from them. A terrible emptiness spreads through me. All along, she was just a puppet for the real monster.

Somehow I lower her body to the floor and fall back, hitting the ground on my hands and knees and retching. The smell of blood surrounds me, a red haze.

Until the sound of Roan's cry cuts through it.

I raise my head. Past the body of the Queen, Roan is moving, his chest heaving as he stares at the Queen's disarranged form. And Caro stands behind him. In one swift motion, she twines one hand in his hair, tipping his head back, and holds her bloodied knife to his throat. I freeze where I'm kneeling over the Queen, afraid that even a blink will provoke her to use it again.

"You've made it so easy for me, Jules," she says. "Everyone's seen the way Lord Gerling looks at you. No one will doubt my story: you're a traitor who seduced him. You convinced him to let you into the Queen's chambers. And then you murdered them both."

Roan's eyes dart to me, then helplessly to the side—he can't turn to look at Caro, not without cutting himself on her blade. What Caro's saying must make no sense, but he understands the danger he's in. "Caro, please," he croaks.

"And *you*." Caro presses the knife in slightly, drawing a trickle of Roan's blood to mix with the Queen's on the blade. "You beautiful fool. You brought the real Alchemist right to my feet." My whole body tenses. "You made a mistake coming back here, Jules," she says, the hint of a laugh in her voice. "If you'd stayed in Crofton, been content to love Roan Gerling from a distance, I might never have found you."

But I scarcely hear her. My eyes are locked on Roan's as his frantic gaze shifts between the Queen's corpse and me. Memories crash over me—memories of sun filtered through the leaves of an oak tree, of breathless fights with wooden swords, of untamed laughter with never a thought of being lesser than. Roan today might be a coward and a fool, but he doesn't deserve to die like this.

"Please," Roan says quietly. He swallows, his skin moving against the knife, and blood trickles down onto his collarbone. "Please, Caro, I'll do anything."

I cut him off. "I don't love him." Out of the corner of my eye, I see Roan blink. "And he doesn't love me." I stare at Caro, hoping with everything I have that she'll believe me, see this one truth. *Please*—

For an instant, I think I see doubt flicker in her eyes. But it's too late—was always too late. I know Caro, know that her desire to break me has burned away everything else in her mind.

"If you wanted me to have mercy," she growls, "you shouldn't have taken my immortality."

And she draws a deep red line across Roan's throat.

I open my mouth to scream, but nothing comes out. All the air in my lungs has turned to lead. Someone has their fist in my chest and is pulling my heart out.

As Caro steps back from him, Roan lifts his hands to his throat. His brow furrows, and he looks bewildered at the blood seeping between his fingers and spilling down his chest. His mouth closes and opens and closes again; silent, helpless words that are lost to me, lost to everyone living.

Then he tips forward, landing facedown beside the Queen, and is still.

For a long moment, I think that time has stopped again, and I will it to turn back, will all of this to be undone.

But there's blood spreading over the floor. Time hasn't stopped. It's just that the room is utterly silent, as silent as the tomb it has become.

Caro stares at me, waiting—for me to break, for power to flow back into her. But nothing happens. And nothing happens. She tilts her head to the side, a small frown twisting her face— an expression of contained disappointment.

A spark of rage like I've never known in my life ignites in my chest. The fury sears through me as I stagger to my feet. It tells me that I am alive—and unbroken.

"You really didn't love him," Caro says. "It doesn't matter. I'll find the one to break you, if I have to kill every single person in Sempera. And in the meantime, you'll be caged again at Everless. How fitting."

At these words, the rage pushes me into motion. I leap toward Caro and throw my hands out, willing time to freeze

Caro in place long enough to lock my fingers around her throat. Power surges up through me and spills out, catching the air in the room, but only in strange bubbles. As the bubbles race toward her, I see Caro raising her hands, too, her head thrown back in laughter.

Her power and mine collide with a *boom* that seems to shake the world off its axis, and I'm blown backward onto the floor, my ears ringing. All around us, books fall from shelves, paintings crash to the floor. Glass shatters somewhere, and as I roll painfully up onto one elbow, dozens of jewels spill from the Queen's dresser and rocket across the floor.

As the ringing in my ears gradually fades, I hear screams in the distance, and the heavy drumbeat of footsteps coming toward us. I haul myself into a sitting position as the door bursts open and Everless guards pour in. The first of them skids to a halt and cries out at the pool of blood on the floor, the bodies.

"Help!" Caro shrieks. I turn my head to see that she's on her feet, pointing at me, her face a mask of horror. Ivan, silent and staring at Roan Gerling's body, is by her side. *Five minutes*, I realize, *when she wanted the guards to bear witness*.

She keeps screaming as the guards converge on me, as they grab my arms and haul me upright. I don't even try to fight. All the space inside me has been taken up with swirling horror and sickness, with no room left for resistance.

As they drag me away, Caro stops screaming long enough to smile, never once breaking my gaze.

EPILOGUE

Drip.

   Drip.

   Dri—

The drop of water freezes in midair, halfway through its journey to the floor. In the almost-pitch-black of the dungeons, I can hardly see it. But there it is, hanging in the air, a tiny globe reflecting torchlight from the hall. A small thing, like a jewel—pretty and useless.

I release my hold on time and let the drop fall to the ground. It adds to the patch of dampness on the stone that's slowly spreading toward me, will eventually reach me where I sit huddled in one corner, shivering, my arms wrapped around my knees. My facility with time is worse than useless now. I can play with the drops of water in my cell, or make the torch outside pause midflicker. But I can't make this cell any warmer, and I can't escape.

I can hold time in my hands, but no matter how much I concentrate, I can't make it flow backward. I've tried what seems like a thousand times.

The name *Antonia* sits in my mouth like a cavity. Something sweet once, now rotten. The Alchemist's name, my very first. I finally know who I am, and I can feel the knotted mess of power and history locked inside me—but that only makes it more bitter that I will die here, that Caro, the Sorceress, has bested me. I have failed Antonia. I have failed all the past selves without even knowing who they are, how hard they fought. I've failed Roan, the boy I once loved. I've failed Sempera—leaving the land in her power, and Ina at her mercy.

My stomach clenches at the thought of Ina. My sister.

She must hate me, despise me with every fiber of her being. And why not? I've heard the guards whisper—I know the stories Caro has spread about me. That I'm the *witch* who seduced Roan, and used him to gain access to the Queen. That I murdered the Queen, and then Roan, too, when he tried to stop me. That Caro stumbled upon me there, standing over their bodies with the knife cast at my bloody feet.

For a moment, I consider letting my mind consume me. I could close my eyes and lose myself in a vision, fall into memories that are as pure and real and plentiful as an endless string of pearls. But I press my hands against the cold stone floor, trying to anchor myself to the present, this cell and nothing else. If I lose myself in pleasant memories, I might never return—but if I think about Roan's blood on the floor, or imagine Ina's face when she learned he was dead, despair will unwind me.

It would only be a further betrayal of Antonia and all my other selves to fall apart now. Instead, I focus on what I know.

Caro needs me alive, or I'd be dead already. She needs my heart to break to get at the power hidden somehow inside. This should comfort me, but I don't trust my heart, already ragged with the loss of those I love the most.

Somewhere in the dark depths of my mind, a voice whispers that I should hope to die before she can break me. But the idea of giving up life now—when I finally understand who I am, when I can feel my power hovering just beyond my fingertips— makes every fiber of my being wail in protest.

No. I refuse to die.

The sound of boots on stone rings out in the cold, damp hallway. It grows louder with each step toward my prison. I don't move. There's no point—the guards never get close enough to the bars for me to reach them and grab the keys.

But something is different. The footsteps sound lighter than normal, and hesitant. They pause at intervals, as if someone is stopping to peer into cells.

I look up just as Liam comes into view. When he sees me, as his eyes widen and he rushes to my cell door, my heart—wounded and exhausted as it is—swells and beats a little stronger.

But no. Liam cannot be here. The image flashes behind my eyes of Roan, trembling with Caro's knife to his throat; and then Roan on the ground, wide-eyed and lifeless with his blood spreading around him. If she discovered Liam was helping me, she'd do the same to him—or worse.

"What are you doing?" My voice is hoarse from lack of use. I get shakily to my feet as he wraps his hands around the bars. He looks terrible, his face drawn and paler than normal, throwing the dark circles beneath his eyes into sharp relief.

"Jules," he says softly. "Are you all right?"

"You can't be down here," I snap, trying to hide my fear. "Caro will—"

"I know what Caro will do," he cuts in. His voice is heavy with grief; I remember that his brother is dead. "I should have seen what she was. If I had—" He breaks off, looking down and away, and I think I can see the glimmer of tears in his eyes.

"I'm sorry about Roan," I say, as gently as I can. Even if the brothers didn't get along, I can't imagine what it would be like to see my sibling cut down like that, for no reason other than cruelty.

My fists clench, thinking of Ina. I push my fear away.

"Roan is just the beginning," Liam says thickly. "While Ina prepares to take the throne, Caro has the estate locked down. She's rounding up everyone with any connection to you and questioning them."

My blood turns to ice. *Lora. Hinton.* "She has to break my

heart," I say, half to myself. "She's looking for anyone I love."

Liam finishes my thought for me. "You have to get out. Before she starts killing them." His hands tighten around the bars, his scarred knuckles whitening. "We have to go. We only have a few minutes."

I squeeze my eyes shut, trying to calm my racing mind enough to think. Images of the people I love float through my mind, a silent chorus. Swallowing down my terror at the thought of more falling victim to Caro's wrath, I meet Liam's gaze and approach him.

When I put my hands over Liam's, he shivers at the touch but doesn't move. His skin is warm, the only warmth I've felt in days, and I savor it. "Close your eyes," I tell him. I close mine, too, and call on the power inside me, willing the current of time around us to stop.

The cell and the hall outside it are so bare that when I open my eyes, I'm not sure if it's worked. Then I notice the sound of dripping water has stopped and the torch behind Liam is frozen midflicker.

But Liam is with me, breathing heavily though everything else has stilled. My body trembles with weakness; with little food and sleep, I feel the weight of time in my limbs. Still, I manage to squeeze Liam's hands in mine. In response to the pressure, he opens his eyes. He blinks slowly, in wonder, as he realizes what's happened.

I take my hands from his—ignoring the regret that seeps

through me—and point down the hall. "The guards are down there. They have keys."

Liam understands immediately. He steps back, pausing for an instant to gape at the still flame of the torch, and then he's off, striding with sure footsteps down the hall. My hands shake with fear for him.

But in a few minutes, he's back, the key clenched in his fist. He fiddles with the lock, and I wait, my heart racing. The door comes open faster than I expect, and I stumble forward, unused to standing on my own. Liam catches me against him, and for a moment we stay like that, with his arm around my shoulders and my cheek pressed against his chest. Warmth surrounds me, and for a moment I feel almost safe. But I know we can't stay like this. Time is frozen down here in the dungeons, but upstairs— for Caro, for Ina, for everyone I love—the seconds tick on.

Liam steps back first, dropping one of his hands to enfold mine. "I know a back way out," he says, his voice low and urgent. "Follow me."

He tugs me along down the hall, careful not to outpace me, though I can tell he's itching to run. Liam leads me down narrower and narrower hallways, the air cold and heavy and smelling like water. At first, I count down the seconds until the moment we'll be pursued—but soon, it's all I can do to keep putting one foot in front of the other, between my weak body and concentrating on holding the time freeze for as long as I can. Before long I have to let it go or collapse.

Eventually, we reach a narrow, spiraling staircase that seems to rise and rise. But finally we do come to the end, and emerge into a small hut lit with an oil lantern. I glance out the window and see the lake, and the castle beyond that—we must be in one of the guards' warming huts by the northern wall. There's a cot and a table cluttered with supplies, and a door across from us, edged in gray twilight.

I let go of Liam's hand and sink onto the cot, drawing in as much fresh, aboveground air as I can fit into my lungs. All my limbs feel weak, watery. I watch Liam as he gathers the supplies on the table, thrusting them into two knapsacks, then turning and holding one out to me.

"Addie can hide us tonight," he says. "Then tomorrow we'll get as far away from the estate as we can."

His face shines with earnestness, and looking up at him makes my body ache. He's risking his life for me at this moment, and about to give up everything he's known.

I can't let it continue.

"Caro killed Roan because she thought I loved him," I say.

Liam's eyes flicker. "But you didn't."

A needle of pain stabs through my chest. "Maybe not. Maybe just not enough. That's not the point." I stare straight into Liam's eyes, willing him to understand, to feel the danger swirling around us. "You can't come with me, Liam. It'll only get you killed."

His mouth twists. I wait for him to argue back, but he just

stares at me for a long moment and then, finally, nods. A mix of relief and disappointment floods me.

"If I had trusted you sooner . . ." he says at length. His voice splinters, and he takes a deep breath before going on. "If I had told you what I knew, none of this would have happened." The words he leaves unspoken hang between us. *The Queen would still be alive. Roan would still be alive.*

"And none of this would have happened if I'd gone to Ambergris like you asked," I counter softly. "We can blame ourselves all we want, but that doesn't help stop Caro now." My voice catches on her name.

Liam holds my gaze as I reach out to take the bag he's packed. "Wait." His fingers brush the back of my hand, then pull away. He opens a drawer under the table and takes out a small, battered book bound in leather. The sight of it plunges me into memories—cold nights in our cottage, sitting on Papa's lap while he read stories from the book. Opening the cover on my own and tracing the words there, knowing they belonged to me, even though I was too small to read. And other memories too, mine but not mine, the minds of Antonia and all my other lives, my other selves, their memories and hopes and loves and terrors laced through my blood and bones. This is what my father sought in the vault, what he gave his life for.

"I hate the thought of you alone," Liam says softly.

For the first time in what seems like centuries, I feel a spark of hope. "I'm not alone," I tell him as I take the book. I couldn't be alone, not with the words of my past speaking to me from these pages.

Liam watches me, holding his hands stiffly at his sides like he wants to reach out again but won't allow himself to. "What are you going to do?" he asks quietly.

"I don't know," I admit. "Hide. Learn about myself. Then try to face Caro, when I'm ready."

"It's not too late to disappear," he says. "You could change your name. Leave Sempera. She'd never find you."

"She would find me," I say with certainty. "You don't know her like I do. But I won't disappear. I won't leave you— leave everyone under her thumb forever." I reach out and grab his hand, and he blinks. "Stay here, at Everless," I tell him. "I'll need you before this is over."

Slowly, slowly, he nods. "I'll help you in whatever way I can. And I won't say goodbye, Jules," he whispers. "Now run."

I take one last, long look at him—this boy who I hated for so long, who's been protecting me since he was a child himself. His eyes are dark hollows, brimming with yearning and fear. For an instant I want to kiss him—but hold myself back, remembering that my touch is a mark of death.

"Thank you, Liam," I say.

Then I turn my back on him and walk into the night, the past weighing heavily on my shoulders, toward a future as wild and unknowable as my own heart.

Don't miss the sequel to
Everless

Coming January 2019